S0-BZA-443

THE SENIOR PARTNER

THE SENIOR PARTNER

George Hammond

Library of Congress Number:		99-90481
ISBN Numbers	Hardcover:	0-7388-0406-1
	Softcover:	0-7388-0407-X

The Senior Partner is the story of four crucial months in the life of Stuart Emerson Craxton III, a senior partner at Tilden & Hayes, a very conservative, and fictional, Manhattan law firm.

All characters in this novel are also fictional. Any resemblance to real persons is due to the minimal variety in lawyers' personalities.

Names, characters, places and incidents either are the product of the author's imagination or are used fictitiously, and any resemblance to any actual persons, living or dead, events or locales is entirely coincidental.

Originally copyrighted in 1994 as *The Partner*. However, since John Grisham's unrelated novel *The Partner* was copyrighted and published in 1997, the title was changed to *The Senior Partner*.

Pyth Press and **Virtually a Publisher** are service marks owned by Pyth Press LLC, a New York limited liability company.

This book was printed in the United States of America.

To order additional copies of this book, contact:
Xlibris Corporation
1-888-7-XLIBRIS
www.Xlibris.com
Orders@Xlibris.com

CONTENTS

Chapter One

Stuart watched his daughter Ashley through the library's bay window. She was playing in the backyard with Shogun, their golden retriever, causing the few snowflakes which were falling to swirl about in the brisk January air. But Stuart's unaided eyes could only see blurred streaks of blond, pink and a yellowish brown, the remnants of Ashley's hair, her skiing outfit and Shogun's jumps in the air, so he settled back into his chair to read. His half-glasses were tilted slightly to the right in their accustomed place on the bridge of his nose.

Stuart read *The New York Times* carefully, gleaning information about European attempts to encourage Iraq to withdraw from Kuwait and about Baker's offer to meet Saddam Hussein in Geneva, but Stuart remained impatient for the fighting to begin. The necessity of using force appeared so inevitable to him that he even wondered why some of the younger partners, still in their 40s, did not see that inevitability clearly.

As always, Stuart simply assumed that each of them had had his or her mind muddled by having been a teenager during the '60s. And, as always, he was pleased that he had escaped a similar fate by just a few precious years. But Stuart Craxton also prided himself on his restraint and had privately chided the senior partner who had suggested over lunch that the United States just "nuke 'em all".

When he had finished the paper, Stuart folded it carefully and walked over to the kitchen. The only indications that the paper had been touched were two penciled-in stars over Russell Baker's essay on pushups being required of reporters in the Gulf, Stuart's usual way of letting his wife Catherine know that she might enjoy an article.

As he set the paper down on the counter, Stuart noticed an open bottle of white wine. He returned to the library with a glass of that wine, picked up a recent spy novel and resumed reading on page 73.

Several minutes later a stifled scream from Catherine's bedroom caused Stuart to jump, losing his place.

Hysterical, he thought momentarily as he leaned over the edge of the chair, trying futilely to reach his favorite bookmark without getting up.

But then a second scream followed, a crescendo of intense maternal pain that invaded every nerve of Stuart's bent body.

It was Saturday afternoon, January 5, 1991. Violence had visited Stuart E. Craxton III's family for the first time in 70 years.

Chapter Two

Takahiro Nishizaki raced furiously through his elegant, small home on the outskirts of Kyoto, searching for something he believed he could never lose. He clutched a piece of paper tightly, crushing it in his anger, but smoothing it out every few minutes to stare at it, to attempt to destroy its reality by force of will.

He threw open a window in his son's small bedroom and searched through the garden for the tenth time with his eyes. The quick movements of several branches of a large bush brought a surge of hope, but the brisk January breeze that was their cause soon reached Takahiro, increasing the pressure in his temples.

"Kaoru!" he silently screamed in despair before falling back on his son's bed, quietly sobbing his only child's name over and over again.

When the pressures in his head finally subsided, Takahiro smoothed out the crumpled paper carefully once again and set it in front of him. He stared for a long time at the rip in the corner he had caused when he had grabbed the paper too hastily from the spokes of the deserted bicycle.

When he finally looked up he saw the framed picture of Michiko which Kaoru kept near his bed, but he was still unwilling to comprehend the obvious. Several more minutes passed before his unwillingness began to dissolve. Takahiro had successfully avoided facing reality for so long that he had begun to imagine he would never have to.

"Michiko, I beg your forgiveness," he whispered to his dead wife, and then left for his office to make the necessary arrangements to fulfill the note's detailed instructions.

Chapter Three

Stuart Craxton stood over Shogun's lifeless form, still out of breath from his quick but fruitless search of the neighborhood. He held Catherine back, to prevent her from touching anything, as they stared at the small pool of blood forming beneath the golden retriever's head. A few drops of blood shone near his ear in the late afternoon light.

Catherine was the first to notice the rolled-up note tied to Shogun's collar, but when she grabbed for it Stuart continued to hold her back. She could not speak. She just pointed in fear. He saw the note immediately.

Stuart took a clean white handkerchief out of his pocket, covered his hand with it, and tried to remove the note, but it was tied to Shogun's collar too tightly. Without being asked, Catherine ran inside to get a scissors. She returned with a small nail clippers and gave it to Stuart.

When he snipped the string, the note slipped out of his handkerchiefed grasp. One edge dipped into Shogun's blood before he grasped it again. Stuart then carried the note carefully back to the kitchen, as if it were a bomb that might explode if handled recklessly.

Stuart spread the note, one edge tinged red, on top of the newspaper sitting on the kitchen counter. He unconsciously dropped his handkerchief as they read the untouched note:

> I was in your neighborhood and needed a playmate. One million dollars wired to account 230-17647865 in Zurich within 36 hours and *absolutely* no contact with the police will ensure her safe return. You can trust me.

> I will trust you. Call 337-9690 immediately to accept this outstanding offer.

Catherine began to cry. She sat down at the kitchen table and buried her face in her arms, crying without reserve or shame. "If only we were poor," escaped her lips more than once.

Stuart was relieved she was crying, and not screaming, as he picked up the phone. He had already pressed 337-96 before Catherine looked up and screamed.

"What do you think you're doing?" she yelled.

"Accepting," Stuart said calmly, but was prevented from doing so by Catherine's quick rush to the phone. She had terminated the call before he could shield the phone from her assault.

"I thought you were calling 911," she said coldly, "until I realized—"

The rest of her sentence hung in the air as a silent reproach.

"We can't call the police, Cath. Didn't you read the note?" Stuart was excited, but his acceptance seemed so obvious a course of action that he had not imagined his wife would think otherwise, and he was slow to comprehend that she did.

"Were you just going to accept without even discussing it with me?" she asked.

"We have no choice."

"But we do. We can call the police and have them find out where this phone, 337 whatever, is located, and then—"

"And if Ashley is with her? Then what?"

"Then—her?"

"Whoever! What you don't seem to understand, Cath, is that this lunatic must know we can get him the funds. Must know. Why else would he use 36 hours, and not 48, or something more reasonable for a weekend?"

"What?"

"36 hours from the time this note was left is about 4:15 Monday morning, but that's already 10:15 in Zurich. The banks will be open. The wire can be made in time. And he must know I can make it."

"Are you telling me we have a million dollars sitting around just waiting for this to happen! And that someone else knows that and I don't!"

"No. Of course not, Cath," Stuart said after a moment. He tried to be reassuring, but his pause had been slightly too long to succeed. "But you are forgetting Mohadi Sukemi. We are always transferring money in and out of his Swiss bank accounts. Whoever planned this must know that."

Stuart thought a moment longer. "Maybe it's that legal assistant I had fired last year," he said, but he was actually thinking of his discovery last summer that a woman in night steno was certifiably crazy. She had been the substitute for his regular secretary, Christine Lava, while Christine was on her annual Wilderness Club vacation.

The moment Stuart had finished reading the note he had remembered what's-her-name, quite a crazy name which he couldn't recall. He was sure she was responsible for this outrage. She knew his Scarsdale address, had had access to all his personal information, and had even worked on a Swiss wire transfer for his client Mohadi Sukemi. And that one word, "outstanding", had convinced him that he was dealing with a lunatic.

But he hesitated to tell Catherine. He didn't want her to know that a crazy woman had kidnapped Ashley. It was better for her to think it was simply someone after money. That could be dealt with more easily.

"Why did you have him fired?" Catherine asked, seeking clues as to why this particular form of revenge had been sought by a former legal assistant.

"Total incompetence," Stuart said quickly. "But that's irrelevant now. We can solve this problem with money. We have the money. And we are going to solve it that way. We can think about pursuing the jerk later, after Ashley has been returned."

"And if he doesn't return her?"

"He will. He will. He'll have a million dollars, won't he? What more could he want?"

"But the police—"

"Ashley's not the police's daughter. She's mine."

"But—"

"Monday afternoon will be soon enough to tell the police if the money does not succeed. Anyway, Grandpa trusted the police, and look where it got him. I'm not willing to take that chance with Ashley."

Catherine gave up. She unconsciously folded her hands in her lap and squeezed them tightly together. She had seen Stuart like this many times before. He made decisions quickly and stuck to them. And most often he was right.

In any case, his reference to Grandpa had made it perfectly clear that he would not be shaken from his decision, that it had become a matter of principle and family tradition.

On a cold November night in 1920, Stuart's grandfather had relied on the police. The textile factory Stuart Emerson Craxton had owned in Massachusetts was being unionized against his will and he had attended a workers' meeting to plead his cause. Mr. Craxton had been a relatively generous employer and was confident that he could sway the group. But he had also accepted a police escort due to the threat of violence which had been made by one of the union organizers. As Mr. Craxton had stepped onto the platform to speak, a small bomb had exploded.

Several days later, when his oldest son, Stuart E. Craxton, Jr., investigated the incident, he discovered that only his father had been affected by the blast. No one else had been close enough to the platform, not even his father's police escort, to have been even slightly hurt. But Stuart Emerson Craxton, then 47 years old, had been killed instantly by the blast.

Stuart Junior, then 22 years old, had quickly decided to sell the factory, had accepted an all-cash offer for 85 percent of its value, and had left Massachusetts with his mother, a younger brother and two younger sisters without looking back or ever returning.

Stuart Junior was not indecisive. He had never once regretted that he had not gotten in on the boom of the '20s, and was pleased that the Depression had proved him right. When the crash came in 1929, Stuart E. Craxton, Jr. was already a rising young corporate lawyer at Tilden & Hayes in New York. And in 1938, the same year his wife Anne gave birth to their only child, Stuart E. Craxton III, Stuart Junior was appointed Managing Partner of the white shoe firm.

Over the years Stuart Junior had expanded his hatred of unions until it included all Democrats. He had never once voted for Roosevelt, even during the war, and then stopped voting completely when Truman upset Dewey in 1948.

And in 1963, long before such retirement at age 65 would have been mandatory under the firm's partnership agreement, Stuart Junior had retired as Managing Partner of Tilden & Hayes so that his son could join the firm upon graduation from law school.

Stuart Junior had never regretted his relatively early retirement either. He had taken up golf, conquered the game and continued to play to a four handicap until his death of a heart attack, on a Florida course, on March 15, 1974.

His name, career choice and hatred of Massachusetts, unions and Democrats were among the legacies Stuart Craxton's father had passed on to him. But even more obvious to Catherine was his decisiveness. Twenty-three years of marriage to Stuart had made that abundantly clear.

Stuart hesitated a moment, choosing carefully what to reveal, and then explained his plan to Catherine.

"I will call Sukemi tomorrow—"

"Tomorrow?" Catherine interrupted.

"It is a dead certainty he will agree. There is no advantage to disturbing him in the middle of the night in Jakarta."

"Oh."

"Cath, listen, I'm certain we can transfer one million dollars out of one of his accounts as soon as the Zurich banks open on Monday. Then I'll sell a few of our investments over the next few weeks and pay him back. It will not be difficult."

Catherine was aware that between their two inheritances, and savings from Stuart's annual income, they had over $5 million invested, but she was still astounded at the ease with which her husband spoke about huge sums of money. Her own father had also been rich, but he had never been at ease with money. The difference, though, was not based on character so much as on habit. Multimillion dollar transfers had been part of Stuart's job for 28 years.

"It's that simple?" Catherine asked.

"That simple," Stuart said, and tried to smile reassuringly. This time he was more successful.

"All right. Go ahead," she agreed, realizing that argument was futile with Stuart once he had reached this level of detail in one of his plans.

Stuart picked up the phone and pressed 337-9690. The phone rang 12 times before someone picked it up and waited in silence for Stuart to speak.

"I accept," Stuart said as firmly as he could. There was another moment of silence and then the line went dead.

Chapter Four

I have no character, Takahiro Nishizaki thought as he drove to his Kyoto office. His father would be ashamed of him, he knew that. He also knew that there was no reason to tell his father, and he never would, but he would feel the shame every time he visited him in the hospital, feel the disgrace he had brought on his family, and his father would somehow know this.

But he would never tell him. Never explain. Because that would break his father's ailing heart, and one father's broken heart was enough.

Takahiro did not need an explanation for why the yakuza, those gangsters, had never bothered his father. His father was unapproachable in that way. He would have spat in their faces and they knew this. And they also knew that Takahiro would not have dared to ignore them. After many smaller demands, each of which Takahiro had protested but complied with, they had now made his complete servitude clear by kidnapping Kaoru.

Takahiro thought of Kaoru again, hoping that he was old enough to behave courageously. He was mature for a boy of 12, having become more serious after his mother died in June of 1989. He was a bright boy, too, both in his studies and when playing with other children, and Takahiro had reason to hope that Kaoru would eventually cover his personal shame with reflected glory.

Takahiro also had reason to hope that his son would be released unharmed by the yakuza if the 20 million yen ransom price was paid promptly. But Takahiro knew that the yakuza would continue to demand part of Nishizaki International's profits for the rest of his life. And they would always know exactly how much he could give and that he would always give it. It was infuriatingly inescapable.

The loss of the money he could bear. The loss of character he found very difficult. But the loss of Kaoru was impossible for him to imagine. And somehow they knew that too.

Takahiro's grandfather had passed his stubbornness down to Takahiro's father, but Takahiro felt that he had not inherited any of it. His grandfather had been thoroughly disgraced late in 1937, having been ejected from the civil service, but this was a point of family pride, not shame.

His grandfather had worked in the agricultural ministry, somewhere near the top of the hierarchy. The activities of the Japanese military in China were not his business. But, during an executive conference on agricultural trade policy in Tokyo in late December, his grandfather had stood up and publicly expressed his shame over the brutal use of force in Nanking.

The other ministers had all turned away, or hung their heads, and had refused to talk again until Takahiro's grandfather had left the room. He had never returned to his job. Although that had meant poverty for them until well after the war, Takahiro's father was always very proud of this incident.

"If only you could grow up to be such a man!" Takahiro's father had often said to him when he was a boy. And when telling the same story to Kaoru about his great-grandfather, Takahiro had always used the same words. But he knew now that he himself would never be such a man. Never.

Takahiro was prepared for this crisis, but not in the way his ancestor had been prepared. At the suggestion of a business acquaintance, he had purchased gold bars and an office safe after his yakuza troubles had begun. And now he was prepared to meet the ransom demand, to deliver 20 million yen in gold bars to five different locations within the same hour.

The yakuza's methods had thoroughly intimidated Takahiro Nishizaki, just as they had intimidated thousands of other businessmen. He was now fully prepared to make annual contributions to the river of gold which surges through Japan, a river which neither creates nor nourishes, but simply influences the outcome of important decisions by virtue of whose private vaults the gold currently inhabits.

Chapter Five

Stuart Craxton sat down on a chair near the kitchen counter, exhausted. He touched the newspaper on which the kidnapper's note rested, but he ignored the note. Unconsciously he began to read those parts of the articles which the note did not cover, only vaguely aware that he was avoiding Catherine's gaze. The day had started so normally that Stuart found it hard to grasp that an enormous chasm had just been jaggedly cut between his past and his future.

He had gone to work as usual for a few hours in the morning, driving his Acura sedan into Manhattan as was his Saturday habit, and then had returned home with the same mixed feelings of pride and contempt he often felt on Saturdays. Pride in himself, contempt for others.

Only two other partners had been in the office that morning. Associates had been there by the dozen, but their relaxed weekend dress code had become far too relaxed, in Stuart's opinion.

The traditions at Tilden & Hayes, one of the oldest New York law firms, had recently taken a beating. More like a one-two punch, Stuart had decided. First had come the extravagantly profitable '80s, followed by the current sluggish uncertainty. Both had had a profound effect on the principled practice of law, as many of the younger partners at Tilden & Hayes had developed a taste for extravagance not easily set aside.

Stuart detested the vanity of those who maintained a Fifth Avenue apartment, a Dutchess County weekend estate and a South Carolina oceanfront condominium. He thought such conspicuous consumption was undignified. They were not investment bankers, he was fond of saying to those partners whenever he had the opportunity.

Stuart could not imagine why owning so much real estate, plus two or three expensive European cars, was so desirable to these younger men. He felt certain that the two women partners, Carolyn and Lois, were not so foolish, but he had no real idea what their possessions were like.

His own five-bedroom Tudor home satisfied every need Stuart had in a residence. He could have afforded more, of course, but his home was right for his family. Right for the firm image.

But in the late Saturday afternoon light, his Scarsdale home looked quite different to Stuart. It had failed to protect his family.

The peacefulness of Catherine's Saturday routine had also been shattered. For the last five years, from the time Ashley had turned three, Catherine had cleaned the house on Saturday mornings while Stuart was in Manhattan. He had vetoed her decision to let the cleaning lady go when she had first proposed it. But he had acquiesced six months later when, after a traffic jam had spoiled his desire to go to the office, he had returned home to find Catherine listening to the Beatles full blast over the roar of the vacuum. It was only then that he discovered she had ignored his veto, having assumed he would never know the difference.

Catherine enjoyed the control she had acquired by that dismissal, and had eventually also taken over all the other tasks, including the care of their garden, which she had previously delegated to hired help. Her two sons no longer needed nor wanted any more mothering, and Ashley was easy to care for.

Although Stuart was well aware that Catherine often spent Saturday afternoons alone in her bedroom listening to classical music while she read, he still had no idea that she was only four credits shy of completing her M.A. in Art History at New York University. Catherine had been secretly planning to get a job in a museum once Ashley was a little older ever since Ashley's first day of kindergarten. Now her fear was that Ashley would never get a little older.

Catherine felt frustrated that the control over Ashley's fate had just slipped out of her hands, but she knew that her ceding of control during crises was unavoidable. After two years of uncertainty early in their marriage, she had realized that she would never have joint control with Stuart over anything. So she had made their relationship a pleasant one by dividing up their lives into areas he controlled and areas he didn't.

But she was not willing to be kept in the dark about the details of Ashley's fate. So she watched Stuart patiently, waiting for him to explain, hesitating to interrupt his thoughts. He would tell her. He always did eventually. But she was alarmed as she watched Stuart's exhaustion set in, draining his face of color.

"Cath, Cath, what have I done?" he finally sighed.

"We can still call the police," Catherine said quietly.

"No, I don't mean that. I think—I mean—"

Stuart lapsed into silence again.

Catherine waited a while longer. "What did they say?" she finally asked. "Was it a man or a woman? When will we see Ashley?"

Stuart turned to her and whispered, "they didn't say a thing. Not a thing. But they heard me. I know it."

"So what do we do now?"

"All we can do is wait," Stuart insisted.

"It's awful not knowing."

"It certainly is. But I do know one thing for sure, Cath. And that is that one million dollars will be in that Swiss bank account first thing Monday morning, even if I have to fly to Switzerland to make it happen."

"Will that be necessary?"

"No. It wouldn't make any difference."

"Then stay here with me."

"I will, Cath. I'm not going anywhere."

Stuart stared at his feet. He could not escape the idea that he was responsible. He kept trying to remember something he might have said to what's-her-name to infuriate her. Or maybe Ray Callari, the Personnel Manager, had let it slip when he had fired her that Stuart was the one who had demanded it. But that was unlikely. Callari knew his job. He would not have made that mistake.

While Catherine waited for an explanation, she walked to the window and stared out at the too empty lawn. "What are we going to do about Shogun?" she finally asked to end the silence.

"Well, we can't just let him lie there, can we? Shouldn't we call the vet?"

"And how will we explain his death?" Catherine was surprised to discover that she was prepared to lie if necessary. She was also surprised that she had not yet thought about Shogun or his quick but violent death.

"He wasn't old enough to die," she added quietly.

"The vet will probably think I shot him," Stuart said, ignoring her comment on Shogun's age.

"Why should he think that?"

"Who else could have done it? One of Tim's crazy friends?"

"They aren't that crazy."

"You're right. They're probably not *that* crazy. But what are we going to do? Bury him in our backyard and not tell anyone?"

"Well we do have to tell Stu and Tim. And we have to tell them right away. About Ashley."

Stuart was not pleased, but he knew he had no choice. His sons had a right to know about their sister.

"OK, Cath. I'll call Stu and you talk to Tim when he gets home. Do you know when he's expected?"

"No, I don't," Catherine said apprehensively.

"Why isn't that kid more responsible?" Stuart nearly shouted. "It's just incomprehensible to me. And what's taking your son so damn long to decide wh—"

"Our son! *Our* son, Stuart! But let's not fight about Tim now. We haven't insisted that he tell us his schedule, have we? I'm sure he'll be home for dinner."

"So am I. He's happy enough to eat here but—"

"Stuart!" Catherine demanded, silencing his criticism. Tim fell completely within her area of control.

Stuart did not say another word. He walked out of the kitchen slowly, deliberately getting himself back under control.

Catherine shared Stuart's concern about Tim, but she felt very differently about their second son. She did not mind the strange black clothes, with so much dangling metal, so many zippers and skeleton heads, or even the wild haircuts and pink streaks in his hair. What bothered Catherine was that when she looked at pictures of herself at 19, in beads and blue jeans, she could see the same pain in her eyes that she now saw in Tim's. And she didn't want Tim to hate the world forever, as she had been so afraid she would in 1964.

But Catherine also knew that, to Stuart, Tim was "incomprehensible". Catherine doubted whether Stuart had ever felt such pain as a teenager, but even if he had, she assumed that by now he had totally forgotten the sickening feeling brought on by the sudden awareness of the corruption and lies of adult life.

As Catherine sat at the kitchen table she slowly realized that she had been thinking about how Ashley's kidnapping was only going to make Tim's situation worse. She immediately felt guilty that she had been thinking of Ashley's trauma in terms of its effect on Tim, rather than on Ashley.

Ashley the Accident, she thought affectionately, remembering Stuart's secret nickname for their daughter. And then she remembered Stuart's comforting her after the difficult birth, telling her over and over again that although Ashley had been an accident, she was definitely not a mistake. Catherine began to cry again, softly this time.

Minutes passed before she felt a strong hand on her shoulder. "It'll be all right, Cath. You'll see."

Catherine looked over her shoulder at Stuart. He had a roll of dark green trash bags in his hand.

"Want some help?" she asked.

"Yes I would."

The only difficult part was dragging Shogun's body onto one of the trash bags. Neither felt comfortable touching him, but together they managed. Just in case a neighbor might be looking, Stuart covered Shogun with another bag. Then they dragged his body behind the garage, next to the wood pile. Stuart set several heavy pieces of the firewood on the edges of the top trash bag so that it would not blow away.

"Shogun'll be fine right here until Monday," Stuart said. "We'll decide what to do with him then—when we know."

He put his arms around Catherine's shoulders. They walked back to the house together without talking.

Stuart had difficulty reaching their first son, Stu, at his New Haven apartment. Stu had returned to Yale on January 3rd to get a head start on his last semester. After an hour and half of trying to get through, Stu finally answered.

"Son, it's Dad," Stuart started, and then had no idea how he was going to break the news, so he said, "we're going to have to get you an answering machine. I've been trying to get through for hours."

"I was in the library," Stu said blandly. He was not about to feel guilty about not being in his apartment on a Saturday evening. "What d'ya need?"

"I have some bad news. It's about Ashley."

"Well for God's sakes what happened? Has she been hurt?" Stu was immediately excited.

"No. Well, we really don't know. She's—missing."

"Missing? What do you mean missing?"

"We can't find her and we think that maybe, just maybe, she's been kidnapped."

"What?"

"Kidnapped, son. That's what we think. We think she's been kidnapped."

"How?"

"From out of the backyard. She was playing with Shogun. And now Shogun is dead."

"Tell me what's happening Dad! Stop being so damn vague!"

"We don't know much. We just know Ashley is missing. Shogun was lying in the backyard dead. And there was a note."

"Well what the hell did the note say?"

"They want money. On Monday. And I'll get it to them. I don't want you to worry about this—"

"Dad, Dad, cut the crap. Where's Ashley?"

"I don't know. I've told you that. We have no idea. She disappeared from our backyard about 4:15 this afternoon. And Shogun was left lying there. Dead."

"And what did the note say? Read me the note, Dad." Stu had learned over the years that he never got his way with his father unless he was rude and demanding.

"It just asks for money. Says she'll be safely returned if we send the money."

"Read me the note, Dad."

Against his better judgment Stuart read the ransom note to his son. When he had finished Stu was even more excited.

"She's been kidnapped by a lunatic. Can't you see that? Are there any clues? Any idea where she is?"

"No. None."

"What did the police say? Have they got any ideas? Did they find out where that phone number is?"

"You heard the demand. No police."

"You haven't called the police?" Stu couldn't believe that was possible.

"No. We haven't. And we're not going to unless Ashley hasn't been returned by Monday afternoon."

"You're just going to pay a million dollars—"

"I'd do the same for you, Stu—"

"That's not what I meant and you know it. I just want to know why you'd trust an obvious lunatic for more than one second."

"Because I think I know who kidnapped Ashley. That's why."

"Who?"

"Someone I fired."

"Well that's just—"

"Stu," Stuart said firmly, taking back control of the conversation, "that doesn't matter anymore. All that matters is that we get Ashley back safely. After that we'll call in the police and go looking for the jerk. But until then, until Ashley is back home, I don't want the police involved. Remember what happened to your great-grandpa—"

"That was 70 years ago! And this is a kidnapping! Of an eight-year-old girl! What else are the police going to do except help?"

"They might mean well—"

"Damn it, Dad. Ashley is my sister, and there's a lunatic somewhere out there with her. I want him found. Now."

"It's not that easy."

Stu was very angry, both with his father and with the senselessness of the whole situation. Why his sister? And what was this obsession his father had with great-grandpa's death? He couldn't understand either. But he did understand that when his father had made a decision, there was no way to move him. Stu was just the same way.

"So," Stu said after letting his anger subside a little, "what do you want me to do?"

"Nothing. We'll know Monday by noon whether the money worked. There's nothing anyone can do until then except wait."

"Do you want me to come home?"

"What do you think?"

"I think if we all wait together none of us will survive."

"That's not true."

"I exaggerated, you're right. So how does Tim feel about all this?"

"I haven't talked to him yet. Your mother is doing that right now. He only came home about 15 minutes ago."

"Then have Tim call me, OK? He'll let you know if I'm coming home."

"OK."

"Good luck," Stu said and hung up the phone.

Stuart was angry with himself for letting Stu talk to him that way. Stu was the only person who ever got away with it. But he was a bright, decisive boy. His rudeness would be smoothed out soon enough, Stuart thought. He did not realize that Stu was only rude with him.

Stuart shifted in his chair, uneasy about his conversation with Stu, and then noticed the spy novel lying open on the floor where he had dropped it two hours earlier. He stood up, picked up the bookmark and placed it inside the book before setting the book back on his desk. Then he walked slowly up the stairs to Tim's bedroom.

He paused and listened outside the door. As an undercurrent to the loud sounds of an old rock song he could hear Catherine talking to Tim in an intimate tone. He imagined her sitting cross-legged on Tim's bed, and Tim sitting on the floor, like a much younger child, but the talk was not childish. It was about pain. Then he heard Catherine start to cry as a new song began. Once he recognized the song, he decided to come back later.

Stuart's imagination was not far off. Catherine was sitting cross-legged on Tim's bed, but Tim was sitting on the other end of the bed, not on the floor. And the song that Stuart wanted to avoid, the one that always made Catherine cry, played on her emotions with reinforced power. The words, "what if you knew her and found her dead on the ground?", that had always hit her hard, hit her even harder. Catherine was very worried that that was how she would find Ashley.

In spite of her tears, Catherine was trying to explain to Tim once more that, although she had been 25 years old and already a mother when *Ohio*, the song about the Kent State protest deaths, had been released, she had always felt it expressed best the anguish she had felt at 19 when she realized how many lies she had been told as a child. And, though Tim never quite understood why, President Kennedy's death was always part of his mother's explanation.

Catherine also tried to explain that she had done everything she could not to lie to Tim. So it made her very upset to see the same sadness in him that she had felt.

"I am my mother's son, not my father's," Tim had told her many times, trying to let her know he was attempting to understand. But today he was struck by her statement that nothing as bad as Ashley's kidnapping had ever actually happened to her before. She had been afraid of what she had read about, and seen on TV, but she had not experienced it. Not personally. Her parents had both died peacefully in their 70s, her two brothers and their families were healthy and her own children—"well, that's obvious," she had said.

Tim found it incomprehensible that his mother had escaped so much real suffering. When Tim was 15 his friend Andy had been killed in a car accident. Steve, another friend, had been the driver and had been drunk. Steve was still devastated.

And when Tim was 17 he had been partying with a group of his friends down in the East Village on Halloween when they had been attacked by a gang with knives. Tim had helped carry his girlfriend, Sandy Blair, to the hospital, where she had needed 15 stitches to close an ugly gash on her right breast. He had burned his bloodied clothes afterward.

Six months later, on a Monday morning, Tim's senior classmates at Scarsdale High had each found a photocopied poem in his or her locker. The poem was called *Sandy's Life*:

I peeked early under the tree,
And took into my own hands,
What Santa had waiting there for me.

Sandy had committed suicide early in the morning, the day before, all alone on an East Village street. The knife she had used and five copies of her poem were found in her coat pocket. She had not left a copy at her parents' house.

And then, because the Blairs' parish priest would not say the Mass, Sandy had not even had a funeral. Since there was no doubt that Sandy had committed suicide, her parents had given up right away.

Feeling his mother's emotional pain reminded Tim of Sandy, but it also reminded him of how strange it felt to be less naive than his own mother. He felt more strongly than ever the need to protect her from the harshness of life.

Tim had attempted to fulfill that need by neither telling her about the Halloween fight nor talking about Sandy's death. And he had not told his father in order to avoid hearing the word "incomprehensible". So Stuart often blamed Tim's moodiness, and his lack of ambition, on Catherine's excessive influence. All Stuart knew was that Tim had finished high school with near straight A's a year and a half ago, and had not yet decided where, or whether, he wanted to go to college. So far all he had done was hang out with his crazy punk friends.

Stuart only waited until *Ohio* was over before he returned to Tim's bedroom door and knocked lightly. He had hesitated about intruding on their conversation, but his conviction that he did not want his son reacting to pain with immobility, as Catherine often did, overwhelmed his caution. He wanted Tim to learn to react to pain with actions. Actions which minimized the pain.

Stuart felt certain that this crisis could be of some use in waking Tim out of his lethargy. And even if Tim didn't listen to him, he just might listen to Stu. Although that probably meant Tim would want to go to Harvard, Stuart was even willing to violate the family ban on living in Massachusetts to get Tim to go to college.

He knocked again a little louder on Tim's bedroom door and then opened it slowly. Catherine and Tim both looked up at him. Stuart sat down, uncomfortably, on the floor. Catherine turned the music off.

"I believe that Ashley will be all right, son. I really do," Stuart said quietly.

"How can you be so certain?" Tim asked sullenly.

"Because I think I know who the kidnapper is. And I think one million dollars is all he's after. I don't think he'll harm Ashley. I really don't. He might be greedy, but I don't think he's the violent type."

Stuart told Tim the same comforting lies he had told Catherine, in the same tone of voice. Without realizing it, Stuart had stopped talking that way to his older son, Stu, years ago.

"It's not just money people are after. It's not all economics," Tim lectured his father.

"That doesn't sound Marxist to me," Stuart said, not being able to help himself. He almost always got angry when talking to Tim.

"I'm not a Marxist," Tim said. "It's just that—"

"Stop it," Catherine interrupted.

"OK," Tim said, "but if we are going to use Sukemi's money to free Ashley, I want to know how he made it."

"What difference does that make?" Stuart asked, finding the question irritatingly irrelevant.

"A lot," Tim insisted. "You said at dinner once that he's got more than half a billion dollars invested in the United States, didn't you?"

"I suppose I did."

"Well, how does someone honestly make that much money? That's what I want to know. Even Madonna doesn't have that much money."

"Tim, I've never asked him. I just don't know." Stuart was trying hard to be patient.

"Well, guess, Dad. Guess!"

"It's none of my business."

"You know perfectly well that no one can make that much money legitimately."

"Sure they can. You just don't understand business. Maybe if you tried studying it—"

"Well I have studied *Who's Who*. So I know that Sukemi is president of the Indonesian Oil Refinery Company."

"And he has been the president for more than 20 years. People make a lot of money in oil."

"Especially if they own the company."

"That's right."

"But Dad, Sukemi's president of a government-owned company. There aren't any private owners. None."

"Then maybe he inherited his wealth. He probably had to be

wealthy to get that position in the first place."

"Do you believe that?"

"I really haven't thought about it," Stuart said defensively.

"That's even worse. Would you have thought about it if Ferdinand Marcos had asked you to oversee a billion dollars of his investments?"

"I'm just a corporate lawyer. Not an investment banker."

Tim ignored Stuart's evasion.

"How about Idi Amin? What if he had asked you—"

"Son, you really don't know how Mohadi Sukemi made his fortune, do you? And I don't either. So let's just leave it at that. We're going to borrow money from him for just a week or two. And I'm sure you're not telling me you want us to risk Ashley's life simply because you don't know where Sukemi's money came from, are you? Where do you think Swiss Bank Corporation's money comes from? Heaven?"

"Don't you care? Don't you care at all?"

"Right now I only care about Ashley's safety. And I have no evidence whatsoever that Sukemi made his money other than perfectly legitimately. He's a very smart man."

"No evidence. No evidence! If we lived in this house and you were a garbageman, would that be enough evidence?"

"No, Tim. It wouldn't. Both your mother and I inherited money from our parents, just as Sukemi could have—"

"You're not listening to reality, Dad."

"This is reality," Stuart erupted angrily, "and you'd better get used to it, son."

Tim ran out of the room and down the stairs. After the front door slammed shut Catherine looked up at Stuart. His face was buried in his hands. She touched his right shoulder softly as she was leaving the room.

"Please tell Tim when he comes back that Stu wants him to call," Stuart said quietly.

"I'll do that," Catherine said, and closed Tim's bedroom door behind her.

Chapter Six

An hour before dawn on Sunday morning, January 6th, Takahiro Nishizaki stood on the front steps of his Kyoto home, looking at his watch. It was almost time to leave.

His car was waiting for him in the driveway, but Takahiro was reluctant to move. He was prepared, but he found it difficult to accept. The first step was always difficult to accept.

Takahiro looked at his watch again. He had to leave. Kaoru was out there, somewhere. And he would see him soon. That hope eased his reluctance. He walked to his car and backed it onto the street.

He drove about 400 meters down nearly deserted streets and parked across from a bus stop. He opened the trunk and took out a bright orange child's backpack and walked over to the bus stop, where he left it sitting on the bench. He walked back to his car, not turning around. As he drove away he could see, in his outside mirror, that the backpack had already disappeared.

He drove another 250 meters to a school, where he left a bright yellow child's backpack on the playground. Another 700 meters brought him to a library, where he left a large black canvas duffel bag just outside the front door.

Takahiro then drove another kilometer and parked outside the local police station. He opened the trunk and took out a new black alligator briefcase. He hid it carefully under a bush in a small park directly across the street from the station. The street lights along that edge of the park had been turned off early.

Takahiro looked at his watch again. He had enough time. He drove back toward the large park near his home as the sky began to lighten. He parked on the street and took a plastic shopping bag out of his trunk. He walked through the park to the rock garden where he had strolled with Kaoru many times. And with Michiko too. He begged her forgiveness one more time, but he knew that he did not deserve it.

Takahiro stepped onto a stone in the middle of a small brook and knelt down. He took a gold bar out of the shopping bag and placed it on the stepping stone. Then he folded the bag and slid it into his jacket pocket. He took the gold bar in his hands and stretched forward, bowing his head as he knelt on the flat stepping stone in the middle of the brook.

He did not look up when he heard someone approach. A Japanese man, about 30 years old and almost six feet tall, wearing an expensive, British-tailored pin-striped gray wool suit, and maroon Gucci loafers, stepped onto the flat stone in front of Takahiro. Takahiro could only see his shoes.

"You are scum," the man said loudly in Japanese before reaching down and taking the gold bar out of Takahiro's hands. Then he kicked Takahiro into the cold water of the shallow brook.

Takahiro never raised his eyes as he resumed kneeling in the middle of the brook. He remained there, silent and shivering, for several minutes after he had heard the man leave. Then he raised his eyes and looked around.

No one was there. He stood up and stepped out of the brook. As he tried to wipe some of the water off his pants he looked around again. He didn't see anyone, but he felt he was being watched.

He took off his soaked jacket and decided to run to his car. He was very cold. After two steps, though, he turned around again, sure that he was being watched. He saw a pair of eyes in a nearby bush and his heart nearly stopped.

"Kaoru!" he yelled triumphantly, but Kaoru didn't move from his hiding place in the bush. His eyes were fixed upon his father with an anger Takahiro had never seen before.

"What have they done? What have they done?" Takahiro cried as he ran toward Kaoru. He untied Kaoru from the trunk of the bush and then undid his gag. He seemed unharmed, as they had promised.

But Kaoru still did not move. He did not respond to Takahiro's caresses. He just stood there, immobile.

"Kaoru, say something. Say something to me," Takahiro pleaded with his son.

"I want to die," Kaoru whispered, the tremors of shame permeating his voice.

Takahiro slumped to the ground, oblivious to his cold wet clothes. He now understood the source of his own father's courage, but it was too late. For the first time in his life he would have preferred to be dead.

Chapter Seven

Later that same Sunday, just after 11:00 in the morning in Scarsdale, Stuart stood on a ladder outside his home. With a hammer, pliers and screwdriver as weapons, he was attempting to remove their Christmas lights. Three wreaths and several strings of lights already lay on the front porch. One wreath had been considerably mangled by the process.

The Craxtons, like most of their neighbors, considered January 6th the last permissible day to leave Christmas decorations up, just as the day after Thanksgiving was the first permissible day to put up such decorations.

Stuart was removing the decorations himself because Catherine and Tim had refused to help. They both thought Ashley would want to see all the decorations still up when she came home on Monday.

Stuart had convinced them of that much. Ashley would definitely be home tomorrow, he had told them, because everything was set in Switzerland for the bank transfer. Mohadi Sukemi had even refused to take any interest for the short term loan of a million dollars. Stuart told them he had not even had to explain to Sukemi why he needed the money. Sukemi trusted him that much.

That trust had impressed both of them, and Stu indirectly. After talking with Tim for the third time since yesterday evening, Stu decided he'd stay put in New Haven unless Ashley had not been returned by Monday afternoon.

Stuart Emerson Craxton III was often this persuasive. But he could not make any of them see the necessity of taking down the Christmas decorations so that the neighbors would not notice that something was amiss. No one but Stuart imagined that that one day difference would be noticed.

But it would have.

Stuart did not mind. He was not handy with tools, not at all, but that caused the work to distract him thoroughly. He carried on his small war against the decorations as if they had been responsible for Ashley's kidnapping.

Tim had decided to drop out of the decorations discussion by volunteering to bury Shogun. I have a good idea, he had told his father, and Stuart thought it best just to agree for once. He had helped Tim get Shogun's body inside one of the trash bags, after taking off the identification tag. The body was already cold and hard. To Stuart it no longer seemed related to the pet they had played with for the last four years.

Tim had pulled the old Volvo station wagon out of the garage and they had loaded the bag, a large shovel and the wheelbarrow in the back. It was the same Volvo Tim had been embarrassed to be dropped off at school by when he was 14. His friends had all been dropped off by Mercedes and BMWs. He had changed his ideas considerably since then.

Tim had told his father he'd be back in several hours, at the earliest, when he had driven away. That was two hours ago. While Stuart was struggling with the lights, Tim was digging a hole deep into one of the dunes at Jones Beach. The sand was hard, but not frozen. A strong, cold wind blew in off the Atlantic. The beach where Shogun, Ashley and Tim had often played together was deserted.

Tim fought against his memories of those days of sunburn and laughter as he slid Shogun's body out of the bag and into the grave. He covered it quickly, hating the reminder of having buried Ashley in the sand, up to her neck, so many times. Then he threw the shovel into the wheelbarrow and pushed it back to the Volvo. He revved the old engine, as a tribute to Shogun, before taking the long way home.

Catherine had spent those same two hours reading, trying to avoid fighting with Stuart over the decorations. When she finally gave up, she came out onto the porch and watched Stuart struggle with the fasteners holding the lights in place. About half of the last string of lights hung down limply as Stuart worked on the next fastener.

"Can't you just leave one string up? Just one?" Catherine begged.

"Then we might as well have left them all up. We can leave the stuff up inside, but—"

"You're so stubborn!" Catherine said in frustration, but both of them vaguely realized that the decorations were irrelevant to the tension between them. In a rare burst of intuition, Stuart was the first to grasp this consciously.

He came down off the ladder and took off his gloves, swiping them together as if they were dirty. "Let's leave it like this for now. I'll finish up later," he conceded. Catherine hugged him tightly.

"You must be cold," she said. "Let's go inside. I'll make us some tea."

As the front door was closing behind them they heard the footsteps of someone running up the sidewalk. Catherine was the first to glance out the window next to the door. She immediately thought she must be imagining the scene. Ashley had run up onto the porch right behind them. They opened the door again quickly.

"What are these lights doing hanging here like that?" Ashley asked slowly, out of breath after a three-block run.

Catherine grabbed her and lifted her up, holding her tightly while Stuart ran down the sidewalk to the street, searching vainly for evidence of Ashley's kidnappers.

After he reluctantly returned to the porch, Stuart stood still for a full minute, staring at Ashley, seeing the tears of fear in her eyes, and listening to her labored breathing, but not quite believing that she had been returned. Then he stepped forward and gently stroked her hand. He waited for his turn to hug her, but it never came.

After several more minutes of desperate hugging, Ashley was seated on her mother's lap in the living room, still held tightly in her arms. Stuart got down on one knee next to them and held Ashley's hand.

"Are you all right, dear?" Stuart asked in a tone Ashley felt treated her as if she were much younger than eight.

"I think so, Daddy," Ashley said, more shaken by her parents' reactions to her return than by her actual ordeal. "Roo said it was all a mistake."

"A mistake?"

"Yup. Roo told me to tell you that. He told me to say 'it was all a mistake, Mr. Craxton. Please forget all about it.' All about what?"

"It's a long story, Ashley," Stuart said, "I'll tell you some other time."

"OK, Daddy," Ashley said. She knew this meant she'd never know unless she could get Tim to tell her.

"Darling, did he really say 'forget all about it'?" Stuart asked. He was thoroughly baffled.

"Yes, sir. He said it was all a mistake."

"Well, young lady, you've been very brave. But before we forget all about it, I want you to tell us where you've been."

"With Roo."

"Who's Roo?" Catherine asked.

"He's this clown."

"A clown?" Stuart found this incomprehensible.

"Yup. Roo's a clown. He was very nice to me."

"The whole time you were gone?" Stuart asked.

"Yup."

"Well what did you do with all that time?"

"Mostly we played cards."

"Cards?" Catherine asked.

"Yup. First we played War, and then Hearts, but Roo's favorite was Concentration, so we played that mostly. He always won," she said, disappointed.

"Where were you?" Stuart asked.

"In a white house with a really big backyard."

"Bigger than ours?"

"Much bigger."

"Did you play in the yard?"

"Nope. Roo said it was too cold to play outdoors."

"He did huh?"

"Sure did."

"So you only played indoors?"

"Yup. Roo didn't have any other games so we just played cards."

"No TV?"

"No TV. But it was fun to play with Roo. Except that he always won at Concentration."

"Did you get any sleep with all this card playing?"

"Sure I did. Roo asked me what my bedtime was, so I told him. Well, I told him 9:30. And then right at 9:30 he made me go to bed."

"Where did you sleep?"

"Upstairs."

"Where was Roo?"

"Stuart!" Catherine said angrily, but Stuart silenced her with a cold glance. He turned to Ashley and tried hard to smile.

"Where was Roo, darling?"

"Downstairs—I think."

"What do you mean you think?"

"Well that's where he was when I woke up. He was sleeping on the couch."

"Did you see what he really looked like then?"

"What?"

"I mean, did he have his clown makeup off? Had he washed up?"

"No, Daddy, he was still a clown."

"With a big red nose?"

"With a big red nose and a white and black face. But he never made any jokes."

"Did he ever laugh?"

"Nope."

"Did you ever try to run away?"

"Nope. Roo told me, in his funny voice, to be patient. He said it was a mistake, but that I had to be patient, just like you always say. He promised he'd take me home this morning."

"Were you afraid?"

"Sure! I was mighty scared when he grabbed me."

"Tell us exactly how that happened, dear."

"Well, I was playing with Shogun in the backyard and once, when I turned around, there was Roo. First thing he did was put his hand out to shake mine and then asked me if I'd ever met a real clown before. But when I started to shake hands he grabbed me and covered my mouth with his hand."

"Where was Shogun?" Catherine asked.

"Shogun was right there and he barked and then Roo—"

"What did Roo do?"

"Roo shot him. Is Shogun better yet?"

"No, darling. Shogun is dead," Stuart said.

"But Roo said he didn't really hurt him. He just put him to sleep," Ashley said and started to cry.

"He told you that?"

"Yup. He told me Shogun would be all right, just like on TV when they catch the elephants."

"He lied to you."

"Roo wouldn't lie like that."

"Well Roo did about Shogun," Stuart said. "He was a bad man."

Ashley cried a bit more. "But he was nice to me."

"I'm very happy to hear that, darling," Catherine said.

"But he was," Ashley protested, feeling that she wasn't being believed.

"We're glad the clown was nice to you, darling, but how do you know he was a man?" Stuart asked. More than ever he thought the kidnapper must have been the lunatic, what's-her-name, from night steno.

"'Cause he's a clown."

"Not all clowns are men."

"Well Roo is. He has a deep, funny voice. At first I couldn't understand him, but then I realized he was telling me not to be scared, to stop crying. If I would stop crying, he said, we could have a little fun together, like in a circus, and then I could go home."

"No," Catherine moaned.

"Did Roo hurt you, darling?" Stuart asked. He was furious but under control.

"No, Daddy, Roo's a clown."

"Clowns can hurt people too," Stuart said.

"Not Roo. He was nice to me. Why don't you believe me?"

"We believe you, darling, it's just that—"

"We had pizza," Ashley interrupted her mother, hoping she would then be believed.

"Pizza?"

"Yup."

"Did someone bring it to the house?"

"Nope. It was a frozen one. Roo said we were too far away from the stores to get a fresh one."

"He did huh?"

"Sure did. And he made me bacon and eggs for breakfast, too."

"So where is this house full of pizza and bacon and eggs?"

"I don't know. Roo said it was a game not to know that. I had to wear a blindfold until we got there and I had to put it back on when we left. Roo let me take it off this morning when we got to White Plains—"

Catherine stood up and picked Ashley up in her arms. "Well you're home now, darling," she interrupted. "Let's go see what kind of food *we* have for you."

"But I'm not hungry," Ashley protested, squirming in her mother's arms. She felt she was too big to be carried, but Catherine held on tight.

"Are you sure Roo didn't hurt you?" Stuart asked as Catherine carried Ashley away.

"I told you, Daddy, he was a nice clown."

"Nice clowns don't kill dogs," Stuart said bluntly.

"That must have been a mistake. Roo said the whole thing was a mistake."

"Well did Roo ever—" Stuart started to ask, but Catherine's

angry glance cut him off. She walked out of the living room carrying Ashley as if she were a baby.

Stuart knew Catherine had good reason to be angry with him, but he couldn't help himself. He had to know. And now he was thoroughly confused.

A few hours later, while Ashley and Tim were watching a football game together in the basement gameroom, Stuart asked Catherine to join him in the library. When the door was shut he spoke very firmly.

"I want a doctor to examine Ashley tomorrow. I want to find out why this clown kidnapped her."

"No," Catherine said quietly, but no less firmly.

"What's wrong with you? Can't you see your approach has failed us. Miserably."

"I don't want Ashley to be afraid of everyone. I don't want her jumping whenever someone unfamiliar comes by. I don't—"

"We both know what you don't want. And now, thanks to you, she drives off happily with a clown. And still thinks he's nice."

"I don't believe he abused her. And what's more important, Ashley doesn't either."

"She could be just blocking it out."

"Well there's no indication—"

"How would you know?"

"I made her hot soup and had her drink lots of water. Then I gave her a long bubble bath. She had to pee while I was there and she did not seem to be sore. There are absolutely no indications Ashley has done anything but play cards with a clown and eat pizza. And I don't want a bunch of doctors and therapists changing that for her."

"If she shows any sign—"

"I'll keep my eyes wide open. If her behavior changes or she starts talking about it differently, I'll agree. But otherwise absolutely not. I am not going to help create a trauma that I've been trying to avoid for eight years. And as far as I can see, there is no reason to believe she's been abused. This Roo character must have been awfully nice to her to get her to believe Shogun's death was a mistake."

"Then what the hell was that all about?"

"That's what I want to know, dear. Some day maybe you'll tell me."

"What?"

Catherine walked over to Stuart and held his hand.

"Stuart, I feel like I don't know something important. And you do. But Ashley is back and that's all I care about right now. Still, I'd appreciate it if you told me everything. Some day. And the sooner the better."

"But Cath!" Stuart protested.

Catherine walked out of the library without responding. She had regained control of Ashley's fate. And she had no intention of letting it slip away from her again.

Chapter Eight

At 7:58 Monday morning Stuart walked down the Scarsdale station platform and stopped at the spot where the first door of the first car of the 8:02 Express to Grand Central would open. Catherine had asked him to stay at home an extra day, but Stuart was too eager to investigate the few leads he had. And he was expecting a call at 11:00 from Mohadi Sukemi which he couldn't miss.

He had not been able to tell Catherine that Mohadi Sukemi had been traveling since last Wednesday on his way from Jakarta to Zurich, with stops in Bahrain, Jeddah and Cairo to discuss oil strategies in light of the imminent Gulf War. Catherine assumed that Stuart had spoken with Sukemi early Sunday morning, since that is what he had told her. But it was not yet time to tell Catherine the truth.

Stuart was impatient for that time to come, both because he had trouble keeping track of his white lies and because he wasn't completely successful at telling them. But he felt the surprise would be worth it.

Catherine felt vaguely uneasy still, both about Ashley and about Stuart. She did not yet want to let Ashley out of her sight. So Stuart had suggested that Catherine and Ashley visit Catherine's brother in Connecticut for two or three days so that they could both settle down before returning to their routines. They were all packed and set to leave directly from the Scarsdale train station when they dropped Stuart off.

A casual observer would have seen just another middle-aged couple kissing goodbye, with a blond child in the back seat, scrambling out and into the front while her parents kissed. The child was perhaps a little young to be his, but probably too old to be her granddaughter. She must be his second wife, that observer might have thought to explain the apparent discrepancies satisfactorily, because Catherine still had a reserve of beauty in her face, her long dark brown hair and her kind brown eyes which, in dim light, often made her appear younger than 40. She was in many respects a fortunate woman. And her grateful awareness of that fact enhanced her beauty.

A keen observer, however, would have noticed that Stuart's thinning gray hair and serious blue eyes contributed to the illusion that his wife was at least 15 years younger than he, when their difference was only seven years. He would also have noticed the tension in Catherine's smile, the nervous way she broke off the kiss when she heard the car door open, and the intensity with which she watched Ashley move into the front seat and put her safety belt on. He would have wondered slightly at Catherine's reaching over and unlocking and then relocking Ashley's door, and her making sure three times that Ashley's safety belt was securely fastened. And he would surely have noticed the distress in Stuart's eyes as the car pulled away and his wave was not returned, and how his slightly stooped shoulders, undoubtedly the result of decades of desk work, sagged almost imperceptibly when the car was out of sight.

But there were no keen observers at the Scarsdale train station that morning. It was January 7, 1991, the first Monday morning after the holidays, and no one was paying any attention to his fellow sufferers.

Stuart waited patiently for the train, surrounded by well-dressed businessmen and women, but he still stood out. His dark gray wool overcoat, expensive deep blue suit, red print silk tie and white silk scarf were not unusual, nor was his erect, almost military posture, other than those shoulders, remarkable in this crowd. What made Stuart stand out was his face.

Almost everyone else's face showed the wear and tear of insufficient sleep, of too much concentrated effort and of too much indulgence to forget the pain. But Stuart's serious eyes were always alert, even early on a Monday morning, and his face, though somewhat ascetic, was neither flushed nor gray. It had a healthy undertone to it, the undertone of an energetic man. And a 53-year-old energetic, alert and intelligent face stands out in a crowd, even in a crowd of successful businessmen and women, if it is early enough in the morning.

The 8:02 Express arrived seven minutes late and pulled to a stop a few yards further up the platform than normal, so Stuart was no longer first in line to go through the doors when they opened. This annoyed him slightly, but what annoyed him much more was that the young woman he had allowed to step through the doors in front of him had taken his usual seat.

The Metro North train cars which serve Scarsdale have five seats across, two on one side of the aisle and three on the other. Sitting in the middle of the three-seat side is avoided by commuters whenever possible, as one then has to rub shoulders with two strangers, not just one.

Even better would be none. That is why heaven for nearly every commuter is to get the aisle seat on the three-seat side as long as the middle seat remains vacant.

Stuart's years of commuting experience on the 8:02 Express had led to the conclusion that the fourth row aisle seat of the three-seat side of the first car provided him the ideal combination of seating comfort and a quick getaway upon arrival at Grand Central Terminal.

Originally Stuart had preferred sitting in the aisle seat of the second row because there are only two seats in the first row, allowing him to stretch his long legs out during the 35 minute ride. Ever since he had become the first Craxton to exceed six feet tall, Stuart had been proud of those long legs. But he did occasionally worry that the time was coming when the quarter-inch margin of success he had enjoyed for so many years might disappear.

If pressed, Stuart would have had to admit that he had not looked at the height measurement his doctor had written down during his annual check-up for the last three years. There had been some doubt, during his annual checkup when he was 49, about how much, if any, of that quarter-inch was still left.

But it had only taken Stuart a few months of commuting to discover that sitting on the end of the second row made him the prime target for abuse by clumsy passengers and their carry-ons. Stuart had made up his mind to try another row shortly after an umbrella's sharp point had drawn blood from his ankle the day after a swinging briefcase had hit his shin.

Having quickly discovered that the third row is the most popular with those forced, when the train is crowded, to choose a middle seat, Stuart had settled for the fourth row aisle seat. He had been sitting there for so many years now that he more or less believed he had the right to sit there.

The young woman did not know this. She smiled sweetly at him, as some women do when relics from a previous, more polite era unaccountably appear. He passed by her to the fifth row, silently fuming.

But he felt much better a few seconds later when a broad-shouldered man sat down in the middle seat of the fourth row. His good fortune in narrowly avoiding riding shoulder to shoulder with the large man induced Stuart to wonder if maybe the fifth row wasn't better after all. But his experience at Grand Central upon arrival reconfirmed his belief in the fourth row. Leaving the train took a crucial 20 seconds longer and the exit ramp was already crowded.

Stuart walked through Grand Central to 42nd Street and then two blocks further to the imposing glass entrance of the office tower at 101 Park Avenue. He took the elevator to the 43rd floor, barely registering the greeting from the night watchman who was still sitting at the reception desk. The 43rd floor receptionist who was supposed to take over at 8:30 was still getting her coffee.

Stuart breezed right through to his corner office, overlooking Park Avenue from high above 41st Street, and motioned to Christine Lava, his secretary, to follow him in.

As he took off his overcoat, he dictated her first assignments.

The tone of his voice revealed his annoyance, but since Christine knew that he always felt annoyed if he arrived after 8:45, even if only a few minutes after, she ignored his tone.

"I want Callari on the phone right away. I have a question about—say, what was the name of that night steno girl who substituted for you last summer when you took one of those ungodly long vacations?"

"I don't remember. It was a weird name, though. But Robert will remember."

"Why do we always have to ask Kim?"

"Because he always remembers?" Christine asked rhetorically.

"Yeh. OK. Ask Kim. He'll know. And tell him I want to see him in my office at 9:30 instead of 10:00. Also, remind him that we have our conference call with Sukemi at 11:00."

"He remembers. He already mentioned it to me this morning."

"Great," Stuart said, hanging up his suitcoat next to his overcoat in his office's built-in closet. He took a small piece of notepaper out of his shirt pocket and continued. "Then I want you to get Accounts Payable to wire $100, deducted from my personal account, to account number 230-17647865 in Zurich. That's all I know about it. Just test the number to see if the wire will go through. And tell me right away what they find out. Interrupt anything except the call from Sukemi."

"Got it."

"Then find out where (914) 337-9690 is located. My guess is it's a public telephone. Catherine got a call from an old friend and he left that number for her to call at 9:00 last night, but no one answered. Do you think you can get that information?"

"If it's a public phone, sure."

"Great. That's all," Stuart said and sat down at his desk. When he looked up Christine was still standing there.

"What are you waiting for, applause? Get me Callari. After you get that name from Kim."

"Mr. Craxton, you know perfectly well that administration

doesn't get started before 9:30. And Mr. Callari is never the first one in."

"You're right. So as soon as he gets in, have him call me. And don't do that again."

"Do what again, Mr. Craxton?"

"Take such an ungodly long vacation. What do you want to go tramping through the woods for anyway? Waste of time, if you ask me. Two hours of that should be enough for any sane person."

"I'll make sure Mr. Callari calls," Christine said while leaving his office, ignoring the usual nonsense from Stuart. She always got her long vacations. He couldn't work half as quickly without her and she knew it.

Christine had started working for Stuart just months after her arrival at Tilden & Hayes 12 years ago, fresh from secretarial school. She had developed a harder edge in many of her conversations as a result, but that only fooled the unobservant.

Christine used her telephone's intercom to call Robert Kim, although he was only two offices away. Stuart didn't like it if she wasn't at her desk when he wanted her.

"Robert, it's the usual, plus he wants to see you at 9:30 instead of 10:00."

"I'll have to reschedule my meeting with Jim, then. Can you let him know I'll drop by as soon as I'm done with Stuart?"

"Sure," Christine said, thinking about how often James Berner's patience was tested in this way. Because Jim had only been a partner for five years, he always had to wait if Stuart needed Robert.

The seniority system was still in full flower at Tilden & Hayes. One week's extra seniority, even after 25 years, could still make a difference as to how large a partner's corner office was.

"And Robert," Christine continued, "Stuart also wants to know if you remember the crazy name of that night steno woman who substi—"

"Bounteous Love."

"That's her. Bounty. What ever happened to her?"

"She's a floater over at Skelly Adams & Neff."

"Floating describes her perfectly," Christine said. She could hear Robert's laugh in stereo, over the phone and directly from his office. But she didn't laugh out loud. Stuart didn't like it.

"Gotta go," Christine signed off.

"Later," Robert said.

Robert Kim never regretted that one year earlier the Managing Partner of Tilden & Hayes, E. Theodore Swaine, had announced a new cost-cutting policy that required each secretary to work for at least two lawyers. But the senior partners who were used to having their own secretaries were very upset, and Stuart had had several allies in his two-month fight against the new policy.

Stuart had wavered in his opposition after Robert Kim was the other lawyer assigned to Christine, since Robert did 80 percent of his work for Stuart, and Christine already did most of that work anyway. But Stuart had only surrendered after Ted Swaine had also agreed to eliminate the exception for his own secretary.

Christine Lava actually liked working for two lawyers instead of one. As long as she was busy, and no one screamed at her, she was happy. Christine couldn't stand screamers, even for the one or two days they were in T&H's offices for a closing. Fortunately, no one at Tilden & Hayes was an habitual screamer. It was as socially unacceptable there as it was a badge of seriousness and intensity at Skelly Adams.

In any case, no one boss could ever overload Christine. She was too fast, too organized and too conscientious for that to happen. And since Stuart's and Robert's work was often the same, she now had an even better idea of what was going on, because Robert explained things. Stuart just commanded.

After terminating the intercom connection, Robert Kim sat at his desk and wondered why Stuart wanted to start their meeting a half an hour early. Maybe it was just to keep him on his toes.

Robert had assumed correctly that the 10:00 meeting had been scheduled to discuss the annual analysis of Sukemi's U.S. investments. He had had to make this assumption because Stuart rarely told him the exact subject of their meetings in advance. That was also designed to keep Robert on his toes.

After eight years of working together, it had become an unnecessary game. Robert was always prepared. But Stuart had never stopped playing and Robert had never complained. Still, although he was thoroughly prepared, Robert was nervous about this meeting. He wondered how Stuart would react to one of his conclusions.

At exactly 9:30 Robert walked two offices over, around Christine's dark mahogany triangular secretarial station, custom-built to create a dramatic entrance to Stuart's office, and through Stuart's open door. He sat down in one of the chairs in front of Stuart's desk and waited with his chart and his papers on his lap. Stuart continued to read a contract for several minutes. Then he looked up at Robert, peering over his half-glasses.

"So, how do things look this year? Nothing embarrassing to tell Mr. Sukemi, is there?"

Stuart smiled. He knew the estimates they had received for 1990 were way above average. They would be satisfactory even if the economy had been much better.

"It looks like his average return on investment should exceed 12 percent for 1990. And if he hadn't dropped $23 million into a hole called Garuda Oil, he'd be closer to 16 percent."

"And he'd be barely breaking 10 percent without the Nishizaki restaurants. It's just stunning what Sydney Brewster has done with them."

"True, but—"

Christine walked in and interrupted. "I've got Mr. Callari on the line."

Stuart picked up his phone and motioned for Robert to stay put in his chair. "Getting in earlier every year, aren't we, Ray?"

"It's a good thing no one forces me to keep your hours, Mr. Craxton. Not at my age. Besides, I don't have any friends in Jakarta."

"And you never will getting up so late."

"I can live with that," Ray Callari bantered. Ray had been the Personnel Manager for more than 35 years. Stuart's father had created the position, and had hired Ray, to relieve the Managing Partner of the burden of firing employees.

"Look, Ray, I've got a question about Bounteous Love. Remember her? That little pixie in night steno? Her nickname was Bounty, right Robert?"

Stuart mentioned Robert's name to let Ray know that Robert Kim was in his office. Stuart's simultaneous wink let Robert know that Stuart acknowledged that Robert was the source of Bounty's name, even though Ray Callari would never know that.

"Sure I remember her. She was a real Lulu."

"Crazy as a loon," Stuart agreed, "but something came up this weekend and I was wondering what happened to her after she left here."

"I hear she's at Skelly Adams & Neff," Ray said.

"Robert thinks so too. Apparently they'll take anyone there."

"Well, Bounty is a fast typist," Ray said in her defense. As far as the night staff was concerned, Ray personally went easy on character issues. But he had so often been put on the defensive by a partner's moral outrage over some uncovered indelicacy that he had almost stopped using the justifiable, but rarely soothing, explanation that "this is New York, after all."

"I'll bet over at Skelly they probably haven't even noticed she's got a screw loose," Stuart suggested.

"Could be. I've never once gotten a call asking about her. But they hire by the bushel over there."

"Bushel of nuts."

"More like apples," Ray said. "There are always a few rotten ones."

"Well, I have one more question about this rotten one, Ray. What did you tell her when you let her go?"

"The usual, Mr. Craxton. Not enough work for night steno. I mean, they always have some downtime, so—well, that's what I say to 'em."

"You didn't mention my name?"

"I'd never do that, Mr. Craxton, you know that. I'm not that old."

"That's what I thought, Ray, just had to ask. My wife got a crazy call this weekend from a woman she didn't know and the only crazy one I could think of was Bounty."

"You haven't met many women, have you Mr. Craxton?"

"I guess not, Ray. Anyway, I had to ask. But I knew what your answer would be. Thanks a lot."

"Sure. Anytime," Ray said, and paused a moment before adding, "as long as it isn't before 9:30 or after 6:00."

They all laughed as Ray hung up. The T&H lawyers all had Ray's home phone number. And used it.

"So where were we?" Stuart said, getting right back to business.

"Well, 1990 was a very good year for your client," Robert said. "Mohadi Sukemi increased his personal U.S. holdings by another $45 million, bringing his total investment to just under $597 million. About half of that is in oil, mostly in preferred stocks and high interest bonds, just over 30 percent is in real estate now that the purchase of the Houston office tower from the RTC has been finalized, and the balance is in his Chase Manhattan-managed portfolio of common stocks and bonds. That is, other than the chain of 30 Japanese restaurants he owns with Nishizaki International USA, Inc. As you know, his holdings in that chain nearly doubled last year."

"Sure they did. It's his best investment. And Sydney is predicting the return in 1990 will exceed 28 percent."

"Well, take a look at this," Robert said, nervously pushing the chart he had prepared in front of Stuart. "Sukemi now has $49 million invested in his 50 percent interest in the Nishizaki joint venture. But at the end of 1989 he only had $28 million invested, in 1988 only $12 million and in 1987 only $5 million.

"And if you look over here," Robert continued, pointing to a separate box on the chart, "it shows that the original four restaurants opened in 1987 cost $2.5 million each to buy and furnish. Now, just three years later, with very little inflation, the 12 new restaurants Sydney opened averaged $3.5 million each."

"The new ones are classier. And make even more money," Stuart said. "Besides, the eight restaurants opened in 1989 cost even more. About $4 million each."

"I wasn't going to mention that."

"Sounds like a lot to you, does it?"

"For Japanese restaurants? Yes."

"But for Korean restaurants it would make sense?"

"Even less," Robert Kim said. Unless he was very tired Robert never swallowed Stuart's bait.

"Well, Robert, you don't need to be an investment banker to know that price follows performance. Sukemi's interest in the Nishizaki restaurants is already worth millions more than he paid for them. And that's all that matters. Even a Picasso is worth $15 million only because several other fools out there are thinking about paying $16 million for it. And we're talking real cash flow here. Investors would pay a lot of money to get their hands on the $25 million a year those 30 cash cows are producing. But if someone buys Sukemi out, they'd better make sure Sydney Brewster is part of the package, because she's the one primarily responsible for milking them so well."

"But think about it, Stuart," Robert said, not giving up yet, "$100 million for 30 Japanese restaurants?"

"That's where Sydney has an edge. Top end of the market in 27 major cities, with two each in New York, Chicago and LA. Economies of scale that are hard to match. And now we're going to take the profits coming and going. Nishizaki International in Japan has agreed to sell five of its food processing plants to our U.S. joint venture for just $10 million so we can supply the restaurants ourselves."

"When will that sale take place?" Robert asked. It was the first he had heard of the latest expansion.

"Soon. Sydney said we can inspect the factories on site in Japan near the end of February."

"She never stops moving, does she?"

"Never. She's always thinking, and always thinking bigger and smarter. And you'd think, with her father, that she would never have worked a day in her life."

"I guess she inherited his workaholic gene. Senator Brewster was certainly no slouch."

"Look who's talking."

Robert smiled. That was as close as he had ever come to receiving a compliment from Stuart.

"Speaking of workaholics," Robert said a moment later, "have you heard anything yet from Sukemi about his meetings in Jeddah? The price of oil is continually being squeezed higher by the uncertainties of the Gulf situation and—"

"Not yet. But I doubt if he'll mention anything when we talk to him. He doesn't discuss strategy with me."

"Or you'd be as rich as he is?"

"Probably."

"Have you ever asked him how he does it?"

"Does what?"

"Make so much money. Judging from the little I know, he's clearly a billionaire. But he never gets mentioned in *Forbes*."

"He considers the media a nuisance, just a bunch of boys showing off who has the most toys."

"I see. So how did Mr. Sukemi collect all his secret toys?"

"I've never asked him that, Robert."

"I can understand your professional discre—"

"Maybe his father is wealthy," Stuart interrupted.

"Is his father named Suharto?"

"Well, why don't you just wait another hour and ask Mr. Sukemi that yourself."

They both laughed. Even Stuart realized he did not have to give Robert an order not to ask *that* question.

Chapter Nine

At 10:35 Stuart left his office impatiently. He wanted to talk to Christine, but she was tied up on the phone and wasn't answering his intercom beeps. He leaned over the edge of her secretarial station and stared at her. She looked away and took down the information. When she hung up, Stuart was still standing there.

"You didn't answer my beeps!"

"Special orders override standing orders," she said, quoting one of his rules for her.

"And what's that supposed to mean?"

"I was on the phone with Accounts Payable. Other than Sukemi's call, you implied that that had top priority."

"Right. Well?"

Christine found Stuart's otherwise infuriating habit of never acknowledging he was in the wrong tolerable only because he also quickly forgot about it whenever anyone else had been in the wrong, so long as his business was being taken care of efficiently.

"The wire didn't go through. The bank code 230 is the Union Bank of Switzerland's head office in Zurich, but their account numbers only have six numbers, not eight."

"Let me see that number again."

Christine showed it to him: 230-17647865. "It looked a little longer than usual to me too," she said as Stuart checked the number against his written note.

"It is too long," Stuart agreed. He had not noticed that before. Robert and Christine almost always took care of the details of Mohadi Sukemi's Swiss wire transfers.

"And I've tracked down that telephone number for—"

"How long have you been sitting on that information?"

"Approximately three minutes. Want it?"

"Of course."

"It's a public phone, just as you guessed. It's located at the Sprain Lake Golf Course. Your wife's old friend must be a fanatic to play golf in January."

"At 9:00 at night."

"No wonder no one answered."

"Right. So, that's that. He must have left the wrong number. Now I want you to get Bounteous Love on the line for me. We think she's at Skelly Adams."

"Right away, Mr. Craxton," Christine said as Stuart walked back into his office. But she relaxed for 30 seconds first before starting the process of tracking Bounty down. Stuart rarely stood over her like that, but it was always unnerving. She could tell it was going to be one of his few very bad days. They were always intense.

About five minutes later she had Bounty on the line. Floaters, those secretaries who fill in for absent or vacationing secretaries, are often hard to locate.

"Hello, Bounty," Christine said, "please hold for Mr. Craxton." Then she used her intercom to let Stuart know that Bounty was on the line waiting for him. Stuart picked up right away.

"Hello, Bounty," he said, "how's it going?"

"I can't talk right now, Mr. Craxton," Bounty said. "This phone is not secure, if you know what I mean. I'll call you back within five minutes from another phone."

"Have you still got my number?" Stuart asked nervously.

"Of course I do. But more talking now is not safe," Bounty said and hung up.

Stuart stretched back in his chair. The lunatic, he thought, how dare she intrude on my family this way. He could see her in his imagination, standing at a public phone at the deserted Westchester County golf course, waiting for his humiliating phone call.

A petite blond woman, not more than 24 years old, Bounteous Love had given Stuart nightmares the summer before when he realized she was crazy. And was working for him. He had forgotten how efficient a worker she was. Not like Christine, of course, but she was an excellent typist. And she was even somewhat organized, a skill rarely found in a substitute. A little scatter-brained, that's all he had originally thought, until one day near the end of the three weeks she had launched into an explanation of the Universe that depended on crystals and skyscrapers and waves of purification she was creating that would destroy sin. And approximately 95 percent of the human population as well. He remembered she had told him he would be safe.

Stuart called Christine in. "Bounty will call back in a few minutes and when she does I want to take the call right away. If Sukemi is already on the line, I'll take her call in Robert's office. If Sukemi calls while I'm on the line with Bounty, have Robert take the call in his office and tell him I'll join him there as soon as possible. Got that?"

"Got it." Christine didn't ask any questions. But she was astounded. Nothing had ever exceeded the priority of a call from Mohadi Sukemi before.

At 10:54 Bounty called back. When Stuart picked up the receiver, he heard her say, "the Goddess smiles upon you."

"What?" Stuart asked. He was very nervous and couldn't quite believe his ears.

"The Goddess smiles upon you, Mr. Craxton." Bounty emphasized words in a way that let you know they should be capitalized.

"Oh, *that*," Stuart said in frustration. He remembered the last conversation he had had with Bounty and wanted desperately for this one to be over. But he needed to know first.

"Well, She sure didn't this weekend," he said to humor her.

"You experienced the Turbulence too? I thought you were beyond that stage, Mr. Craxton. But it was frightful, wasn't it?"

"What?"

"I saw the work you did and it was amazing. But I thought you did it from beyond the Turbulence. Now I'm even more impressed. I just love working with you on this Clarification. It's much more fun than the last one I worked on in the Andromeda Galaxy. Those folks were really messed up out there."

Stuart tried very hard to stay calm. He thought that that was the only way he might get through to her.

"Bounty," he said in a whisper, as if he were part of a conspiracy, "do you know if any of those folks out there made a mistake this weekend?"

"Always. They're always making mistakes, Mr. Craxton."

"But I mean a special Mistake. One that affects me personally."

"They all affect each and every one of us personally. That's why the Clarification work we are doing is so important, so crucial to Human History."

"Bounty," Stuart said, nearly losing his temper, "I mean a Very Special Mistake. One that involves one of My Children. Do you know anything about it?" Stuart had unconsciously begun to capitalize words too.

"I can ask the Goddess. She will tell me."

"That's not necessary Bounty. I can ask the Goddess myself. I just want to know if you personally know about that special Mistake."

"I'm very sorry, Mr. Craxton. I was so busy with the Clarification this weekend—"

"That's all I wanted to know," Stuart said and felt relieved.

"I'm truly sorry I didn't notice, Mr. Craxton," Bounty apologized. "It's just that I was concentrating on the good work we were doing together. No mistakes for us, right? I'd say, with Mother Nature's Support, that we'll have another three levels cleared out by the end of January. But it's just like those Luciferians to try to distract you, our best worker, by attacking your Chil—"

"Bounty, it was wonderful talking to you, but—"

"I know how busy you are, Mr. Craxton. That's why it's so amazing what we get done, don't you think? A First Class Team. That's what the Goddess calls us."

"First class?"

"And that's not all. I've been working on Mr. Adams and I think he'll be joining us soon. But only if his Double doesn't take over. It's heavy going for him still. He can't keep hold of his own body for more than three hours at a time, but I think he'll be with us next Saturday afternoon."

"That's good to hear, Bounty. Now I've got a call on the other line—"

"If it's Mr. Adams let me know."

"I will. Goodbye Bounty."

"As the Goddess wishes."

Stuart hung up quickly and stared at the phone. When he had recovered from the shock of the crazy conversation, he called Christine in and told her never to accept another call from Bounty, no matter what the circumstances, and to make sure that the front desk in the lobby and each reception desk was immediately informed that Bounty should be prevented from ever entering the T&H offices again.

When Christine left, Stuart reconsidered his assumptions about Ashley's kidnapping. He no longer had any idea as to who had kidnapped Ashley or why they had done it. But when he briefly considered completely giving up his attempts to solve the mystery, an unfamiliar and very uncomfortable feeling that he was losing control seeped through the outer edges of his awareness.

Stuart responded immediately to that subtle threat by plunging back into the details of his daily life with an even fiercer self-absorption than usual.

Chapter Ten

About two minutes after Bounty had hung up, at exactly 11:00, Robert Kim joined Stuart in waiting for Mohadi Sukemi's call. They briefly discussed the points each wanted raised in the conversation and then ran out of topics.

"What time is it?" Stuart asked. Robert looked right past him, out the north windows of Stuart's office, and read the huge digital clock under the *Newsweek* sign.

"11:12," Robert said.

"You can read that?" Stuart asked.

"Sure. With my glasses."

Stuart looked over his half-glasses at the huge clock near the top of the 40-story office building. He could only see a blur.

"Well, I can't," Stuart said. "My reading glasses are of no use when something's that far away."

"Then you probably need bifocals," Robert suggested.

"Bifocals are for old men," Stuart said contemptuously.

"Not really. My father has been wearing them since he was 27."

"You must be kidding," Stuart said, mildly surprised, and then, wanting to change the subject anyway, decided on the spur of the moment to ask Robert if he had any thoughts about Ashley's strange kidnapping, in the roundabout way he had devised, but had previously decided against using.

"Did you see that kidnapping movie on TV last night?" Stuart asked Robert. "I forget the name."

"No, I didn't. Was it any good?"

"It was awful. The usual. But the basic plot was quite puzzling and I'd like to know what you think about it. A ransom note demanding one million dollars was left when the little boy was taken on a Saturday afternoon. And the note specified payment into a Citibank account within 48 hours. But the boy was returned to his family on Sunday night before the money had been paid—before the money could have been paid. And the boy was told by his kidnapper that he should just tell everyone it had been a mistake. Now, what do you think of that?"

"Was there any gratuitous sex in this movie?"

"No."

"And there were no hints that the kid had been abused?"

"Well, the ransom note did mention something about needing a playmate."

"So. There you are. The boy had been kidnapped by a homosexual, or a woman with strange age preferences, and had been abused. And the ransom was just a cover for that. Right?"

"No. The kid was fine. He had been treated well."

"So what was the purpose?"

"That's what I couldn't figure out."

"And that was it? Dumb movie."

"Real stupid," Stuart agreed, "as if a lunatic had done it."

"Then maybe it was a neighborhood prank by some teenagers."

"Maybe. But it was more than a prank. The kidnappers shot the family cat's head off."

"Did they burn a cross on the lawn too? Some suburban kids are into that."

"No. Nothing like that. It was all ridiculously boring. Except for the family, of course."

"And there was nothing else in the ransom note?"

"Well, there was the usual line about not contacting the police."

"And did the family contact the police?"

"No. They didn't."

"Could the kidnappers know that?"

"If the family was being watched—"

"And the show ended with the unexpected return of the boy?"

"That's right."

"Then I'd guess there will be a sequel."

"A sequel?"

"Sure. Or maybe it was a lead-in to a weekly series. Sounds like the start of a cat-and-mouse harassment game to me. They probably just kidnapped the kid to see if the family would go to the police. And they didn't. So now the cat has the mouse trapped."

"But why?"

"It doesn't have to make sense, Stuart, it's TV. It just has to have a happy ending."

"Well that's good to hear," Stuart said, but he was very eager to change the subject again. He hated it when Sukemi made him wait like this.

To pass the time Stuart asked Robert how his parents were doing. Robert explained that his father was considering retiring early from his engineering job at Hughes Aircraft in Los Angeles, but that all was well. Both his parents were eagerly awaiting the birth of the fifth grandchild his three younger sisters had produced.

Stuart seized the opportunity to tease Robert about when he planned on starting his own family. Robert had always wanted to answer such questions, which his own parents, and his wife Lily's parents, and all their aunts and uncles, kept asking, by pretending to break down and sob out that they just couldn't have children and to plead pitifully for everyone to stop reminding them of their misery, but he didn't believe he could pull off the lie. And it was never a satisfactory answer just to say that they didn't have that desire. Not yet anyway. Robert was only 34 and Lily wasn't even 31 yet. They had lots of time. And they lived in a small Manhattan apartment.

Instead, Robert parried the tease gracefully and then asked Stuart how Ashley had enjoyed the holidays. Stuart was explaining how she was unfortunately getting too old for the excitement previously generated by the Santa Claus myth when Christine interrupted.

"Mr. Sukemi is on line two," she said, and then closed Stuart's office door.

"It's about time," Stuart said to Robert and then pushed the button on his phone that flipped Sukemi's call onto the speaker system.

"How were the slopes today, Mr. Sukemi?" Stuart asked.

"All in all, quite respectable," Mohadi Sukemi replied in British-accented English. He had graduated with a First in English Literature from Oxford in 1964 before obtaining a doctorate in Petrochemical Engineering at the Zurich Polytechnic Institute. It was while he was a student in Zurich that he had acquired his taste for winter sports. Mohadi Sukemi was calling from St. Moritz.

"I just had to make one last run," he said. "Sorry if I'm a little late."

"We're just sitting here reviewing your 1990 estimated returns," Stuart said, politely letting Mr. Sukemi know he would be paying for their waiting time, "but before we get into that, how were the slopes in Jeddah on Saturday?"

"You've heard me say it before, Stuart, but things there have been all downhill ever since '86, when the King gave Sheik Yamani the boot. I have to admit I'm prejudiced, as I personally miss the old fart, but I also think he would have played this game against Saddam Hussein more cleverly."

"Well, our forces are in place—"

"Oh, the war doesn't bother me nearly as much as what comes after. And I don't think even Mr. Hussein knows what a bloody mess he's gotten us all into. But the fact is, he is ruining everything. And by everything I mean—well, what the hell. It's just money. So talk to me about my investments. Are we still in business?"

Stuart gave him a quick rundown of the annual estimated returns they had collected and told Mr. Sukemi that he would receive all the details by Federal Express on Wednesday in St. Moritz.

"Good, good," Mr. Sukemi said, "but you haven't mentioned that septic tank Garuda Oil—"

"It's the Japanese investments that are doing the best," Stuart said to head off Mohadi Sukemi from focusing on the one big loser.

"The joint ventures with Nishizaki International are gushing cash like Old Faithful—"

"Come, come, Stuart, I know all about your enthusiasm for Nishizaki International and things Japanese. But what I want to know is, how much did the loss come to on Garuda Oil?"

"If you will indulge me, Mr. Sukemi," Stuart said, "before we leave the Nishizaki investments I'd like your sign off on the purchase of five Japanese food factories for $10 million. Your share is $5 million. And the current cash flow is nearly $2 million. Nishizaki Japan is willing to sell all five to our joint venture so that we can supply our 30 restaurants directly. That should push the current return over 20 percent because we'll get the profits coming and going. I'll send you the details."

"Great. I'm signed off. Now let's get back to Garuda Oil."

"As you know, the news isn't pleasant. Robert's calculations show nearly a $23 million loss in 1990."

"Then that's it for J.P. and his prevarications," Mohadi Sukemi said in a polite but intense tone, clearly angry with the situation. "I found out in Cairo yesterday that the word on the street is that J.P.'s been using an astrologer to decide where to drill all those useless wells. And I am confiding in you gentlemen right here and now that I personally have absolutely no intention of throwing millions more into the North Sea without gaining control of Garuda Oil first. So tell me, how do I do it?"

"You want to buy out the Krishnanda brothers' entire 55 percent interest?" Stuart asked.

"No. I just want to get control. I have no say over that idiot J.P.'s decisions and I need it. He clearly hasn't figured out yet that his first and only successful drilling was a fluke."

"Well, the Garuda Oil Exploration Company partnership agreement does give you certain rights—"

"Look, Stuart, I need to veto J.P. whenever I want to. That's what I need."

"Unless you buy their controlling interest—"

"I'd rather they bought my 45 percent than that. I'm not too keen on laying out $85 million or more to buy them out. But even that would be better than being forced to ante up a couple million every month to support J.P.'s idiocies."

"Well you can always initiate the buy-sell process under Section 10.3. You just set a price per percentage interest and then notify the Krishnandas you'll either buy their interests at that price or sell your interests to them at the same price. 180 days later one or the other deal has to be completed."

"But they'll bleed me dry during those 180 days and I won't be able to do anything about it. I don't like that scenario because I don't trust these chaps."

Robert distracted Stuart, motioning that he wanted to speak. Stuart nodded that that would be fine.

"Mr. Sukemi, this is Robert Kim," he began. Robert had only begun to sit in on the discussions with Mohadi Sukemi two years earlier and had rarely talked to him directly.

"Good evening, Mr. Kim."

"Good morning—from New York," Robert said somewhat awkwardly, and then launched into his idea.

"There is a provision designed to give you exactly the veto powers you want. But it has a high price tag. As you may recall, when the Garuda Oil Exploration Company was formed 22 months ago to buy Texaco's North Sea rights, all three Krishnanda brothers were under a pall from the whispers about their involvement in the Bofors scandal of the Gandhi Administration."

"Quite right."

"And so you insisted on having a particularly strong remedy in case you disagreed with their management decisions. Since the Krishnandas desperately wanted to expand outside their real estate empire into the oil business, and since they needed your experience, your connections and your money, you forced them to give in, in spite of their attorneys' strenuous objections."

"Quite bluntly put."

"As you may also recall, we inserted that strong remedy into our usual 'Inability to Agree' provision. That's Section 10.7 of the partnership agreement, in case you want to review it."

"Now I remember."

"Good. The conflicting interests that needed to be solved then were that the Krishnandas wanted complete control over the operating decisions and the additional capital calls, and you needed to be able to prevent a run on your capital if their decisions proved to be unprofitable."

"Right. So what is the remedy?"

"You send them a notice invoking Section 10.7 and for 90 days no management decisions can be made without your approval. You gain a complete veto over all of J.P.'s decisions."

"R.P.'s and M.P.'s too?"

"There's no loophole for them," Robert said. "And if any of them dares to ignore your veto rights during that 90-day period, they have to pay heavily. 100 percent of any related losses would be their responsibility and 100 percent of any profits from any unauthorized act would go to you. That effectively cuts out all their incentives for ignoring your veto powers."

"I thought I remembered something about a veto. And that's exactly what I need now."

"But there is a price for exercising that right. Or you would have invoked it immediately."

"I should have."

"I doubt it," Robert said, "because if you are not able to come to an agreement within that 90-day-period, Garuda Oil must be legally dissolved and its assets liquidated within 120 days. And that could cost you dearly. The equipment owned is worth less than 20 percent of the value of the company as a going concern."

"And I suppose I can't sell the employees upon liquidation?" Mohadi Sukemi asked facetiously.

"Not here in America," Stuart said.

"Not in Indonesia any more either. It's a crying shame."

"Things just aren't the same as they were in the good old days,"

Robert added to the banter, "but one thing is still the same—a fire sale is never good for the seller."

"That is clear. But what's worse is that right now, with the price of oil soaring, Garuda Oil hasn't got a single proven well in the pipeline to sell off. All thanks to J.P.'s superstitions."

"If you feel that way about it, then you need your veto. Invoking Section 10.7 will definitely stop him in his tracks."

"And force us to liquidate Garuda Oil for about 20 cents on the dollar?"

"Perhaps, but it's unlikely—unless a buyer can't be found quickly."

"That's likely."

"Then there's quite an incentive for the Krishnanda brothers to agree with you, isn't there?"

"Quite."

"Of course," Robert added, "you could amend the partnership agreement during that 90-day-period to change the remedy. For example, the buy-sell provision Stuart mentioned could kick in at the end of the 90-day-period, instead of the forced liquidation provision. But if the Krishnandas won't agree to your demands during that 90-day-period, they might not agree to amend the remedy either. That's why there's such a big risk in invoking Section 10.7. You're going to have to decide if things have really gotten that bad."

"Right you are, Mr. Kim. I'll think about it and get back to you both."

"Then we'll wait for your decision on Garuda Oil and start the process for buying the Japanese food factories, right?" Stuart asked.

"Quite right. I'll call you when I've made up my mind on Garuda Oil. 'Til then."

After Mohadi Sukemi had hung up, Stuart stared across his desk at Robert. "How the hell did you remember all those details? And I take it for granted you wouldn't have opened your mouth if you weren't 100 percent sure you had it right."

"Oh, I was sure all right. Don't worry, Stuart. That's what's in the agreement."

"But we've—"

"I suppose I remember that provision so well," Robert interrupted mischievously, "because we had to create it, not just crib it from somewhere else. And it was rather fun making the Skelly Adams attorneys swallow something they knew was a very poisonous pill."

Robert Kim had actually just reviewed the remedy sections of the Garuda Oil partnership agreement that morning, assuming Sukemi would be angry about an investment which was losing so much money.

"I see," Stuart said, but he had his doubts. They had created hundreds of similar remedies over the years with minor variations in each of them. And although Robert had an excellent memory, it was close to impossible for anyone to keep the number of days for each period, and the rights connected with them, straight even a few months after a deal had been put to bed.

"Well you'd better not breathe a word of this to anyone," Stuart continued. "The employees at Garuda Oil's headquarters in Houston are antsy enough about how Sukemi and J.P. have been fighting."

"Not to mention the men on the drilling rigs in the North Sea."

"No one will be happy."

"Especially Sukemi—after he calculates how many paychecks Garuda Oil will have to print each week for idle employees if he decides to fight."

"That's one reason I don't think he will," Stuart said. "My own guess is that about 20 employees in Houston, 12 in Frankfurt and 100 to 130 on the North Sea rigs will still be on the payroll."

"But he really didn't like that astrology rumor—"

"Would you? No one wants others to think his money is being wasted by a fool."

"Then why did he ever get hooked up with J.P. in the first place?"

"From what I've heard, the Krishnanda brothers and Sukemi

have had joint interests in a Jakarta hotel for years."

"And Garuda Oil?"

"J.P. apparently was very clever. He found out that Sukemi wanted to get into North Sea oil, so he bought an option on Texaco's rights, and then went to Sukemi for more capital. Sukemi delayed, and the Krishnanda brothers shopped around, but no one else wanted to get in bed with them, so Sukemi eventually got his 45 percent at what looked like a good price."

"And now we know otherwise."

"Graphically."

"I also noticed Sukemi's not too enthusiastic about the Japanese," Robert cautiously ventured.

"I didn't hear him say that," Stuart said defensively. "He just takes these Nishizaki investments a little too much for granted. They are his best invest—"

"I just meant that maybe you shouldn't go overboard emphasizing the Japanese elements of the investment."

"What do you mean?"

"Well, the Indonesians, like the Koreans, can be a little wary when it comes to the Japa—"

"I thought you told me all four of your grandparents were Americans. How would you know what the Koreans think about the Japanese?"

"I read."

"Glad to hear it."

"Stuart, it's just like those brass rubbings you made during that London business trip a few years back. I pay attention to my ancestral home too, even if I am a third-generation American."

"Can't argue with that."

"Good. Just thought I'd mention it."

"Anything else?"

Stuart was annoyed that Robert had advised him how to talk to his own client, and Robert realized that he probably shouldn't have brought it up.

"Yes, I do have another question," Robert said, attempting to dilute Stuart's annoyance.

"Shoot."

"Why are the Krishnanda brothers known by their initials?"

"They started that themselves. I guess it sounds British to them. Besides, their middle name is something ghastly, like Priyahabinadaba, and their first names are no better, as I recall."

"That sounds just like J.P., starring in the Krishnanda show live from Frankfurt, but I still haven't got the slightest idea what M.P. and R.P do."

"From what I've heard, M.P. oversees the family real estate empire from New Delhi and R.P.—well, R.P. lives in Madrid. For now. The rumor is he's chasing a V.I.S. in Rome and might move his office there."

"A V.I.S.?"

"A Very Important Skirt."

"Oh."

"Supposedly an Italian movie star."

"Pursued by an Indian playboy?"

"Exactly. The maharajahs may be history, but they have left behind a high standard which R.P. is constantly trying to exceed. And J.P and M.P. aren't far behind."

"In that case," Robert said, "to keep these maharajahs straight, let's call them Jack, Mike and Ralph."

Chapter Eleven

A week later, on Tuesday, January 15th, Robert Kim walked into Stuart's office at 4:10 in the afternoon and sat in the chair on the right in front of Stuart's desk. Stuart was busy reviewing a partnership agreement Robert had recently drafted for Prudential. It contained the terms of a proposed joint venture with Charles Hutchins, one of the few New York real estate developers still actively seeking financial support for new construction.

Stuart did not look up for ten minutes. Just as he preferred not to set a book down unless he was at the end of a chapter, he preferred to complete his review of each contract provision without any interruption.

When he finally looked up, Robert was waiting for him. "So, how does the letter of intent look?" Stuart asked. The letter outlining the basic terms of the proposed $10 million investment in the Japanese food factories had been sent over by Sydney Brewster that morning.

"Good. It's the usual," Robert said, but there was something in his voice that Stuart noticed right away.

"But you don't like it, right?"

"Right."

"May I ask why?"

"Sure. With a net cash flow of almost $2 million, you'd think the price tag for the five factories would be way over $20 million. So it makes me uncomfortable that Nishizaki International is willing to sell them for only $10 million."

"But they're our joint venture partner. They'll still own 50 percent of the factories after the sale. And they want to make sure our 30 cash cows are well-fed."

"I know that. But it still doesn't add up."

"So, what's bothering you? Something else is clearly on your mind."

Robert hesitated, but decided to take the plunge. "Nishizaki's signature."

"What?"

"He signs his name like a schoolgirl would. Take a look at this," Robert said as he handed Stuart a copy of the letter of intent. It was signed at the bottom by Takahiro Nishizaki as President of Nishizaki International, Inc.

Stuart looked at the signature. "That's how he signs his name, Robert. I've seen it a hundred times."

"So have I. But it still bothers me. Look at those little circles over each i. Just like a schoolgirl would copy an e.e. cummings poem."

"What?"

"Nothing. But have you ever seen a businessman, one who signs his name often, use such precise, schoolgirlish handwriting?"

"I didn't know you'd become a handwriting expert," Stuart said sarcastically. "Don't you think you're skating on thin ice with this one?"

"Maybe. But I don't feel good about this deal. Or the signature."

"It's just the Persian Gulf deadline, Robert. It has us all on edge."

"Could be."

"Then let's just forget all about those little circles for now, OK, and give me a good business reason why Sukemi shouldn't invest in a 20 percent return his joint venture partner is handing him."

"Well, I hate to look a gift horse in the mouth—"

"That's exactly what you're doing—"

"—but the Japanese are accustomed to much lower rates of return. And if the sales price is too low for an American deal, it is much too low for a Japanese one."

"It's an inside sale, that's why. To keep the 30 restaurants supplied. How many times—"

"But—"

"You'd feel a lot better if you knew Sydney Brewster personally, I can assure you. Don't you remember that profile on her in *International Investor*?"

"Sure I do."

"Well, do you remember it mentioned that her connections in Japan go way back, and include this Takahiro Nishizaki, owner of one of the biggest food production empires in Japan?"

"Sure."

"And how Mr. Nishizaki told Sydney about five years ago he wanted to enter the United States market, so she developed this plan for him?"

"Yes, Stuart."

"Well, everyone can see she's executing that plan marvelously. The early restaurants performed beyond expectations and we've now expanded to the full extent of that market. Next on the agenda, from what I hear, is a chain of Japanese food stores. It should be clear even to you how these factories make sense for supplying both the existing restaurants and the future stores."

"It does sound good—"

"It's not just good, it's great. But you need courage to pull these things off. And, although I hate to use the vernacular, especially in this case, Sydney Brewster has balls. She's so sharp with money it makes your head spin. She even has programmed into her computers the last day that each invoice can be paid without penalty, and that's the day the check is sent out. That maximizes her float—"

"But if she is that sharp with others—"

"Look, Robert, we are lawyers, not investment bankers. We are not paid to analyze investments. If we were, we'd get paid like them. And that's a hell of a lot more than we get paid, as you very well know."

"Sad, but true."

"Well, then, relax."

"I can't. Something about this just doesn't make sense to me.

And Sydney Brewster's great success is part of what is making me nervous."

"Finally you've said something that makes sense to me, young man," Stuart said, "but next time I talk to Sydney I won't bother telling her you're jealous of her success."

"Right."

"I seriously suggest you examine your conscience on that one—but on your own time, Robert. Right now I want to know what's happening on Garuda Oil."

"I faxed that draft notice you reviewed to Sukemi this morning. He's still in Zurich."

"And he still wants that veto. I just wonder if he's willing to pay the price to get it."

"What are the current odds?"

"Frankly, I'd be surprised if he went ahead with the fight. But something he said yesterday makes me think he just might. He really does not like the effect he imagines those astrology rumors are having on his business reputation."

"He'd risk millions just to refresh his reputation?"

"When you have billions, why not?"

"I didn't think of that."

"There are lots of things you don't think of, Robert. I just want to make sure that an ambiguity in Section 10.7 isn't one of them."

"It's watertight. You've read it."

"Pretty stark end game, isn't it?"

"Absolutely."

"And not a single ambiguity?"

"We drafted it."

"Then let's hope for once we weren't perfect."

Chapter Twelve

Robert Kim slipped quietly through the front door of his one bedroom condo at about 11:30 that night. The ten minute walk from his office to the 21st floor of 630 First Avenue usually cleared his head of thoughts about work, but he was still anxious as he shed all his clothes before slowly turning the knob on the bedroom door.

Although he tried to be silent, in the dark his shoulder hit against the door frame. Light suddenly filled the room.

"I recognize you," a female voice purred seductively from the bed, almost successful in its attempt to imitate Lauren Bacall's whistling instructor's voice.

"Let's hope so," Robert said. "I haven't worked every minute of the last eight years."

Lily Kim laughed as she slid the covers back and Robert crawled into bed. "Not every minute. That's true," Lily agreed, continuing one of their common marital jokes. "And I've never complained once about my tiny allotment, have I?"

"Right. Never."

"Never," Lily emphasized while stifling a yawn.

"Sorry I woke you up. I tried not to."

"I know, Bobby. I was still awake anyway," Lily lied.

"Thinking about your thesis again?"

"Not exactly," Lily said to buy time, and then decided to dip into her even larger concern about the value of her doctoral studies in Cultural Anthropology at Columbia. She actually didn't lose any sleep over the topic, but it seemed that way to Robert.

"It's just that I keep questioning the value of studying and preserving some of these extinct cultures," she continued.

"So why don't you just tell me what happened today to remind you of that," Robert said, realizing that he would be told anyway.

"It was Professor Ostrum."

"Again?"

"Again. I stopped by the department during pre-registration and he collared me. He wanted to make sure I'd be taking his seminar on Central American Cultures. To persuade me he described the Mayas' bloodletting practices and human sacrifices in all their gory and, to him, quite fascinating details. And then he started in again on his theory that the Mayas' ancient rituals demonstrate their closer attunement with the cycles of Nature, their sympathy for and understanding of Mother Earth's impenetrable secrets. Or something like that."

"Bounty would love this guy."

"She sure would. But I find it very hard to keep from laughing. It's a good thing it's my last semester of classes. I wanted to study science, not be initiated into some mystic Nature worship cult. The next thing Ostrum'll have us do is study the entrails of a bull to discover the future. As revealed by Mother Earth, no doubt."

"At the expense of one of her prize bulls."

"Precisely," Lily agreed. "I figure if she wants us to know the future she can just send a letter. We are civilized now. We know how to read."

"It's true we know how to read."

"But that's not quite enough to make us civilized, right?" she asked, putting her hand on his shoulder.

"Apparently not."

"So what happened to you today, Mr. Gloom and Doom? It doesn't sound too cheerful."

It was obvious to Lily that something else was bothering Robert. She had forgotten how personally he was taking the hourly build up of tensions in the Persian Gulf. It would be hours, and maybe even days, before anyone would know if Saddam Hussein would pull back his troops before the bombs started to fall. But Robert, not wanting to remind Lily of the deadline's approach, spoke about his concerns at work instead.

"I'm just worried about SEC. Something isn't quite right with these Nishizaki investments. I can't put my finger on it, but I don't like them. And SEC either tunes out or gets defensive whenever I bring my doubts up."

Lily and Robert referred to Stuart E. Craxton as S-E-C whenever they discussed him because Stuart was one of the twelve senior partners at Tilden & Hayes who were known as the Initials. Lily had found it so amusing that they took such a title seriously that Robert indulged her by almost always referring to the Initials by their initials.

"You'll be out of there soon, Bobby. One more year, maybe two tops. It's SEC's problem. Let him worry about it."

"His and Sukemi's. But that's another thing. Sukemi wants to fight with the Krishnanda brothers over the way they're running Garuda Oil and I'm supposed to supply the weapons. If it were just money—but there are a hundred employees out in the North Sea exploring for oil, and Sukemi wants to shut down the whole operation until J.P. gives in."

"Can't you just lie and tell him that it can't be done?"

"I can't lie to SEC's client. Besides, it's perfectly clear to SEC it can be done. He only wants my input on the details, the mechanics. Anyway, it might even be good for Garuda Oil. According to industry rumors, J.P. has been using an astrologer to help him drill wells, and it's costing Sukemi millions. The first well hit, so J.P. is a firm believer, but none of the others have."

"And what was that you were saying about our being civilized now?"

"That was you," Robert said. "The thin veneer always looks translucent to me."

Snuggled next to him, Lily could feel Robert's anxiety knotting the muscles in his legs. She knew from experience that talking about a distracting idea would work best to relax him, so she quickly thought of a good one.

"Bobby, what do you think? Should I change my dissertation topic to a study of 19th century Manhattan law firms? I'm already tired of studying exactly how much the Minoan culture influenced the Etruscans anyway, and I haven't even started writing my thesis. It would be much more fun to determine how much Tilden & Hayes influenced Cravath during their formative years. And I'm sure there are records I could sift through."

"I have an even better idea," Robert said, catching the fever of his wife's manufactured interest. "Why don't you study the incentives and outcomes of the current cultures of several prominent firms. You could probably get a lot of young associates to talk to you."

"Wouldn't they be biased?"

"Of course they would be. Victims always are. But you could probably get some of the retired partners to discuss firm culture at length, too. For them the culture worked. The comparisons could be quite interesting."

"Ostrum would never approve—"

"So what? Professor Blackburn loves bright ideas for research projects. He'll push it through for you. And he'll be your advisor on it, too, I'm sure. He told me once he had toyed with the idea of becoming a lawyer himself before he decided on his PhD in Anthropology."

"Now there's a nice range of choices."

"It helped that his father was a partner at Lord Day Lord."

"I didn't know that."

"You should pay more attention at the faculty parties you drag me to, dear."

"Of course, dear," Lily replied. Neither Kim ever used the word 'dear' without making it sound slightly ironic.

"But I mean it, Lily. You could, for example, study the hierarchy of cheating on the dinners lawyers have at their clients' expense. There are plenty of lawyers whose moral outrage boils over when discussing colleagues who charge extra chips and soda to be stored for a rainy day, but they themselves never get to work before 11:00 so that they are always still there working when the free dinners become available at 9:00."

"But I thought you guys were always entitled to free dinners."

"Not really. At Tilden & Hayes that perk is limited by a written rule that says you can only charge your dinner to a client's account if you stay past 9:00 due to work for that client."

"Well that sounds reasonable enough. After all, they certainly can't let their slaves starve."

"True. And it is a lot cheaper to feed a lawyer than it is to pay for her time to—"

"Bobby, I just love it when you use 'her' like that."

"Why do you think I do it, dear?"

Lily laughed. She could feel her husband's legs starting to relax. Talking about a new idea almost always did that for him.

"Anyway," Robert continued, "it makes sense, but some lawyers don't follow the spirit of the rule, even if they do follow the letter. Of course, lawyers are trained to use rules to their own advantage, so no one should be surprised. But the rule clearly implies that you've been working hard all day and have to stay late at night due to a deadline imposed by the client. Right?"

"Right."

"But many lawyers routinely come in late. Others dawdle or socialize in order to stay long enough to qualify. And the irony is that all that energy and distortion of routine is undertaken to save $10 a day. By attorneys making more than a hundred grand a year."

"They're just seeking the full extent of their perceived entitlements," Lily laughed. "Maybe I could compare the inevitability of expense account fraud to the inevitability of welfare fraud."

"And maybe you would just have too much fun stepping on our tender toes."

"Yours too?"

"Nah. I was trained by SEC. He hates that stuff. His personal rule is to only spend a client's money the way he would spend his own."

"Does he really stick to that rule?"

"I can only remember one time I disagreed with him, and it was a gray area anyway."

"What shade of gray?"

"Oh, a couple years ago he took the Concorde to London for a meeting, saying it would save his time, and therefore his client's money, but mainly I think it was because he'd never flown the Concorde. Other than that—"

"Just a thousand or two."

"Right. It sounds like a lot."

"It is a lot."

"But we deal with millions all the time. It doesn't look that way—"

"Did I find some tender toes?"

"Oh, shut up and go to sleep, dear."

"This project is sounding better and better all the time."

"Well, since it's obvious you want to wallow in the dregs, I suggest you study the firm culture of Skelly Adams & Neff. I could tell you stories—"

"Please do."

"I'm sure you could learn a lot more by moving into their offices at Chase Plaza. You could study them there as if they were an aboriginal tribe on New Guinea. And there are plenty of lawyers who think they're even less civilized."

"Less civilized?"

"Well, mostly that's hurt pride talking. It still galls some of the T&H partners that Skelly Adams swallowed up, in November 1983, all five floors we used to have at Chase Plaza. And that was just three days after we moved to 101 Park. Last I heard, Skelly has the equivalent of more than 18 full floors in bits and pieces all over Chase Plaza. And that's only their New York office.

"Back in 1983 Skelly Adams probably only had about 230 lawyers. At that time T&H had about 150. Now, just eight years later, they're pushing 800 and we're still hovering around 180. Skelly Adams is still behind Skadden, Baker & MacKenzie and Jones Day, but they're growing faster than anyone else. So everyone wants them to take a tumble, to do a Finley Kumble."

"A Finley Kumble?"

"That's a law firm that imploded through its own excesses. They borrowed money from banks and paid it out to their partners. But they got caught and it's going to cost the Finley partners millions."

"They distributed borrowed money? Like, outright theft?"

"Well, most of the partners there claim they didn't know what was going on. They're blaming it all on their Management Committee. But just imagine a 50-year-old corporate attorney claiming he doesn't understand his own firm's finances."

"Well maybe some don't."

"Maybe. But that should be even more embarrassing. Anyway, Finley Kumble is history. And Skelly Adams is still booming along, making fistfuls of dollars for its partners. Of course, the partners at the white shoe firms enjoy making money too, but it's like the difference between erotic and vulgar. And Skelly Adams is definitely considered vulgar."

"I didn't realize law firms were so sexy," Lily said, running her fingers down Robert's thigh.

"They're not," Robert said abruptly. Although Lily was already getting tired of hearing about lawyers' foibles, she realized Robert hadn't yet talked enough to really relax, so she patiently let him continue.

"Still, I suspect that what really irks the T&H partners is that one of the associates they passed over 12 years ago, Daniel Metzger, is now on Skelly's Management Committee. And he is supposed to be the brains behind Skelly's rapid growth, so they sometimes wonder—"

"There but for the grace of God—"

"And an open partnership slot—"

"Go I."

"Right. And since Skelly, Skadden and Jones Day keep getting more and more press, and more and more of the big clients, it worries the T&H partners that they might be missing out on the future by not becoming bigger themselves. Still, if you ask me, those Skelly attorneys pay a stiff price for flying high so fast."

"You're not exactly taking it easy yourself, dear."

"What I do is nothing. How many times did I work past midnight in '90? Can you remember?"

"About 15 to 20 times?"

"Well, not more than 20. And how many times did I work two days straight without sleep?"

"Last year? Only twice."

"Right."

"But in '86 you had that awful December—"

"Lily, that awful December was only 315 billed hours. That is mere training mush for new Skelly associates. I read the other day in *The New York Law Journal*, in an article about a Skelly bankruptcy bill being judicially trimmed, that the judge had determined it was impossible for a female associate to have worked over 100 hours in just five days. But a Skelly partner was quoted as saying, 'oh, yes, she could have done that. She's a relatively hard worker.' Relatively? What are their very hard workers like?"

"Like you, dear."

"Oh no, Lily, I'd be a wimp there. I've never billed more than 2600 hours in one year, and I've heard that at Skelly Adams anything below 3000 is considered substandard."

"That's insane," Lily commented.

"I certainly think so. And there's no question that Mark Berman is."

"You mean that twerp who refused to change even one comma in a contract in reliance on Skelly Adams' traditions—when he had only been there five weeks?"

"I see you remember Berman too."

"How could I forget him? You complained about him nightly for three months straight—"

"Did I?"

"Yes, dear."

"Sorry."

"It's OK. But if I have to set up my observation tent in their library just to study the behavior of Mark Berman and his kind, I'm afraid I'll quickly lose interest."

"Don't give up yet, Lily. Skelly Adams is also home to a few entertaining eccentrics. Stella Lambert is one. You rarely see one of her kind in a large law firm at all, much less in New York. But she's a gem, so they tolerate her. I mean, at 60, with her excessive makeup, she looks much more like Ethel Merman than like a tax lawyer. But she's got New York's complicated real property tax laws down cold. And she's also got a great sign hanging in her office. It says, 'Sexual harassment occurring in this office will not be reported, but will be graded.'"

"I think I'll start my interviews with Stella. I want to find out your grade."

"I flunked."

"That's a shame."

"No it's not. You don't know Stella."

"Not yet."

"That's right. Not yet, professor. But if you want to meet a real eccentric you've got to interview Herbie Altilano. He's a short, pudgy man, nearly bald at 45. He represents the Krishnanda brothers, but, other than that, is actually quite likable in many ways. Still, he's way too excitable, especially by money. And when he gets excited, well, you'd think sometimes he's about to have an orgasm."

"Literally?"

"Literally. I remember once, at 4:00 in the morning, when we were waiting for a side conference to break up during our negotiations to set up Garuda Oil, Herbie was talking to me about KKR's $25 billion LBO of RJR Nabisco, and the legal fees it had generated, and he got so excited that he could have been impersonating Michael Jackson on stage."

"You mean he grabbed his—"

"Not exactly grabbed. But it sure explained the sheen on the crotch of his pants."

"Did anyone say anything?"

"Nah. Even the women could see he didn't realize what he

was doing."

"How embarrassing!"

"You would think so. But I've seen it several times. Mostly businessmen from the boondocks who have their dreams of wealth all tangled up with sex. But never in New York. That is, except at Skelly Adams. Like I said, they're considered vulgar."

"I see you're not planning on going to Skelly Adams if T&H doesn't make you a partner."

"What do you mean 'if', Lily? You know 'no way' is more like it. It's been two years since Joseph Houseman made partner and there won't be another open slot until ETS retires. And the rumors are that ETS has asked the partners to revise the T&H partnership agreement so he can stay on as Managing Partner past his 65th birthday."

"Is it that much fun to be a partner?"

"Fun? Not really. The money is great. The work is occasionally challenging. But the hours are awful."

"Then why is everyone but you dying to make partner?"

"Because the hours didn't use to be so awful. And the others haven't caught on yet," Robert argued once again. He had been rationalizing his diminishing ambition in this way for nearly three years, ever since he realized that his chances of making partner at Tilden & Hayes were close to nil. But Robert's realistic appraisal was still tinged with hope that new circumstances could alter that otherwise inevitable outcome.

"Don't you think the money has *anything* to do with it?" Lily asked suspiciously.

"Oh, I suppose it does. That and a fact I forgot to mention. You're also granted power over a few personal slaves."

"Always a popular perk."

"Especially with Houseman. He'd probably even have bought a whip to use on his if that were still allowed. The Harvard men claim that's because he's trying to make up for having attended Cornell. And maybe they're right. After all, he is the first T&H

partner in 44 years who hasn't graduated from either Harvard, Yale or NYU."

"That's incredible."

"Some traditions are hard to break."

"They broke them for you."

"Among others. But T&H was forced to expand its hiring practices to include Columbia, Cornell, Chicago, U Penn and our beloved Stanford due to the high demand for new lawyers in the early '80s. That's hardly a sign that T&H has become iconoclastic."

"So you're actually serious about Houseman feeling inadequate because he went to Cornell."

"Let me put it this way. Joseph has loosened up tremendously in the last year—ever since *The Harvard Law Review* published his article on tax-free transfers. Last month I even heard him tell the story about Barbara Sexton's weekend dress code violation. And I couldn't believe it when I heard him laugh about it. It had infuriated him so much at the time."

"Is that the Barbara I met at the Tavern on the Green party a few years ago?"

"That's her. Back then she had already begun her personal campaign to lower T&H's weekend dress code. But she really overdid it one Saturday morning and it nearly cost her her job."

"Come on."

"No, really. Lack of judgment, they would have said. It's a good thing for Barbara that Joseph needed her for that article or I'm sure he would have canned her. I've never seen him madder."

"And her offense against propriety was?"

"Apparently Joseph had gotten a call from some potential clients he'd been wooing. They wanted an immediate presentation on tax-free transfers—to test him, no doubt. And undoubtedly he wanted to impress them, so he said he'd be there in ten minutes. But at that time he was still dependent on Barbara's research, so he went to her office to bring her along, and there she was, sitting at her desk, wearing a pair of ripped jeans and a punk rock T-shirt."

"Were the rips in her jeans indecent?"

"Oh no. Quite decent."

Lily laughed and leaned back to look in Robert's face, squeezing one of his legs between hers. "So it was the T-shirt that bothered him?" she asked.

"Good guess. Apparently he hadn't looked closely at it before they left. But soon after the meeting was underway he realized that the five male executives were continually being distracted by her T-shirt. Her presentation on how their company could save millions in taxes was essentially wasted."

"Was it that indecent?"

"Quite. She was wearing that famous 'Strate 'Em T-shirt. You know, the one that has the nude picture of Mama Cass lying on a blanket on the front."

"I haven't seen that one."

"It's something. 'MAMA CASS' is printed in bold black letters above the picture and 'Dedicated to the One We Love' is printed below. But to get the full impact you have to read the front together with the back. Ironically, since Joseph only complains about the execs being distracted by Mama Cass, I figure he still has no idea of the full extent of Barbara's indiscretion."

"So what's on the back?"

"The name of the female punk rock group, 'STRATE 'EM, is in bold black letters over a picture of four dowdy housewives standing around an operating table, knives out, about to relieve a man of his family jewels."

"I take it that Sexton is a lesbian," Lily laughed.

"She's smart enough to be one."

"And I'm too dumb?" Lily pretended to pout.

"That's not what I meant, Lily. What I meant is that even intelligent men can be such fools when it comes to women that I can understand how some of the smart women refuse to tolerate them. I'll bet Barbara still laughs about how easy it was to distract those execs."

"Bobby, you child! You don't have to be smart to know that.

Every woman knows that. Instinctively."

"They sure hide it well from me."

"That's because you look like the enemy."

"Genghis Khan?"

"He's history. Men aren't."

"Not yet."

"Not ever. If I can help it."

"Dear, are you raising forbidden topic number one?"

"I see no need to raise it," Lily whispered in his ear.

"I really don't think now's—"

"Well, then, tell me what I really want to know," Lily said, backing off gently once more. "Is she one?"

"One what?"

"One lesbian."

"Oh, Lily, I don't know," Robert shrugged.

"You don't know or you don't care?"

"Both. She's damn smart, has a nice smile, is fun to work with and—"

"And what?"

"And I don't need to know. One conjugal relationship is obviously all I can handle."

"For a while there I thought you were about to fumble even that."

"Lily, please! You know you're the only one who can arouse my weak desire to be conjugal."

"Why, Bobby, how romantic you can be when you try hard enough."

"Clearly not hard enough for you," Robert complained.

Lily squeezed Robert's now fully relaxed leg more tightly between hers. "I can always fix that," she whispered confidently in his ear.

Chapter Thirteen

One month later, on Friday, February 15th, Stuart Craxton and Sydney Brewster were having lunch in a private room at the Nishizaki restaurant their clients owned. The entrance to the Japanese restaurant was 43 floors directly below Stuart's office, on the corner of 41st Street and Park Avenue.

Stuart and Sydney were celebrating the excellent year the 30 Nishizaki restaurants had had in 1990. Her final calculations had shown a 29.5 percent return on capital.

Sydney was delighted with that result, her best ever. She sat across from Stuart, in one of her most expensive designer business suits, and exulted in the success of her brainchild and what that meant to her family.

"I am going to Cambridge this weekend to buy a condo for my daughter," Sydney explained. "I want to get that done before we leave for Japan."

"Is your daughter really old enough already for a condo?" Stuart hoped his question would come across as a compliment. He actually thought Sydney looked her age, which he knew was 45. Sometimes she even looked older than that, due to the dark makeup she used around her eyes and the strong, almost masculine profile she had inherited from her famous father.

"She's just 17, but she's going to Harvard next year. And I want her to get nice and comfortable there so she'll stay on and go to Harvard Law after graduating."

"Like mother like daughter."

"That's the plan. And so far she's cooperating. Andy and I expect her to be first in her class."

"You must be very proud of her," Stuart said.

"We are. That's why we are aiming to give her only the best in life. The trust fund Andy and I set up for her will exceed $10 million soon—after last quarter's profits from Nishizaki Management are distributed in March."

"$10 million?"

"A little more than that, actually. And we're aiming for twenty. What with inflation and other uncertainties, we want to make sure our grandchildren are well-provided for. And Syd is our only child, so—well, we intend to spoil her. And her children. But Syd doesn't know that yet."

"You know, Sydney, I don't think I've ever heard your daughter's name before."

"I guess I let it slip out. Actually, I'm a little embarrassed about her name."

"But Syd is a pretty name."

"Yes it is. But we named her Sydney Brewster, Jr. Andy was very nice and went along with the whole thing. It was the '70s, you know."

"I don't see what's wrong with that," Stuart said, but he was obviously surprised, so Sydney quickly continued her explanation.

"Of course, our first boy was to be named Andrew Thames, Jr. But we never had any more children. I couldn't after the birth of Syd. Complications." Sydney suddenly looked much older.

"Sorry. I didn't know."

"Oh, it's all right. We're so happy with Syd I don't see how we could have had any love left over for another child. But then, you didn't have that problem with Ashley the Accident, did you?"

"Not at all. There always seems to be room for one more."

Stuart was the one who was embarrassed now. He didn't ever like to discuss love and he had always regretted spilling Ashley's secret nickname to Sydney. Stuart considered it far too personal a revelation for a business relationship.

"And the trust fund you set up for Ashley? How's that going?"

"Beyond expectations. Far beyond." That was all Stuart would say and Sydney took the hint to change the subject back to her own daughter.

"Andy and I are really looking forward to Syd being at Harvard. We're going to buy a large condo, with plenty of room so we can spend long weekends there too. We want to renew our own ties to the Charles River, the brownstones, the Harvard atmosphere."

"I didn't realize you were such a Harvard fan."

"Don't worry. If Yale beats Harvard next fall I won't take it out personally on your son Stu."

"You won't have a fight with him. Stu will have graduated from Yale by then, anyway, but he would probably cheer for Harvard right along with you. That's where he wanted to go."

"It's a shame that entrance requirements are so high there, but they've got to keep up—"

"That's not it. Stu got into Harvard. I just didn't want him to go."

"That's inconceivable," Sydney said.

"There is a good reason."

"Do you care to share it?" Sydney asked skeptically, assuming that no good reason could possibly exist.

Stuart hesitated, but then told Sydney the story of his grandfather's death, and how his father had vowed never to set foot in Massachusetts again.

"And you? Haven't you ever, even once, been in Massachusetts?"

"No."

"Don't you think 70 years is long enough to hold a family grudge against an innocent State?"

The annoyance in Stuart's eyes let Sydney know she might as well not bother continuing with that topic, so she looked at her champagne, sipped it, and then said, "Yale is a pretty good school too."

"Actually, Catherine and I both prefer NYU. My father went to Law School there and so did I. And I went there as an undergraduate too. If we can ever get Tim to go to college, that's where we want him to go."

"Kids these days can be so tough to deal with. If there's anything I can do to help persuade him, let me know."

"Thanks. But Tim's just—well, it's no use bringing all that up here. We're celebrating, aren't we?" Stuart lifted his champagne and touched glasses with hers.

"Here's to NYU!"

"And to Harvard!"

Stuart laughed. "That's another tradition you won't like. At Tilden & Hayes the Managing Partner has always been an NYU Law grad, right from the start. Samuel Tilden graduated from there in 1841."

"Sounds like a stifling tradition to me," Sydney laughed.

"You can laugh, but we thrive on it. And the Harvard and Yale men always concede that each new Managing Partner is the best man available for the job."

"With such hidebound traditions, how did Tilden & Hayes ever decide to move into this beautiful office building?"

"Our Managing Partner made the decision."

"By himself?"

"No. We all discussed it. There were a few partners who live in New Jersey who didn't want to give up our Chase Plaza offices, but for the rest of us this commute is much better. Still, in the end, it was the Managing Partner's decision."

"I take it he doesn't live in New Jersey."

"He wouldn't let that interfere with his decision."

"Right. Where does he live?"

"Greenwich."

"See what I mean?"

"It might look that way. But his job is to make the best decision for all the partners, past, present and future. And he certainly did that with our move to 101 Park. It was Ted Swaine's first big decision as Managing Partner, and it was an extremely good one. These offices should be more than satisfactory for Tilden & Hayes for another 30 years. And that's the way my father designed the position to operate."

"Your father?"

"Yes. He was the Managing Partner of Tilden & Hayes for 25 years."

"And you? Will you be voted in when Ted Swaine retires?"

"Not a chance, for two reasons. One, the current Managing Partner always appoints the new Managing Partner. And two, Ted Swaine and I have not seen eye-to-eye on so many issues that there is no way he would ever pick me. Besides, he made it clear his heir apparent is Jack Kendall when we moved to 101 Park eight years ago."

"Heir apparent? Is this a feudal system?"

"It's not futile at all. It works very well."

"I said *feudal.*"

"I heard you," Stuart said. He was smiling at her. Sydney realized he had been pulling her leg and she laughed.

"Would you like a tour of the castle after lunch?" Stuart asked.

"Your office is good enough. I always enjoy the view."

A half an hour later, after finishing lunch, Sydney and Stuart stepped outside the Nishizaki restaurant onto 41st Street, bundled up against the wind and snow flurries for the short walk to the back entrance of 101 Park. Once inside, they took the escalator up one floor and walked to the middle bank of elevators. There they boarded the next elevator and were quickly carried up to the 43rd floor.

Helen Schumacher, the regular 43rd floor receptionist, greeted Stuart as he walked past, but he did not return her greeting. Sydney smiled apologetically at Helen as she passed by the reception desk a few paces behind Stuart, not realizing that the employees of Tilden & Hayes were used to Stuart's lack of social skills. They simply assumed it was due to arrogance, with which they were thoroughly familiar. In Stuart's case, though, it was more due to his excessive desire to get on with business once he had crossed the threshold of the T&H offices.

Stuart also walked right past Christine Lava and into his office. He assumed Sydney was right behind him. But she had stopped between Christine's desk and the slanting wall of glass that seemed perched directly over Park Avenue. The Empire State Building stood in the exact center of the view. All of lower Manhattan stretched out in the distance.

Sydney chatted with Christine for so long as she took in the view that Stuart finally came back out of his office and suggested that Sydney join him.

"I really envy you your corner office," Sydney said convincingly as they walked into it. "It would have to be redecorated, of course, but nothing can beat your view."

Stuart liked his sparsely decorated office, with simple but expensive mahogany furniture, including the triangular secretarial station outside his door that helped visitors focus on the view and the finely carved desk that placed him in perfect position to enjoy an even better view of Manhattan.

But Stuart understood Sydney's desire to redecorate. Her own larger corner office on the 37th floor of 919 Third Avenue was lavishly decorated with Persian carpets, a large aquarium, bonsai trees, and two huge pink jade statues of buddha which protected the entrance to her private bathroom. Her office even had a decent view of Central Park. But few views of Manhattan can compete with the 270 degree view that the special design of 101 Park Avenue provides for its best corner offices.

"Actually, we don't call them corner offices," Stuart commented. "The twists and turns of 101 Park produce eight corner offices on each floor, not just four, so at Tilden & Hayes every partner has a corner office. Our Managing Partner therefore decided that we should have a special name for the offices with 270 degree views."

"And that is?"

"Power offices."

Stuart would have preferred to resist his impulse to explain these details to Sydney, but their lunch conversation had instilled in him a desire to demonstrate his own success.

"We have 12 of them," Stuart continued. "One for each of the Initials."

"The Initials?" Sydney asked.

"That's the more or less informal title we use for the top 12 partners of Tilden & Hayes. We're identified only by our initials on partnership memos, so the name stuck. There were only ten until we moved to these offices, but, with 12 power offices on the six floors we have here, ETS decided to expand the number of Initials to 12."

"ETS? Do you always talk in code here?"

"ETS are Ted Swaine's initials. Sometimes we—"

"I've got it," Sydney said. "So you are known as SEC?"

"Right. Among the 40 partners."

"And how many lawyers are there altogether?"

"We have about 180. About 140 are associates, like Robert Kim."

"And when will Robert become a partner?"

"Probably never. The T&H partnership agreement—"

"T&H?"

"Tilden & Hayes."

"Of course."

"As I was saying, our partnership agreement specifically limits the number of partners to 40. Only when a partner retires, or dies, does a partnership slot open up. Robert's chances are therefore very slim to nonexistent. He's not even on the short list."

"The short list?"

"It's a list of the five most eligible associates for the next open partnership slot."

"Well, Robert has certainly impressed me. Why isn't he on the short list? Hasn't he been here long enough?"

"He's in the class of 1983—"

"What?"

"He graduated from Stanford Law in 1983. Our associates are known by what year they graduated from law school."

"They stay in school forever? Is that another T&H tradition?"

"No, you know that, Sydney. Almost all law firms in Manhattan do that. Certainly when you were at Mudge Rose they had you classified—"

"As class of 1974. You're right. I'd almost forgotten."

"Was it that painful an experience?"

"No. Just not lucrative enough. But for Robert apparently it is."

"I don't know about that. He seems rather ambitious to me."

"Ambitious, yes," Sydney agreed. "But he doesn't seem hungry enough, if you know what I mean."

"I'm afraid that's just because he's relying on me," Stuart said, not catching Sydney's meaning, "but I've failed each time I've sponsored him for the short list. There's one woman in particular who I think doesn't deserve it nearly as much as Robert does, but she has a lot of support from the other partners."

"Who's she?"

"Jackie Messer. She's bright, but burnt out. Anyway, even if I could get him on the short list, Robert would still have virtually no chance of getting the next partnership slot."

"Why not?"

"Because Sally Thompson and John Fenwick both work for ETS. And it's ETS's partnership slot that should open up next."

"Your Managing Partner is dying?"

"No. But he's 64 and has to retire on his 65th birthday. There is some uncertainty, though, if he'll do that. He's already suggested amending the partnership agreement so he can stay on. But there's a lot of resistance to that idea from the younger partners who all want to keep moving up."

"And you? It doesn't sound like you have enough clout here yourself."

"I'm resigned to my current status until ETS moves on. I think I'll do better with Jack Kendall."

"Better than what? Or maybe I should just ask where you currently rank among the 12 Initials." Sydney was having fun with Stuart's discomfort.

"Somewhere around sixth," Stuart said reluctantly. "T&H has the 42nd to 47th floors here at 101 Park. The Initials all have power offices, either here on the Park Avenue side, or in the opposite corner, over 40th Street. The Managing Partner's office is directly above mine, on the 47th floor. The heir apparent's office is on the 46th floor directly below—"

"So you're in fifth place on the 43rd floor?"

"Not exactly. It's unclear which of the power offices over 40th Street on the higher floors outrank me. I'd say Paul Morgan on the 47th clearly does. There are always rumors that PJM will actually become the next Managing Partner instead of Jack Kendall."

"Why? You told me Kendall has been the heir apparent for years."

"True. But JWK has one big handicap."

"And that is?"

"He's a Harvard man. PJM is an NYU grad. That will be a hard tradition for ETS to break when the time comes."

"I can't believe what a feudal hierarchy you gentlemen have here!"

"I've already told you it isn't futile, Sydney. It works very well."

Stuart was smiling again. The reminder that he probably ranked sixth in one of the most prestigious Manhattan law firms had cheered him up.

"Well, I've had enough of this arcane knowledge to satisfy me for months," Sydney said. "I'm going back to my office and make some more money."

"Wouldn't you like to hear the latest on the Garuda Oil fight first?"

"Sure. If it's not all explained in initials."

"It won't be. I'll call Robert in." Stuart pushed the intercom button on his telephone and asked Christine to come in. When she walked through the door Stuart held up a letter which had been sitting on his desk, unable to resist the opportunity to tease Sydney.

"Ms. Lava, there's a typo in this letter," he said. "You're just lucky you work for me instead of Sydney. She has a huge aquarium filled with piranhas which she keeps starved for just such moments." Stuart then turned to Sydney and asked, "how many secretaries have you lost that way? Five or six, isn't it?"

"Actually, my tropical fish are vegetarians," Sydney explained, ruining Stuart's joke on purpose.

"I didn't know vegetarian fish existed," Stuart said. "I thought fish spent all their time devouring other fish until the moment they themselves were devoured."

"Well, mine don't do that," Sydney said in an unexpectedly emotional manner. "They are like me, playing by a gentler set of rules, where smarts are what counts. My father played rough in the world of Washington politics and I personally think that's enough violence for one family to engage in for several generations."

It was clear that Stuart's joke had hit a sore spot with Sydney. Christine was embarrassed, both for her boss and for Sydney. She stood there a moment wishing she were someplace else when she noticed that Stuart still had the letter in his hand. She walked up to him and took it, and started to walk out of his office.

"Could you ask Robert to come in?" Stuart asked as she left the room.

"Sure," she said as she walked out.

"Sydney," Stuart said a few seconds later to break the awkward silence, "I'm sorry to change our plans so late, but Catherine has decided she doesn't feel comfortable asking Tim to take care of Ashley for three weeks while we are in Japan, so she has decided not to go."

"That works out fine with me, because Andy told me yesterday he will probably have to go to London on business."

"Then we might as well cut a week off the trip and just stick to business," Stuart suggested.

"I agree. I'll have our flights rescheduled this afternoon. Wasting a whole week in Japan on sightseeing was starting to bother me anyway."

"But there's a lot to learn from the Japanese," Stuart said. "Their superb business methods are the wave of the future. And if the Americans and Europeans get any lazier, they'd be doing us a favor by taking over the whole world economy."

"I'm as hot on the Japanese as you are, Stuart, but I'm not so sure everyone would like that takeover. Company songs, bowing to bosses—"

Robert Kim interrupted Sydney's litany by walking into Stuart's office.

"Bowing to bosses?" he asked. "Is Tilden & Hayes considering yet another cost-saving policy change?"

Stuart was amused, but puzzled. "How would that save money?" he asked Robert.

"It's obvious. If we would just bow to our bosses they wouldn't need such big corner offices to establish their status."

Sydney laughed and Stuart smiled. Most often he liked Robert's irreverence.

"I'll make that suggestion to ETS," Stuart said, "but we'll never get Sydney to give up her corner office."

"No amount of bowing could take its place," Sydney agreed.

"By the way, Robert," Stuart added, remembering the news, "you should congratulate Sydney. Her daughter is going to Harvard next year and then Harvard Law four years later. Now what does a Stanford grad think of that?"

"I think it's very unfortunate," Robert said, addressing his remarks to Sydney, "because your daughter will never get to be the Managing Partner of Tilden & Hayes that way."

Stuart laughed. "See what I mean?" he said to Sydney before asking Robert to describe the latest in the fight over Garuda Oil. But Robert hesitated to answer and Stuart understood immediately.

"Sydney's a lawyer, too, she'll keep it confidential," he said to assure Robert. "I've already told her the basics anyway."

"Well, the Skelly Adams attorneys are basically fighting now over just one thing: how to calculate the last day of the 90-day veto period." Robert was still reluctant to go into details, but he realized that one form of bowing to bosses was allowing them to show off occasionally.

"Why is there any question?" Sydney asked.

"There isn't—except in the faulty imagination of a belligerent young lawyer named Mark Berman."

"That idiot is on the Skelly team?" Stuart asked.

"I'm afraid so. He showed up on their ever-increasing distribution list three days ago. And I heard from him yesterday about this, his latest brainstorm."

"Is there any ambiguity in the notice provision?"

"None that a rational person would see. We faxed the notice out to everyone invoking Section 10.7 on January 24th and we sent back-up copies by registered mail the same day. The partnership agreement is clear that all notices faxed become effective when received, that is, immediately, and that all notices sent by registered mail become effective five days after being mailed. But Berman had the brilliant idea that because the notice was delivered both ways, the registered mail provision governs."

"But why?"

"No articulable reason. It's a distinction he can hang his stupid hat on, I suppose."

"And charge time to," Stuart said with disgust. He hated the methods of the Skelly attorneys.

"Anyway," Robert continued, "the question is whether the 90-day-period started ticking on January 24th or five days later on the 29th. Fortunately no decisions were made by the Krishnandas during the five days in question or we'd have to fight about that too. So the only difference Berman's argument could possibly make is if we don't settle before April 24th, which is the deadline every court in the world would uphold, but do settle before April 29th."

"Absurd. I take it we are holding fast," Stuart said.

"Unless you order me on pain of death to give in, I won't. Not to Berman."

"No such order," Stuart said. "Carry on."

Robert gave Stuart a mock salute and left his office, walking past Christine's desk as she was rereading for the third time the letter she had taken from Stuart. She stopped Robert and asked him to review the letter, making sure he watched out for typos. There weren't any, just as she had assumed.

A minute later, as Stuart was escorting Sydney out of his office, Christine gave him one of her ironic looks. "The letter is perfect now," she said and handed it back to him.

Stuart looked at the letter confused for a moment, and then remembered. "In that case you have earned another reprieve from Sydney's vegetarian piranhas. Just see to it that it doesn't happen again," he joked, but his joke fell flat.

As Stuart carried the letter away toward the elevators he noticed it was the one he had written to the principal of Scarsdale High, asking for 15 certified copies of Tim's high school records. The letter was the first part of a campaign he was considering waging to get Tim into college by September and it reminded him of Sydney's offer to help. By the time they had arrived at the elevators Stuart had developed a plan for her to do just that, so instead of saying goodbye at the elevator doors as usual, he got on with her.

"There is something you could do for me," he began as the elevator doors closed.

"Anything," Sydney said.

"Are you really willing to help me persuade Tim to go to college?"

"Sure. If I can."

"Could you give him a cleaning job at your office, with a lot of scut work, so he'll want to go?"

"That's easy. I'll even make the place dirtier if I have to. He'll be ready for something better in no time at all."

"Thanks a lot, Sydney. I'll send him around on Tuesday, after the holiday."

"Good luck convincing him," Sydney said as she stepped off the elevator into the 101 Park lobby.

"I won't need any luck if I tell him he's being offered a ground floor position with great potential for growth in a dynamic international organization," Stuart said. He remained standing on the elevator for the ride back up.

"If you tell him that, you'll need speed in addition to luck," Sydney said as the elevator doors began to close, "because you'll have to escape his wrath when he comes home after the first day of work."

Chapter Fourteen

At about 8:00 that night, just after dinner, Stuart asked Tim if he could talk to him in the library. Tim reluctantly agreed. He assumed the topic would be college. When the library door was closed behind Tim, Stuart unfolded his plan.

"Tim, I want to ask a favor of you."

"What kind of favor?" Tim asked suspiciously.

"Well, you've heard me talk about the Nishizaki restaurants and Sydney Brewster, haven't you?"

"A few times," Tim said politely. He figured a few dozen times was more accurate, but he was being polite because his father had not yet brought up college.

"And I've certainly mentioned my assistant Robert Kim to you."

"Sure."

"Well, Robert has it in his head that something is a little off in their operations. Nothing specific, he's just a little suspicious, basically because they are doing so well."

"I don't get it."

"The restaurants are making a lot of money but Robert still feels uncomfortable about a few things he has seen. Now, I am going to confide in you what no one else knows, if you promise to keep it secret, especially from Mom, Stu and Ashley."

"Will it hurt them?"

"No, it can only help them."

"OK. I promise."

"Well, the truth is I have invested some of the family money in these restaurants because they are doing so well. And, although I think Robert's suspicions are groundless, I want to make sure. I thought maybe you could help me protect our investment."

"How?"

"I'd like you to take a job at Nishizaki's offices, at least for a month or two, and then keep your eyes and ears open."

"You want me to be a spy?"

"No, son. I just want you to stay alert to the office scuttlebutt. Find out what the employees think of Sydney Brewster. That kind of thing."

"What kind of job would it be?"

"Probably cleaning up, or being a messenger, something like that. It won't pay well, but I'll—"

"That doesn't matter," Tim said, as if it were beneath his dignity to consider the income a job would pay. Stuart had to smile. He knew Tim's dignity was based on the comfort his own income had created.

"But it matters to me," Stuart said. "I'm asking you to do this, as a favor to the family, and you should be rewarded. I was thinking of tuition—"

"I'll consider taking the job, but I don't want a reward," Tim said quickly.

"I understand that," Stuart heard himself respond, to his own surprise and to Tim's.

"When do you have to know?"

"I'd like you to start on Tuesday, so anytime before then is fine with me. As you know, I'm going to Japan next Friday and I'd rather have you settled in Sydney's offices before we leave."

"OK. I'll think about it, Dad," Tim said. He slowly drifted out of the library, not quite sure his father had just confided in him, had told him an important secret and had asked him to help solve a family problem.

Stuart left the library about ten minutes later, just as Tim and several of his friends were leaving together. Stuart emotionally recoiled from the threatening nature of their spiked hair and all-black outfits, decorated with visions of skullheads, demonic faces with protruding tongues and swords bathed in fire. But then he glanced at their scared, but obviously rich and well-cared-for, teenage faces and saw no threat at all. Instead, for the first time, he saw them through Catherine's eyes. Perhaps they were just harmless children trying hard to be gargoyles.

The next morning at breakfast, before Stuart drove into work, Catherine was unusually anxious. She wanted to know what he had discussed with Tim after dinner.

"Nothing much. A possible job, that's all," Stuart said.

"You didn't fight?"

"No, actually, it went very well."

"Well *you* might think so but—"

"What's wrong?"

"Tim didn't come home last night."

"That's not the first time."

"But he's always called the other times."

"Cath, I really doubt if it has anything to do with our conversation last—"

"But it does, Dad, it does."

Tim's voice startled them from just outside the back door. Catherine and Stuart turned and stared as Tim walked into the house, smiling shyly. His hair was cut short and neatly combed. He was wearing blue jeans and a flannel shirt under his parka.

"I'd like to take that job you mentioned," Tim said, sitting down at the table. "That is, if it's not too late."

"It certainly isn't," Stuart replied. "In fact, why don't you get some breakfast in your stomach and then come with me to the office this morning. There are some papers there you can read that might help you on the job."

"That'd be great," Tim said.

"Anybody want to tell me what this is all about?" Catherine asked.

"It's a secret," Tim said.

Stuart winked at her. She was confident she would find out from him sooner rather than later.

Chapter Fifteen

Twelve days later, on Wednesday afternoon, February 27th, Stuart and Sydney were waiting in the reception area of Nishizaki International, Inc.'s modest Kyoto offices. Stuart's enthusiasm was at a high peak after several days in Tokyo. The clean and efficient, if crowded, operations he had witnessed on tours with Sydney and their interpreter had left him more firmly convinced than ever that the economic future would emanate from an Asian island, just as the economic past had emanated from a European one.

Stuart enjoyed the simple beauty of the wall hangings in the reception area as he waited, wondering if that Japanese art form would also capture the world's interest, but Takahiro Nishizaki did not keep them waiting long. When Mr. Nishizaki greeted them, Stuart was surprised to see that he was a young man. Stuart had been expecting someone in his 50s, but Takahiro Nishizaki was clearly not much older than 35. Stuart formulated his first compliment based on that observation.

"I am very pleased to meet you after hearing so much about you, Mr. Nishizaki," Stuart said in English, "and I am doubly impressed to discover that all your accomplishments are the work of such a young man."

The interpreter translated Stuart's compliment into Japanese, but Mr. Nishizaki did not seem pleased. He looked a little distracted to Stuart. He even bowed to Sydney Brewster as if he had just met her too, but she treated him informally, as if they were old friends, taking him lightly by the arm as they walked into his office.

The conversation in Takahiro Nishizaki's modest office was brief, but disconcerting to Stuart. He mentioned several points about the success of the Japanese restaurants in America, but each one met with little emotional reaction from Mr. Nishizaki. His brief replies were translated into comments implying that such successes were so commonplace with him that he never gave them another thought. But the overall impression Stuart received was that Takahiro Nishizaki was either bored or depressed.

When the short interview was over and the three visitors were back in their rented car, Stuart was clearly concerned, but their interpreter, Minoru Yoshida, explained. "Mr. Nishizaki apologizes profusely for his behavior. He wanted you both to know that he is not feeling well because his father has a severe heart problem and might die any day now."

"Thank you for explaining that," Stuart said, "as I was quite puzzled—"

"His father built Nishizaki International out of nothing and Takahiro is very concerned about being left without his guidance," Sydney added.

"Shouldn't we be concerned then too?" Stuart asked.

"Not at all," Minoru Yoshida answered. "Sydney exaggerates Takahiro's father's role. Takahiro himself has increased his father's business a hundredfold in fewer than ten years. He is by far the superior manager. He is just currently distracted by a recent setback in his father's health."

"That's good to hear," Stuart said, but he wondered why Mr. Yoshida had answered his concerns instead of Sydney. When they were alone at dinner that evening, he asked Sydney how involved their interpreter was in Nishizaki International's business.

"Mr. Yoshida is interested in everyone's business, mainly because he's never had one of his own. His excellent English has given him access to many top boardrooms, but he too is distracted by family health problems."

"I was going to compliment him on his English," Stuart said, "but I thought it best not to, seeing that that is his job. Still, it's impressive. His accent is so slight even a child could understand him. But he strikes me more as an executive type than—"

"Minoru will be glad to hear that his Harvard MBA still shows after all these years."

"He went to Harvard?"

"I hope you don't mind—"

"Of course not. But why is he still working as an interpreter?"

"He's devoted to his invalid wife. Caring for her has meant he's never been able to hold a steady job."

"You seem to know Mr. Yoshida well."

"Oh, I do. We're old friends. We met when he was at Harvard. And because his wife's illness keeps him from pursuing a career, I always hire him as my interpreter when I'm in Japan."

Chapter Sixteen

Shortly after 10:00 on Friday night, March 1st, Stuart decided to call Robert. It was just after 8:00 in the morning in New York, but Stuart was impatient. He had nothing else to do in his Kyoto hotel room.

Robert answered the call himself.

"You're in very early this morning," Stuart said.

"I left at noon yesterday to make sure I'd be back here in time for your call," Robert joked. "I figured you wouldn't be able to wait to hear the latest about the Garuda Oil fight."

"What's up?"

"Nothing, really. The expensive stalemate continues. And the Skelly attorneys are up to their usual nonsense."

"I thought that matter over the deadline date had been settled."

"It has been. I had to get Herbie Altilano to beat up on Berman so he would shut up, but it worked. Everyone is in agreement that April 24th is the deadline."

"So what is it this time?"

"It's not even worth discussing."

"Try me."

"Well, this time Berman is raising questions about whether Ralph—"

"R.P.?"

"Right—about whether Ralph Krishnanda was properly notified."

"But we sent notices to him in Madrid and in Rome."

"Like I said, it's nothing. It's just a variation on the same old Berman theme. He might think he's brilliant, but—"

"He's not arguing that because we sent it to both places that there is some kind of defect in—"

"Exactly. It's amazing how you can follow his twisted logic so well."

"It doesn't take a genius."

"It certainly doesn't. And I'm sure I will eventually get Berman's boss to squash this one too."

"After Mr. Altilano thinks enough time has been charged to its pursuit?"

"My thoughts exactly. Herbie can be very patient with his subordinates' nonsense when their time is being billed. But I've already told him flat out that we're more than willing to let Mark Berman try any of his arguments before a judge."

"And what did Mr. Altilano say to that?"

"He said he considers it good courtroom strategy to make a judge laugh once in a while."

"That whole Skelly firm should be boiled in oil," Stuart said angrily.

"But that would spoil the oil."

"You're right. I guess I'll have to devise something cheaper."

"More environmentally sound, too."

"Know of any active volcanoes we can use?"

"Not in New York."

"And nothing else is happening on Garuda Oil?"

"Well, I do want to send around a fax verifying that everyone agrees April 24th is the deadline, if you think that's appropriate."

"Good idea. And do it before Berman has another brainstorm."

"I'll send it out today. And I'd also like to remind everyone in that fax just how expensive this stalemate is."

"Your estimate?"

"$125,000 per day. That's the number I got from Houston. And since we've already endured 35 days of this, by tomorrow $4.5 million will already have been wasted."

"Then I agree, Robert. Put it in. I want Sukemi to know just how much this is costing him. And it might even light a fire under J.P."

"OK. I'll fax you a copy. So how is everything going in Japan?"

"Great. We had a wonderful meeting with Takahiro Nishizaki on Wednesday and we are going to visit three of the factories tomorrow and the other two on Sunday."

"On the weekend?"

"Don't be so suspicious. You're starting to get on my nerves."

"I can't help it. And maybe you'd feel differently too if I told you what I found out yesterday."

"I suppose I can't stop you from telling me, can I?"

"Not this. I was looking over the old documents from the 1988 deals—"

"Didn't I give you enough work to do when I left?"

"This was on my own time, Stuart."

"OK. What did you find?"

"The deed for the Atlanta restaurant had a peculiar notarization attesting to Sydney Brewster's signature. It was handwritten, without a notary stamp, by one Gertrude Nihilist. Her authorization supposedly expired on December 31, 1988. Besides being handwritten, that end date of her authorization bothered me. So I called the Georgia Secretary of State and asked her if they kept records of all the registered notaries. They do. But there is no Gertrude Nihilist listed either now or for 1988. And they told me December 31st is never used as the final date of a notary public's authorization in Georgia."

"So? We have a defective notarization. Has anyone challenged the deed?"

"No. But there's no recording information on our copy of the deed either."

"I'm sure that Sydney has the recorded copy of the deed in her files. It happens all the time that we get an unrecorded copy, because the recorded version usually arrives a week or two after the closing, and people forget."

"I know that. And you might be right. But what really bothers me is that all three of the i's in Nihilist are circled, not dotted, just like a schoolgirl's handwriting. And just like in Nishizaki's signature."

"Still on that tack?"

"More than ever."

"Damn suspicious, aren't you?"

"Yeh."

"You don't like Sydney's operations, do you?"

"No."

"Can you tell me why?"

"Basically?"

"Basically."

"Because of Sydney Brewster. She is too hard, too angry beneath her elegant manners. And I assume if she stretches out payments to cheat her creditors, why shouldn't she cheat her partners?"

"Paying them a 29.5 percent return is hardly cheating her partners."

"True. But I still don't like it. It doesn't pass the smell test."

"You worry too much, Robert. I met Takahiro Nishizaki myself just the other day. These Japanese businessmen know what they're doing, believe me."

"Like when they paid too much for the Rockefeller Center?"

"Take it easy, Robert. I'm going to check out those five factories carefully. I'll be cautious. You've got my antennae up."

"But Stuart—"

"Look, Robert, you're obsessed with these i's. Why can't a man use funny little circles? And why can't Gertrude? But as long as you're in the mood, check someone out for me. His name is Minoru Yoshida. Sydney says he has a Harvard MBA. But he was our interpreter. She told me some story about an invalid wife, but I didn't—anyway, I'd guess he's about 50. He speaks excellent English and seems to be very smart. It really makes me wonder why he's still just an interpreter. So check him out for me. Minoru Y-O-S-H-I-D-A. Does he really have a Harvard MBA, or was Sydney just pulling my leg?"

"I'll be glad to do that."

"I thought you would. Now why don't you flip me over to Christine."

"Right away," Robert said and pushed the right button to transfer the call. Like most of the younger attorneys, Robert Kim was technologically literate.

Late that afternoon, after Robert had finished drafting a Prudential stock purchase agreement that had to be distributed for weekend review, Robert began his investigations into Minoru Yoshida. Since the Harvard alumni offices in Cambridge were already closed for the weekend, he decided to walk over to the Harvard Club on 44th Street to see if their records were sufficient for his purpose. As he was putting on his overcoat, the intercom beep sounded and Christine's voice filled his room.

"Tim Craxton is on line one. He wants to talk to you."

"Tim?"

"That's what I said—and I'm taking off now."

"Great. Have a nice weekend."

"You too."

Robert sat back down at his desk and picked up on line one.

"This is Robert Kim."

"Hello, Mr. Kim, this is Tim Craxton. Stuart's son."

"Hi, Tim. Your Dad told me you got some kind of job over at Nishizaki International."

"Some kind is right."

"What is it?"

"Trash inspector."

"So how is the trash?"

"I thought you might like to know. My Dad says you're the one who is suspicious."

"I am. Do you know any reason I shouldn't be?"

"Nope. And I thought you'd like to know that a secretary told me today she thinks Sydney went to Radcliffe, not Harvard. They all think she's inflated her degree to improve her image, to keep up with her father, and all that."

"Have you told your Dad that?"
"He wouldn't give a shit. He thinks she walks on water."
"And you don't agree?"
"Only if slime can be said to walk on water."

Chapter Seventeen

Robert arrived home shortly after 10:30 that night. Before leaving the office he had made sure that his memo on the status of the Garuda Oil fight had been received by Mohadi Sukemi, Stuart, the Krishnanda brothers and Herbie Altilano.

When he walked through the front door, Lily was waiting for him.

"What kept you late tonight?" she asked. The question was part of their regular routine.

"First I had to get a Prudential stock purchase agreement out to everyone before the weekend started and then faxes had to be sent to Frankfurt, Zurich, Madrid, Rome, Jakarta, New Delhi and Kyoto confirming the agreement that April 24th is the deadline in the Garuda Oil fight."

"Who's where?"

"Jack is in Frankfurt, Mike is in New Delhi, Ralph is either in Rome or Madrid, so we sent it to both places, Sukemi is either in Zurich or Jakarta, so we sent it to both places, and SEC is still in Kyoto."

"How come you don't know where Ralph is?"

"His regular office is in Madrid, but he's pursuing an Italian film star, so now he has an office in Rome too."

"Male or female?"

"The office?"

"No. The film star."

"Female."

"I'm jealous."

"Of the film star?"

"No. Of you. It all sounds so glamorous."

"It isn't, believe me. They're just big cities like New York. The European ones have more cobblestone streets, and the Asian ones have more dirt streets, but other than that—"

"But they're so foreign, so exotic. And completely incomprehensible languages are used there. I'd guess that if English is spoken at all, it is only as a second language."

"That's true, Lily. But how does that make them different from New York?"

"You have a point. So what did SEC say? Did he call this morning?"

"Not until after 8:00."

"So you didn't have to go in early after all."

"No I didn't. But it seemed like I had to him."

"Good enough. So what did he say?"

"Nothing much. He's sounds enthusiastic, but at least I finally got through to him with my suspicions. Probably because now he has one of his own. He wanted me to check out their interpreter, Minoru Yoshida."

"Why?"

"So fluent, so smart, I guess. SEC wondered why he was still an interpreter. Especially since he has a Harvard MBA."

"And did you find anything?"

"Yes, but not about Mr. Yoshida. He did get a Harvard MBA in 1965. That checked out. But while I was at the Harvard Club I also checked out Sydney Brewster. Their records made me doubt she is Harvard Law class of 1974 as she claims, so I called a friend at Mudge Rose. It turns out they don't have any evidence she worked there either."

"Doesn't sound good."

"That depends. It sounds good to me if it helps SEC start to doubt her."

"Bobby, I want you to be careful about being the bearer of bad news. You know what they used to do to such messengers."

"Lawyers are always bearing bad news. It's part of our job."

"Just don't bear me any bad news."

"I won't. Actually, that reminds me. I forgot to tell you a story I heard yesterday during a meeting with Jim Berner and a developer he represents. This developer swears he just built an office building in Memphis where he had to build a special bathroom on the third floor. It isn't for men or for women, but for a man who has had a sex change operation. Apparently no one in the office is willing to share a bathroom with him—I mean her. And it cost over $35,000 extra to rework the plans to fit in an extra bathroom on the floor where she works."

"That is bad news."

"Yes. Toleration is not yet here to stay."

"Not that. It just reminds me that I've got to go to the bathroom too. And the bad news is that it's a bathroom I always have to share with a man."

Lily disappeared into their bathroom while Robert picked up an orange and peeled it. He brought it into the bedroom, set it on the bedside table and began to undress.

As he was sitting on the edge of the bed taking off his socks, Lily reappeared in the bathroom doorway, arms stretched skyward as she leaned her petite form seductively against the doorframe. She was only wearing a Tilden & Hayes volleyball T-shirt.

"Are you trying to tell me we missed another game tonight?"

"No, dear. The next game is Tuesday night." Both Lily and Robert Kim were regulars on the firm volleyball team.

"Then what are you trying to tell me?" Robert asked suspiciously.

"For tonight? No prop, just the top."

Robert deftly slid his pants off and tossed Lily onto the bed in one smooth motion. After playfully wrestling for a minute, Robert slid inside her. She relied on his being distracted to flip him onto his back. Then she sat up and leaned forward, applying rhythmic pressure with her strong pelvic muscles.

"I wasn't talking about the T-shirt top," she explained, but she could tell he wasn't paying any attention to what she was saying.

Chapter Eighteen

Shortly before 9:30 on Wednesday night, March 6th, Stuart called Robert in New York. Christine Lava answered the call.

"Robert isn't in yet, is he?" Stuart asked, and then remembered to wish Christine a good morning.

"He's already here," she said, "but he's not in his office just—oh, here he comes. I'll put him right on."

As Robert was walking back to his office Christine motioned to the telephone receiver and formed the word "Stuart" silently with her lips. Robert went right in and picked up.

"Any news?" Stuart asked.

"There sure is. Are you sitting down?"

"Don't be so dramatic, Robert. I can take it if Minoru Yoshida doesn't have a Harvard MBA."

"Actually, he does. He got it in 1965."

"Then it's the Garuda Oil fight—"

"All's quiet on the North Sea front."

"Robert, stop making me guess."

"It's about Sydney. She never went to Harvard."

"Law School?"

"Both. She went to Radcliffe but left during the Spring of her freshman year there—in 1965."

"How'd you find that out?"

"It was in the papers back then. There was a little scandal involved. Senator's daughter and all that."

"What kind of scandal?"

"It involved Mr. Yoshida. That's how I found out when I was tracking him down."

"Tell me the whole story, Robert," Stuart said. "I'm sitting down."

"Well first, I think it's clear that Sydney Brewster is not a lawyer. She is not listed with the New York State Bar, she was not in the class of 1974 at Harvard Law, and, unless she used a different name, she has never attended Harvard Law School at any time after she was 12 years old. What's more, the personnel manager at Mudge Rose claims she was never an associate there. And I figure it's not likely they would forget the daughter of a Democratic Senator—especially not so soon after he helped bring Nixon down."

"Nixon didn't need much help. But you're right. She would have been noticed at Nixon's old firm. I can't imagine why I didn't think of that before. But how can you be so sure she's not a lawyer?"

"I'm not positive. We could call all the other state bars and law schools."

"Don't bother," Stuart said, resigning himself to the unavoidable fact that Sydney had lied. "So what was this little scandal?"

"For one thing, Sydney and Minoru Yoshida wrote several articles which were published in the Massachusetts and Connecticut papers. Basically they were vehemently against the U.S. military presence in Asia."

"Who wasn't back then?" Stuart said dismissively.

"Almost everyone. This was early in 1965 and remember, Sydney was Senator Brewster's daughter. He was one of President Johnson's staunchest supporters. Almost every article about her started out: 'The outspoken daughter of Connecticut Senator Anthony Brewster has once again. . . '. Apparently Sydney got a lot of attention. And it didn't hurt that she sometimes spoke in public with an Asian boyfriend at her side."

"And that's it?"

"Nope. There's more. The most recent article I could find was a 1969 op-ed piece which *The New York Times* published. In it Sydney lambasted the Vietnam War. She was living in Kyoto, Japan then and—get this—the byline she used was Sydney Brewster, followed by Mrs. Minoru Yoshida in parentheses."

"Mrs. Yoshida?" Stuart was surprised.

"It was in the *Times*. I can show you."

"OK. OK. And that's it?"

"Not yet. The hints of scandal reminded me that Chris Manzano was probably at Harvard back then. Turns out he was a senior there in 1965. I figured he would remember a scandal if—"

"If anyone would, Manzano would," Stuart interrupted. Chris Manzano was a corporate partner at Tilden & Hayes who was known for his social connections and for his knowledge of the private facts behind the public story. He was also the only T&H partner who had worked there as a legal assistant before attending Harvard Law. And he had never forgotten from those two years of work that a lot of accurate information could be acquired by chatting with the messengers.

"—a Senator's daughter was involved. And I was right," Robert finished after Stuart's interruption.

"So what did he remember?"

"He remembered Sydney as a wild thing who would have been talked about even if her father hadn't been a Senator. And the scandal that got her expelled from Radcliffe—"

"Expelled?"

"That's what Manzano said."

"OK. What was it?"

"Apparently she had an abortion done at the Harvard Med School. By a friend of Mr. Yoshida's. The rumor was that the fetus was an Asian female."

"Why are you telling me this dirt?"

"It was 1965. Abortion was a felony then. And that's probably why Sydney went to Japan and didn't come back until sometime after '69. The papers only touched lightly on the scandal, but Chris said the abortion rumor was known and believed by everyone."

Stuart was quiet for almost a minute. Finally he said, "the '60s screwed everyone up. Sydney was just a kid then. What I want to know is, what is Minoru Yoshida's status now?"

"Well, he definitely got his MBA in 1965. With honors. But my computer search of the written media doesn't show his name in anything after that 1969 op-ed piece."

"And Sydney Brewster?"

"That *International Investor* article shows up. But not much else."

"Then let's forget it. She's a businesswoman anyway. There's no reason she needs to have had a Harvard education. She's probably embarrassed about having been expelled and has puffed a bit. But she runs the business like a pro. And you should see these factories we are going to buy. So clean and efficient. Almost completely mechanized—"

"There's more," Robert interrupted. He did not want to hear Stuart's enthusiasm for those factories.

"Let me have it."

"That Mrs. Minoru Yoshida in parentheses kept bothering me, so yesterday I tracked down Sam Maloney, a retired Connecticut journalist, at his home in Orlando. He covered Senator Brewster for *The Hartford Courant* from early in 1960, during his first Senate campaign, until shortly after he lost his seat in the 1984 Reagan landslide."

"How'd you find him?"

"Easy. I asked the editor of *The Hartford Courant* who their expert on Senator Brewster was."

"Oh."

"Anyway, Sam remembered that op-ed piece in the *Times*. He told me he had ignored it as a favor to the Senator. He also knew all about the abortion rumor. And he told me he had heard that the abortion had made it impossible for Sydney to have children. In any case, as far as he knows Sydney has never been married, but he's certain that she lived with Yoshida in Japan for four or five years. His understanding was that Yoshida already had a wife and wouldn't divorce her."

"How can he be so sure?"

"He covered a 1978 family reunion for Senator Brewster's 65th birthday. Sydney came alone, but the other three Brewster kids brought their spouses and children. And Sam Maloney told me one of her sisters called him a few days later to gossip, she was still so mad at Sydney for having caused so much trouble."

"And now?"

"Sam told me he stopped paying attention to the Brewster family scandals in 1985, when he retired, but he's pretty sure even now that Sydney doesn't have a husband named Andrew Thames. Or a daughter named Sydney Brewster, Jr."

"Anything else?"

"Yes. Have you met them?"

"Whom?

"Sydney's husband and daughter."

"No. But Sydney hasn't met my wife or children either. So—"

"Just thought you'd like to know what I found out."

"Good work," Stuart said unenthusiastically. "Now get the closing documents for these factories finalized and send them over to Sydney's office so they're on her desk Monday morning."

"But Stuart—"

"Look, Kim, we've got to be realistic. Everyone exaggerates their credentials. Not everyone can be a Harvard grad—or a Stanford grad. But I'd trade plenty of the ones T&H has for Sydney. Almost no one can make money as well as she does. We're lucky to be in on it. It's good for our client and thus for us. I'll ask Sydney about all this, you can be sure of that, but you forget it for now."

"And the forged Nishizaki signatures?"

"They're just your suspicion."

"Not any more. On a hunch I had Christine find your correspondence file from late 1986 and in it I found Sydney's letter of introduction from Takahiro Nishizaki. He signed it using slanting, unclear and exaggerated masculine handwriting. And there were tiny dots over the i's. You almost couldn't see them."

Stuart did not respond for more than a minute this time. Finally he said, "I've met the man, Robert. And he knows Sydney. That's clear. He's the brains behind this whole operation. I just can't believe Sydney would be dumb enough to have his signatures forged."

"Well someone is forging them. That's clear."

"Maybe—"

"Stuart. It's clear."

"OK. I believe you. But if Sydney did have those signatures forged, well, I'd guess she must have been authorized to do it. I'll ask her about it. But have those documents on Sydney's desk on Monday morning. We haven't asked Sukemi to sign them yet."

"All right, Stuart," Robert said, resigned but no longer depressed because Stuart had at least mentioned the possibility of Mohadi Sukemi not signing them. "That should keep Christine very busy."

"You know she loves to show off. She'll probably have them all done by noon on Friday—if you can keep up with her."

"That's a big if."

"I'm sure you won't slow her down much—unless you let your mind wander."

"Sometimes I can't help it."

"Well just don't do it. Focus on your work. And I will on mine. I promise I'll check this all out with Sydney, including those forged signatures."

"And you'll let me know what she said?"

"We'll talk again on Monday when I get in."

Chapter Nineteen

Stuart Craxton felt the heavy weight of his competing responsibilities and interests as he sat in his Kyoto hotel room. He was more than resigned to the fact that Sydney Brewster had lied about being a lawyer. He didn't even care if she was one, since it didn't make any difference in her ability to manage the restaurants.

The personal rumors of her affair with Minoru Yoshida also did not bother him. If she had married him, and then had divorced him five years later, she wouldn't even need to lie about it. Besides, Stuart had always felt truth was one of the first victims of the '60s. Long ago he had resigned himself to the fact that dozens of his younger colleagues would never be willing to tell him the truth about what they had done during their high school and college years, which laws they had broken, which drugs they had taken. He even supposed Catherine had a few secrets he had never heard. But he was lenient. It had been a confusing time.

Nevertheless, Stuart still felt very uncomfortable about his conversation with Robert, mainly due to the recent lies. Did Sydney really not have a daughter? Did she buy that Cambridge condo for a ghost, he asked himself, and then he remembered the pain in her eyes when she had explained that Syd's birth had led to complications. If that reporter was right about the abortion, he thought, Sydney may have been covering the truth with an almost transparent lie.

Stuart decided to assume that that was the real truth about Sydney's personal lies. He felt obligated to his client, and to his family, to find out what Sydney's lies were, but only if they were relevant. He was also loyal to Sydney, since she had provided his client, and his family, with such an excellent investment.

Yet another factor in Stuart's decision to weigh Sydney's lies in the best possible light was his strong distaste for discussing such personal matters with a business colleague, especially a woman. Stuart's behavior was still constrained by the old-fashioned habits of a gentleman.

So Stuart decided that at tomorrow's lunch, when they would again be alone, he would ask Sydney about the op-ed piece which she signed as if she were Mr. Yoshida's wife, without touching on the more painful aspects of the subject, and then he would ask her about the Harvard law degree exaggeration.

He needed to know how she would react to these easier topics first, because he also decided he would confront her about the forgeries of Takahiro Nishizaki's signature.

The next day Sydney and Stuart had lunch together as planned. The five factories were discussed, including the most recent cash flow projections which Sydney's office had just faxed her the night before.

Stuart wondered the whole time if Sydney noticed anything different about him, but it didn't seem that she did. When the final pot of tea was brought, Stuart emotionally prepared himself, and then launched the inevitable discussion.

"I asked Robert to do some research on Mr. Yoshida," he began, "as I found it hard to imagine that someone with a Harvard MBA, and his skills, would still be an interpreter."

"Really?" Sydney asked. He could see he had her undivided attention.

"Robert told me he graduated with honors in 1965."

"That's correct. I could have told you that."

"Well you did. Except about the honors. But Robert also told me something you didn't. He said that a computer search of newspapers and magazines turned up an op-ed piece in *The New York—*"

"In 1969?"

"Right."

"I can explain that," Sydney said calmly. "I was living with Minoru Yoshida here in Kyoto then, and everyone we knew assumed we were married. It would have caused him a lot of pain if I hadn't fibbed a little about that."

"But didn't you mention something about an invalid wife the other day?"

"When his wife got sick in 1970 Minoru left me and returned to her. She was living a little north of Tokyo with their two daughters while we were living in Kyoto. I assume that now she lives with Minoru in Tokyo, but he never talks about her to me. Not anymore."

"How long did you live here in Kyoto?" Stuart politely edited his question to avoid mentioning Mr. Yoshida.

"Almost five years."

"Then how could you have graduated from Harv—"

"So that's it? I thought you said Robert was doing research on Mr. Yoshida." Sydney was angry but remained professional.

"He was. But then that op-ed piece showed you were living in Japan in 1969 and—"

"He accidentally checked up on my Harvard credentials?"

"Something like that," Stuart said defensively.

"Well I don't have any," she said bluntly. "When Mr. Nishizaki asked me to represent his interests in America, he also asked me where I'd gone to college. So the first school I thought of was Harvard. I'd gone to Radcliffe for a year, but Radcliffe isn't known here in Japan, so I just said Harvard. And he asked me, Harvard Law? So I winked and said Harvard Law. Good, he said. It will look very good. So I pleased him. That's it. And I'm very glad that now you know. I won't ever have to wonder anymore about how I'm going to answer your questions about what things were like at Mudge Rose."

Stuart felt quite satisfied with Sydney's bluntness. He was momentarily inclined to ask her if she wanted her daughter Syd to go to Harvard Law because she never had, but he decided to let those more personal lies alone. He did not want to see that pain come into her eyes again. If she were all alone in the world, he was not going to be the one to remind her of that fact. Instead, he decided to be sympathetic.

"Is it hard for you to work with Mr. Yoshida after—"

Stuart's question trailed off. He was not good at asking personal questions.

"Not at all. We're just like old friends now," Sydney said persuasively. "He drinks too much, and grieves about his sick wife too much, but I enjoy his company. And I feel sorry for him. He never has enough money because he has been devoted to his wife, not his career."

"That's very generous of you."

"Oh, I get something out it too. An excellent interpreter." Sydney laughed and Stuart was forced to join in, though he was not in the mood.

"And you get something out of me, too," Sydney continued, "Harvard credentials or no Harvard credentials, right? Of course, I am assuming that averaging a 27 percent return on your client's capital is still something, isn't it Mr. Craxton?"

"It certainly is, Sydney, but—"

"But I lied? Yeh, OK, I lied about going to Harvard. But, to tell you the truth, I liked going along with Mr. Nishizaki's credentials game because I've always thought credentials were nonsense. And now I've proved I was right. My Dad's conformity to such social rules bothered the hell out of me, and I came out of that limelight, out of being the Senator's daughter and all that, aiming to succeed on my own two feet. With no credentials even.

"But I'm not saying my Dad was a bad guy. He wasn't. He was even too nice sometimes. So it makes it hard for me to understand those Reagan kids dumping on their Dad all the time. I mean, every family has its problems. It makes them look childish, too sheltered even—as if he did too good a job protecting them. But I'm sure it wasn't easy for them either."

"I doubt it was."

"It's not easy for any of us, is it? I'll bet your own father—"

"Something else isn't easy for me, Sydney, but I've got to mention it anyway," Stuart interrupted. He was not about to answer Sydney's personal questions.

"What's that?" Sydney asked. She had regained control of the situation so well that she knew better than to offer any more information before being asked a specific question.

"We are under the distinct impression that Takahiro Nishizaki's signature has been forged on the joint venture agreements."

"No!" Sydney's surprise was effective.

"We think so. We are, in fact, certain. We recently checked back in our files and obtained a few early specimens of his signature which are completely different than those we are used to seeing."

"I can't believe it," Sydney said. "Why would anyone do that?"

"We have no idea. But we—"

"I know. Someone in his office is just making life easier on him, but they shouldn't do that. The Japanese are sometimes not as tight about these things as we are. I'll look into it immediately and make sure that it doesn't happen again."

"It really makes a big difference—"

"I couldn't agree with you more. In fact, I'll call his office right away and find out who's doing it."

Before Stuart could stop her, Sydney had gotten up from her seat. She walked over to a telephone booth near the entrance to the restaurant. If Stuart could have seen her push the buttons, he would have recognized it as the direct line of Samantha Michaels, Sydney's secretary in New York. Sydney left a brief message on her secretary's voice mail and then sat in the booth for another two minutes holding the receiver to her ear.

When she returned to their table she explained to Stuart that a secretary in Nishizaki's offices had routinely signed his name for him, but that they now understood perfectly clearly that only Mr. Nishizaki should sign the agreements for the American joint ventures.

Stuart smiled, knowing that Robert would be pleased to find out he had been right all along about those signatures.

Chapter Twenty

After more than 13 hours of typing, Christine Lava's fingers were tired. She had almost been able to keep up with Robert, who was drafting at his fastest on a wave of adrenalin aroused by an early morning voice mail message from Stuart confirming that a secretary in Nishizaki's offices had been signing the documents on Takahiro Nishizaki's behalf. And that Sydney Brewster had personally assured Stuart that that would stop.

It was 9:30 on Thursday night, March 7th, when Christine drifted into Robert's office, her eyes slightly glazed, and told him that she had had enough.

"I'll work another hour or two," Robert said, "but you go home and come in tomorrow whenever you feel rested. We got so much done today that we are way ahead of schedule. At this rate, we should be done by early Saturday afternoon, so there's no reason to kill ourselves."

"Good. I wasn't planning on it," Christine said. "This is just a job."

"Oh, is that what this is?" Robert teased. He often wished that was all it was, but he rarely felt that way.

About a half an hour later, while he was busy drafting the incorporation documents for a Netherlands Antilles subsidiary of Mohadi Sukemi's Swiss holding company, Robert was paged by the night watchman, Sean Murray.

"Rob Ertkim, Rob Ertkim, please come to the front desk." The paging system projected Sean's distinctive voice throughout the 43rd floor of 101 Park.

Sean Murray was on the far side of 40, but he had an irrepressible mischief in his face that made it clear why the Irish had invented Leprechauns while more prosaic folk were content with fair maidens and noble but dull knights. Sean was a recent immigrant from the green isle, but it was unclear to everyone whether he was a legal or an illegal one, basically because Sean preferred confusion.

And he always pretended he was confused about how to pronounce a name whenever he used the paging system. Since where to put the pauses was his favorite form of confusion, he was especially fond of paging two young associates whose names were Frank Rapp and Alice Hitchcock.

Sean Murray was definitely not ready for prime time. But on late night in the Tilden & Hayes offices he was a hit. There were rarely any partners in the office while Sean was on duty, and if there were, he knew it and suppressed his wilder whims.

When Robert realized he was being paged he pushed the reception button on his telephone and Sean picked up.

"What's up, Sean?"

"Your dinner has arrived."

"But I didn't order any."

"You're going to want to eat this anyway," Sean said mysteriously.

"What?"

"Come see what I mean," Sean said and hung up. Robert didn't mind taking a break, so he wandered out to reception, assuming Sean was playing one of his usual tricks.

When Robert rounded the bend just before reception, after walking down his short section of the ever-shifting hallway's vaguely octagonal pattern, Robert understood Sean's message. A young woman, not more than 22 years old, was standing by reception in a dressed-to-kill outfit.

Robert immediately judged her long blond hair to be dyed, but done well enough to make it hard to be sure. She had on a low-cut white blouse, which revealed miles of cleavage, and a fur coat, which was opened wide. A snug black leather miniskirt highlighted her boyishly slim hips. Her black leather boots were laced up nearly to her knees.

Sean Murray took his eyes off her just long enough to explain that this young woman had brought the dinner Robert had ordered.

"But I didn't order any dinner," Robert said again, this time for the benefit of the delivery woman.

The woman looked confused for a second and glanced down at the receipt she had in her hand. "This was ordered for a Robert Kim at 9:35 by someone named Christine," she said.

"Your secretary really looks out for you," Sean said mischievously.

"That was nice of her," Robert agreed. "Go ahead and sign for it, Sean. I'm going to wash up."

Robert walked past reception and into the men's room. Before he had turned the water on Sean had joined him.

"She wants to be paid in cash, Ertkim. It's not one of the usual places where we have an account."

Robert took a $20 bill out of his wallet and told Sean to pay her, but he began to doubt her story since Christine would only have ordered from a restaurant on the approved list, so he added, "and you'd better get right back out there and keep an eye on her."

"I will, sir, I certainly will," Sean said.

Robert took his time washing up. When he assumed that the delivery woman was long gone, he left the men's room and went back to reception. Sean was staring into one of the all-glass conference rooms that overlooked the Empire State Building. Illuminated by white and blue lighting, the top floors of the skyscraper glowed against the dark night sky.

Robert followed Sean's stare and saw that the delivery woman was sitting in the conference room. He stood next to the reception desk and whispered in Sean's ear, "I said to keep an eye on her, not make her your kept woman."

"If only I could afford it, God might be merciful," Sean replied.

"Maybe. But what is she still doing here?" Robert wanted to know.

"She said she has a question she wants to ask you."

"Right."

"That's what she said."

Robert walked into the conference room, where the Chinese food sat in white containers on the table, and sat down across from the woman. She gave an almost unnoticeable toss to her hair and looked straight into his eyes.

Robert leaned back in his chair. "Mr. Murray told me you have a question you want to ask me. Is that true?"

"Yes. You see I'm thinking of going to law school and I wanted to know what it's like to be a lawyer."

"Is that all?" Robert laughed.

"Basically, yes," she said, and then shifted in her chair as if she were uncomfortable. She crossed and then recrossed her legs, each time revealing brief flashes of pink satin and white lace.

"How long an answer do you want?" Robert asked coyly, "because I could use up a year trying to let you know what it's like being a lawyer." He smiled at her, benignly, but amused at her antics.

She leaned forward, putting her elbows on the table, waiting for Robert to continue with the intense interest of a well-paid listener. With a practiced shake of her shoulders she freed herself of the fur coat which had still been draped around her.

Robert successfully suppressed his laughter, causing his face to redden slightly. She misunderstood this blush, unaware that Robert was trying to dismiss the image in his mind of sausages bursting out of their skins when they are being boiled.

"Being a lawyer entails a lot of hard work," Robert continued, "and some of it is very boring, but it has its compensations."

"But you guys are always here so late, so all alone. Doesn't that get to you?"

"It's part of the job. And everyone deals with it differently. Occasionally someone gets caught with their pants down, but not often. Right, Sean?" Robert said slightly louder. He knew Sean was listening in.

"Right, Mr. Kim," Sean said cheerfully, thinking it couldn't ever happen often enough to him.

"Well, I can understand that," the woman said with great compassion. "So much hard work and no relief from all that tension."

"We get used to it," Robert said. "Anyway, Woody Allen wasn't that far off with his joke that those who develop an interest in the opposite sex become heterosexuals, those who develop an interest in the same sex become homosexuals, and those who develop no interest in sex become lawyers."

The delivery woman laughed, a deep, almost horsy, but natural laugh. Robert thought she looked much better while she laughed. He was even tempted for a moment to ask her her name, but as her laughter subsided she quickly got back in character.

"I have just one more question for you," she said, "but I'd rather ask it in private." She nodded in the direction of Sean, still sitting on the other side of the glass wall at the reception desk, in explanation.

"I really don't think I could give you the answer you want," Robert said. "Besides, you don't need any more advice from me about what it's like to be a lawyer. All you need now are lessons in subtlety."

"What do you mean?"

"A good lawyer is always subtle. But other than that you seem to be well-prepared."

"I do?"

"Certainly. You're a prostitute, aren't you?"

The delivery woman pretended to be shocked and offended. She picked up her fur coat and wrapped it around her, dismissing Robert by hiding her almost invincible charms. She walked quickly out to the elevators and waited very impatiently until one arrived. As she disappeared behind the closing elevator doors, she flipped the bird at Sean.

Sean was still laughing when Robert walked past him, carrying all the Chinese food containers into the men's room. Robert flushed the food down one of the toilets, threw away the containers and returned to reception.

"Say, Ertkim, what was that all about?" Sean asked.

"My guess?"

"Sure."

"My guess is that Sydney Brewster is thinking of changing her last name to Barrows."

"What are you driving at, Ertkim?"

"Oh, nothing," Robert said, temporarily distracted by his musings on what motives Sydney could have had.

"Well I don't know who this Sydney what's-her-name is," Sean said, "but I sure can't believe you let that lassie go. She was all over you. And what a brilliant set of knockers she had. Absolutely brilliant."

"Sean, could you please explain something for me?" Robert asked, genuinely intrigued.

"Sure Ertkim, anything."

"What's with this male Caucasian fantasy about huge breasts? I thought I read someplace that your ancestors were hunters and gatherers, not horny dairy farmers."

"You mean ch—uh, Asians don't like knockers?"

"Well, I can't speak for everyone, and I'm not knocking them altogether, but my personal fantasy is quite different—more tightly trimmed, petite, educated, intelligent, witty. Actively entertaining, not passively weighted down and submissive. A sprite—sort of."

"One of them geisha girls?"

"Not exactly, but I can understand the Japanese a lot better than I can understand this." Robert waved his hand dismissively toward the elevator where the prostitute had disappeared.

"Oh man, if you can't understand *that*, you can't understand anything us white boys are into," Sean said.

"You're probably right," Robert agreed.

"Still, that sprite idea doesn't sound too bad either. Is there a place you can get them here in New York?"

"Not that I know of."

"Come on, Ertkim, you mean to tell me you have this fantasy and never indulge it?"

"Oh no. I overindulge it, Sean. I married it."

Chapter Twenty One

Robert Kim arrived at his office just before 7:30 on Wednesday morning, March 27th. As expected, a package of executed closing documents was waiting on his desk, having been delivered late the night before by messenger. Without taking off his raincoat first, Robert opened the package and slid the documents onto his desk. They were the same contracts Christine and he had prepared in a rush three weeks earlier.

He flipped to the signature page of the joint venture agreement and scanned it. Sydney Brewster had signed as President of Nishizaki International USA, Inc., and Takahiro Nishizaki had signed as President of Nishizaki International, Inc., approving the acts of its American subsidiary.

Takahiro Nishizaki had signed using slanting, unclear and exaggerated masculine handwriting. There were tiny dots over the i's.

Robert relaxed. He took off his raincoat and his suitcoat and hung them on hangers on the hook on the back of his door. He went to the 43rd floor kitchen area and poured himself a large glass of orange juice. Then he returned to his office to review the executed documents and to compile them with the counterparts, signed by Mohadi Sukemi as President of AJ Restaurants Five, N.V., which he had received from Zurich several days earlier. Since the factories were located outside the US, Sukemi's interest in them was being held by a Netherlands Antilles corporation.

Within a half an hour Robert had nearly completed his task. It was then that he noticed the extra documents at the bottom of the pile. He picked them up and started to read. A minute later he walked quickly out to Christine's desk and saw Stuart's package from Nishizaki International still waiting for his arrival. He checked his watch. Stuart wasn't due for another 30 minutes.

"One of the documents is missing from my set," Robert said to Christine in explanation as he picked up Stuart's package, "and I suspect it's here in Stuart's copy."

"They ought to be more organized over there," Christine complained. This had happened several times before.

"I'll just check this over and copy what I'm missing. There's no use in getting him excited over nothing."

Christine agreed as Robert walked back into his office. He opened Stuart's package carefully and slid the documents out. Only the closing documents for the purchase of the five factories were inside. The extra documents had not been included.

Robert's first suspicion was that the messengers had switched their packages as a joke, trying to keep up with their more adventurous colleagues on the 42nd floor. Whenever Donna Taranto was heard screaming down there it was assumed around the office that the 42nd floor messengers had misplaced another of her documents. And, although Donna made a supreme effort to make sure her screaming was a rare occurrence, she was such an entertaining screamer when something went seriously wrong that occasionally, especially on an otherwise slow day, the 42nd floor messengers were not above misdelivering her Federal Express packages to the retired partners' office, where they often languished unnoticed for hours. That was usually worth its wait in entertainment value.

But Robert's suspicion of the messengers proved unfounded. He checked the mailing labels and it was clear their packages had not been switched. The mistake, if it was a mistake, had occurred at Sydney Brewster's office.

Robert took the extra documents with him to the 46th floor copy center and had two sets of copies made. He was back down in his office before 8:35. He slid the original set of extra documents he had received into Stuart's package, at the bottom of the pile of Stuart's copies of the closing documents, and resealed the envelope with new tape. Then he put the package back on Christine's desk.

"You're making Sydney look better than she deserves," Christine commented.

"We all need a little help from our friends," Robert joked, and then returned to his office. There he slid one copy of the extra documents into the file of an old Prudential transaction. The other copy he placed in his briefcase, shutting and locking it.

He put his suitcoat and raincoat back on, picked up his locked briefcase, and left his office. He told Christine that he had to attend a meeting, called at the last minute, and asked her to tell Stuart he would be back around noon.

"And tell Stuart that the closing documents are complete. The money can be wired on Friday as planned."

"If you wait another minute or two you can probably tell Stuart yourself," she said.

"I'd love to," Robert said ironically, "but I'm already late. See you around noon."

Robert walked to the elevators quickly and felt relieved when an empty one arrived a few seconds after he had pushed the button. As he descended he had a sinking feeling in his stomach, unrelated to the motion of the elevator.

As he walked out through the lobby, the regular guard told him he had just crossed paths with his boss. Stuart had stepped onto an elevator only a few seconds before Robert had stepped off his. Robert was visibly relieved.

The guard watched Robert walk through the revolving doors of 101 Park and head north on Park Avenue, sympathetic to the pleasure that just missing one's boss almost always arouses.

Chapter Twenty Two

After walking north up Park Avenue for two blocks, and then east down 42nd Street, Robert turned south on Third Avenue and followed a meandering route back to 630 First Avenue. There he surprised Lily by walking through their front door shortly before 9:00. She hid the book on motherhood she had been reading under a pillow while Robert took off his coat.

"Have you been fired?" she asked, keeping her back up against that pillow.

"Not yet," Robert said, clearly upset.

"Then what's going on?"

"That's what I'm here to find out. But I have to study some documents first, in private. Then I'll let you know everything. It should take me an hour or two."

"Do you want me to leave?"

"No. Of course not. I meant in private like being here with you. And not in the office."

"Oh. Sydney Brewster again?"

"I'm afraid it's even worse than that this time."

Robert went into the kitchen to get something to drink. While he was out of sight, Lily suppressed her curiosity about what could be worse than his concerns about Sydney Brewster, slid her book under her sweater and walked over to their bedroom, mentioning to Robert as she passed the kitchen door that she would be studying in the bedroom so that he could use the living room.

A few minutes later Robert laid the documents and charts he had copied out on the living room floor. He picked up the cover letter to Stuart from Sydney and read it again. Then he glanced at the Nishizaki Management Company ownership chart on the floor.

He had never seen it before, but its implications were so clear that he momentarily felt sick.

Nishizaki Management Company was owned by two corporations. 50 percent of its stock was owned by Nishibrewster, Inc., a British Virgin Islands corporation, and 50 percent was owned by A.T. Accident, Inc., a Panamanian corporation which Robert thought he had formed for Mohadi Sukemi four years earlier. But there had been a difference in that incorporation, an unimportant difference which Robert now remembered. Instead of Robert being the incorporator, as was usual, Stuart had decided to be the incorporator himself.

The ownership chart of Nishizaki Management Company revealed why. 100 percent of the stock of Nishibrewster, Inc. was owned by Sydney Brewster. And 100 percent of the stock of A.T. Accident, Inc. was owned by Stuart E. Craxton III.

The cover letter accompanying the chart and documents described the final calculations of Nishizaki Management Company's fees for managing the 30 Nishizaki restaurants during 1990. A.T. Accident, Inc.'s 50 percent share exceeded $2.1 million.

There was also a receipt dated March 20, 1991 included among the documents. It confirmed that the outstanding balance of $727,439 in 1990 management fees which were owed to A.T. Accident, Inc. had been wired to its Swiss Bank Corporation account in Geneva, Switzerland.

Robert also reviewed his copy of the management agreement, which he had worked on four years earlier. He remembered having thought back then that Nishizaki Management Company had been generous since it had not asked for a set three to five percent fee, but instead had asked for 50 percent of all the profits in excess of an annual 20 percent return on capital. Robert had assumed at the time that that was the same as not requiring a management fee at all. Since the management agreement was not an arm's length contract, he had not been overly surprised by those terms.

But now, with all the facts laid out in front of him, he was very surprised. Essentially, Stuart and Sydney were splitting the profits in excess of a 20 percent return with their clients. And there were millions in profits to split.

Nothing could have made it clearer to Robert why Stuart was so unwilling to listen to criticism of Sydney Brewster's operations.

But Robert's detailed analysis of the Nishizaki accounting reports during the next two hours completely revived his suspicions of those operations. Stuart's $100,000 investment four years earlier in Nishizaki Management Company was paying off handsomely, but there were patterns in the numbers and projections which disturbed Robert.

Eventually he focused on the Atlanta restaurant, the one whose deed had already aroused his suspicions. The numbers showed that it was by far the most profitable restaurant, and had been ever since it had opened in 1988. But Robert could think of no reason why the patronage of a Japanese restaurant by Atlanta residents could produce returns in excess of the already stunning numbers enjoyed by the restaurants in New York and Los Angeles.

"Lily," Robert yelled while running through 1990's final accounting numbers again, "I'm ready anytime you are."

Lily waltzed into the living room decked out in black tights and an Edwardian blouse.

"I'm ready too," she teased, but could immediately see how worried Robert was and stopped playing. Robert had not even noticed.

"What do you think, Lily? Could a Japanese restaurant in Atlanta make $2.3 million in profits in one year?"

"How big is it?"

"It seats 125," Robert said, taking out his calculator. "That means that even at a $10 per meal profit—"

"Sounds like a lot to me," Lily said.

"It is, but let's see here—that would be 630 patrons each day, 365 days a year."

"Sounds possible."

"Well, it's not impossible, but it's highly improbable, wouldn't you think? That's more than two full seatings at lunch and three at dinner, and never an empty seat—every day of the year."

"And a $10 profit per meal—you're right. It's not likely."

"It sure isn't. If it were that easy to make money, everyone would be in the restaurant business."

"Are you going to tell SEC?"

"That's what I came home to discuss with you. This morning I got some documents from Sydney Brewster that I think were meant for SEC's eyes only. And those documents explain his reluctance to be critical of Sydney's operations. Apparently SEC and she are sharing in the enormous profits from the Japanese restaurants. And enormous means, in my guesstimation, that over the last four years SEC's share exceeds $3 million. It seems he has it all tucked away in a Swiss bank account in Geneva."

"Is that illegal?"

"Not necessarily. The Swiss bank account and Panamanian corporation, for a U.S. citizen, make you wonder, but—"

"Then why do you look so worried?"

"Because SEC is earning money from one of his client's investments. That may not be illegal, but it is severely frowned on by our ethics codes."

"I didn't know lawyers had ethics codes—"

"Lawyers have codes for everything, even for legal ethics."

"Legal ethics? Isn't that one of those famous oxymorons? Like military intelligence?"

"Good God, Lily, can't you be a little easier on lawyers? You seem to keep forgetting you're married to one."

"I'll try to remember, Bobby. But that could spoil all my fun."

"Thanks a million."

"For what?"

"For thinking that being married to me will spoil all your fun."

"Well, not *all* my fun—"

"Lily!"

"OK—so what you're saying is that SEC is in trouble with the New York Bar?"

"Not necessarily. It all depends on prior disclosure, on whether his client, and the T&H partners, know about it."

"And your guess is they don't?"

"Well I didn't. And I've worked with him for eight years. So—"

"And if SEC finds out you know?"

"That all depends too. But my guess is I'll be gone the next day."

"That's not fair."

"No one ever said life is fair."

"I've heard a few people try."

"Try is right. But fair or unfair, I've got to decide what to do and I need your input—because this will affect you too. And there are several possibilities."

"Number one?"

"Number one is I don't even know if I can trust these documents. Maybe Sydney Brewster sent them to me on purpose. Maybe she's trying to trick me."

"I don't see how that could—"

"Remember the prostitute? I seriously suspect Sydney had her sent over in an attempt to compromise me."

"Why?"

"Revenge for uncovering the forgeries."

"Or an attempt to prevent future investigations?"

"Could be. And now this. How am I supposed to know if it isn't just another trap?"

"In what way?"

"Sydney wants me out of the picture, right? What better way than to make me distrust SEC? Or get me to cause a scene so that SEC distrusts me? He thinks I'm too suspicious anyway. What happens if he finds out I'm suspicious about him?"

"The end of your working relationship."

"Which is precisely what she wants. After all, why was the ownership chart in the package? It's simple enough. SEC didn't need to see it again."

"What ownership chart?"

"Sorry. It just shows how Sydney and SEC own Nishizaki Management Company. Since SEC didn't need to see it—"

"You could be right, but if you want my input, here it is. I think you'd better stop worrying about your relationship with SEC and start worrying about your own career. If SEC is a crook—"

"I just can't believe that," Robert said. "I need more evidence than this to even consider that possi—"

"Then let me consider it. Soon you will be up for partner—"

"That's just not going to happen, Lily, I've told you a hundred—"

"Hear me out. It doesn't matter to me whether you make partner or not, but the last thing you need is to get kicked out now. Just short of the goal. Your problem, Robert, is that you keep thinking of everyone but yourself. SEC would forget about you in a second if—"

"Maybe. But I can't accuse a man I've worked with for eight years of something I'm not sure of. That's just the way I am. And I'm not about to change."

"Then think of me—"

"I always do, dear."

"And our future family—"

"Forbidden topic number one seems to have snuck—"

"This is probably a bad time to tell you this, Bobby, but I think I'm pregnant."

"What? When? How do you know?"

"I don't. But I am late."

Robert calmed down. He'd heard this one before.

"How late?" he asked.

"Two days."

"Don't you think you'd better wait a—"

"But this time I feel it, I know it."

"That's great, Lily. But don't ask me to rejoice in our good fortune for another week or two, OK?"

"OK, Bobby, but I wish you were happier about the—"

Robert looked at Lily with a boyish confusion in his face. It made her laugh, as it always did, as it always was intended to do.

"We'll break out the champagne as soon as your doctor confirms the good news, all right?"

"All right. But I won't drink any—"

"We both know you'll be a wonderful mother, dear, but now do you think we could get back to discussing my dilemma?"

Lily and Robert discussed the possibilities. They decided that it was either a trap set by Sydney or that Stuart had secretly, at least as far as Robert was concerned, been profiting from the Nishizaki restaurants. Still, Stuart's investment, and the enormous profits, could not be faulted as long as Mohadi Sukemi and the T&H partners knew about the arrangement.

Robert insisted upon assuming the best possible scenario—that he had been left out of the loop because Stuart was under no obligation to tell him. But if the T&H partners had also been left out of the loop, Stuart's legal career would be in jeopardy. And Robert was worried that now that he knew, he had an obligation to let the partners know—or else his own legal career would be in jeopardy.

And Robert was also still worried about that Atlanta restaurant.

Lily could quickly see that her role in this discussion was to agree that Robert should allay his major worries by doing something about them. That was the only way Robert ever stopped worrying about anything.

Within half an hour they had agreed that confronting SEC was not wise because, whether the information Robert had received from Sydney was true or false, such a confrontation would severely damage his relationship with SEC and would serve no positive purpose. But since Robert had to be sure that the Tilden & Hayes partners knew about Stuart's investment, he convinced Lily that he should tell Ted Swaine, the Managing Partner, about the documents he had accidentally seen, and should assume, during that conversation, that Ted already knew all about Stuart's investment.

As for the Atlanta restaurant, without telling Stuart, Robert decided to gather all the information he could about it. Lily's only veto was of Robert's suggestion that they spend the next weekend in Atlanta.

When they were done making these decisions, Robert sighed. "If only people would stick to business when they're doing business," he complained.

"Why do you keep wishing that?" Lily asked. She had been trying for years to stop Robert from thinking such useless thoughts.

"Because my job would be a hell of lot easier."

"But irrelevant. Why waste your time hoping our culture will become better than the people in it? Because I can guarantee you that it never will. The Professor Ostrums of this world are far too interested in blood-letting rituals to allow them to disappear."

"I thought I was talking about business—"

"Besides," Lily continued heatedly, ignoring Robert's comment, "aren't you the one who tells the other lawyers to be thankful their clients get so confused so often, because if they didn't there would be no real reason to advise them?"

"I knew you'd throw that back at me some day. Can't you just let me complain? Just once?"

"Sorry. Go ahead and complain."

"Now it's not any fun," Robert complained.

"Sorry I ruined your fun," Lily said soothingly. She really was sorry. He almost always listened to her complaints patiently, but for some reason she could never listen to his without trying to shake him out of his doldrums.

Lily's apology renewed Robert's desire to complain, this time about SEC. Robert needed reasons for going through with his decision to talk to Ted Swaine about the documents he had seen, because Robert was uncomfortable about performing that duty. So he rehashed with Lily SEC's faults, his insensitivity to the feelings of the messengers, secretaries and receptionists at Tilden & Hayes, his occasional jealousy of Robert's popularity at Prudential and his use of associates' round-the-clock labor to make a point at a meeting—often a point that Robert felt could have been made just as effectively with less sweat and tears.

And he told Lily the story one more time about how several months ago Mohadi Sukemi had called on a Wednesday and mentioned to Stuart that he and his wife would be in New York on Saturday and wanted tickets to see *The Phantom of the Opera.* Robert still laughed about how Stuart had called the box office and insisted that they sell him four center section tickets even though they had told Christine Lava they were sold out. In frustration Stuart had complained to Robert that if the legal printers could swing last minute tickets for the big shows, why couldn't he? After all, he was an Initial!

Robert found it hard to believe that Stuart was so naive after decades of working in New York City. Robert had had to explain to Stuart that such demonstrations of cultural "clout" were merely the result of ticket purchases at exorbitant prices from institutional scalpers.

But rather than steeling his resolve to talk behind his back, Robert's affection for Stuart, and his preference for working for him, faults and all, was actually increasing. His faults, after all, were endemic in the profession and at least Stuart never pretended to be excessively kind in an attempt to distract you from hearing the sound of a nearby knife being sharpened for use upon your back.

Lily was surprised at Robert's increasingly generous tone of voice and called him on it.

"For all your complaining, you still sound quite fond of SEC."

"Well, in his own reserved way, he can actually be quite charming when he wants to be."

"Would Christine agree with that?"

"I didn't say he was perfect. And I certainly wouldn't want to be his secretary, but I like working with him. He is principled—"

"Then what's he doing with a secret Swiss bank account filled with millions of dollars?"

"That's what I'd like to know," Robert said. "And I've decided Atlanta is the place to start looking."

After he made these decisions, Robert started to relax.

"Friday is going to be crazy," he told Lily. "Sukemi's $5 million for his half of the Japanese food factories needs to be wired to New York and it's the last business day of the quarter."

"It's Good Friday, too."

"I hadn't even thought of that. With everyone trying to leave by noon, I sure hope his $5 million doesn't get lost in the rush of quarter end transfers."

"Don't worry, Bobby. How could $5 million get lost?"

"It's easy, especially such a small amount coming into New York during the rush hour for electronic transfers."

"$5 million is not pocket change."

"On the wires it is. I've seen it take five hours to find $425 million. And by the time it was found it was too late to reinvest it for the weekend."

"Someone must have been pissed," Lily said, quickly estimating three days of interest in her head. "That's more than $100,000 down the drain."

"That's right. But fortunately it wasn't my screw up. Or we wouldn't even be discussing how to hang onto my job."

"Or become partner. You know, Bobby, maybe your chat with ETS will help get you on the short list after all."

"It'll probably hurt me more than help me."

"You never know. Loyalty to the firm and all that. Just maybe—"

"Don't get your hopes up. The short list is set in stone. And it's only a month until the Anniversary Dinner. They're not going to make any changes at this late date."

"And no one on the list is vulnerable?"

"Maybe Jackie Messer, but none of the others."

"What about Fenwick?"

"John's a front runner."

"I thought you said he was a suckup."

"He is. But he works for ETS and is still neck to neck in his race with Sally Thompson for ETS's slot."

"And the other three are out of it?"

"Well, they don't work for ETS. And it's his decision to make.

Besides, Sally Thompson is a class act. She'll be hard to beat anyway."

"Isn't Sally the one who used to teach Third Grade or something?"

"That's her."

"If she's so good, why is there any question?"

"Never underestimate the power of flattery."

"But the partners have got to be able to see right through that."

"That's not it, dear. Flattery doesn't work because it fools the partners, but because the partners know the 'suckup' is hungry, know he can be manipulated, know he is desperate to get what he wants—in this case a partnership slot. And that means the partners think they will always be able to control that person—if the need ever arises. Which makes congenitally insecure people feel more secure."

"But ETS doesn't strike me as insecure."

"That's true. ETS is a confident bastard, but I know only four other partners who seem to pay no political attention to the weaknesses of their colleagues and subordinates. And they are all Initials."

"Is SEC one of them?"

"Absolutely."

"So Fenwick has a chance?"

"Yup. He's a good lawyer. But I'm still laying 2 to 1 odds on Sally Thompson."

"And the longshots?"

"Mark Aiello is an excellent lawyer, but he has nothing special going for him. That's deadly for a white male right now."

"Then why haven't you played your minority card to get yourself on the list?"

"And Mark Aiello off?"

"I guess."

"Because no one even thinks about me as a minority at Tilden & Hayes."

"What about all of SEC's Korean comments?"

"That's only when I irritate him. I'm sure it doesn't even enter the picture."

"Right. So who else is on the list?"

"Frederick Hirsch. I think he has the best chance besides Sally and John. He's been cultivating his own clients for years, but that also hurts him because, not being dependent on the partners, he has not developed that much support among them. Since the money he brings in is not overwhelming, I assume they'll arrange for Fred to join one of the seven firms that have spun off of Tilden & Hayes over the years."

"And Jackie Messer?"

"I like Jackie. I like her a lot. But she's tired and seems too intent on pleasing partners."

"She's a suckup too?"

"In her own way. But she also works like crazy. I think she put in 3100 hours last year, and has usually come in at over 2700 each year. But her real problem is that she has retained a few mannerisms of the beautiful college girl—a toss of the head to show her hair, leaning over desks inadvisedly, that kind of thing. She's smart enough to do without it. But it certainly was popular. Unfortunately for her, she's 34 or 35 now, and there are younger distractions."

"That's not fair. You men age so gracefully."

"I can show you a million who don't. And, fair or unfair, Jackie relied on her charms when that wasn't necessary. Now she is paying for it."

"But obviously she is paying less than you are."

"Because she's on the short list and I'm not?"

"You got it."

"Jackie is very bright and a very hard worker. My point was simply that if she had relied more on her skills and less on her charm, and had paced herself better, she'd have a very good chance right now. But she still has a chance. You're right. She's on the short list and I'm not."

"Don't worry about it."

"I don't. You know that. I never wanted to be partner. I just wanted to practice law honestly—"

"—collect a nest egg, and then be a professor someplace."

"You've been listening to me after all."

"The hundredth time it sunk in. So when are we headed back to Stanford?"

"Wouldn't you really rather go back to LA? It would be so much easier to find babysitters—"

Lily jumped into Robert's arms and kissed him. That was as close to a yes as she figured she was ever going to get on forbidden topic number one.

As soon as Robert left to return to the office, Lily called her mother in Los Angeles to let her know they were working hard on making her first grandchild.

Chapter Twenty Three

Barbara Sexton walked into Robert Kim's office shortly before noon on Thursday, March 28th. Robert had left a message asking for her help the evening before, after he had failed to contact the Atlanta restaurant.

Robert had called information in Atlanta to get the telephone number of the Nishizaki restaurant at about 8:00 Wednesday night, but was told that the restaurant had an unlisted number. That had thoroughly confused the operator, but her records were clear. Still, she had admitted to Robert that she had never heard of a restaurant having an unlisted number before.

So Robert had looked into his files and found the telephone number that had been listed in the original filings with the Georgia Secretary of State. He called that number. No one answered even though Robert let it ring 50 times.

But Robert had not concluded that the Nishizaki restaurant was just too busy with private patrons to answer its unlisted number. So, on a hunch, he had asked Barbara to help.

When Barbara walked into his office Robert could see that she was in a very good mood. "What's new?" Robert asked, "you sure look cheerful."

"I am. And my landlord is responsible," she said.

"Your landlord cheered you up? What did he do, lower your rent?"

"No. But he told me a funny story. You see, about three weeks ago I finally decided to dump all my old law school books, so I put them in the trash. And then yesterday I hear that my landlord caught his ten-year-old son staying up way past his bedtime, reading my old law books with a flashlight. So my landlord asks his son what he's doing. And his son says he's studying, because he wants to grow up to be a lawyer just like me—and then he looks up at his Dad, worried, and asks, 'they let boys do that, too, don't they Dad?'"

Barbara laughed, wishing every boy could feel gender anxiety at least once in his life, and Robert joined her, but for a different reason.

"What else have you been putting in the trash?" Robert asked her. "This kid probably knows more about you than the FBI."

Barbara was momentarily startled by that thought, but she couldn't think of anything damaging she had thrown away, so she remained calm. But she was more willing to disturb Robert's own serenity because he had teased her.

"Geez, Robert, I thought you'd appreciate that story because it shows there's hope for our future—if we minorities just stick together," she said.

"I thought women were the majority," Robert said, ignoring her identification of him as a minority.

"Numerically, yes. But politically, not yet. But when we are we will remember. And that nonsense I heard about you last week will disappear so fast that heads will sp—"

"What nonsense?" Robert's curiosity was piqued, just as Barbara had intended.

"Just something Mark Aiello said after you left last week. You remember, the lunch where we were discussing the Gulf War."

"Sure I remember. What did Mark say?"

"Just that you probably were too generous to the Arabs because—"

"Because I'm a Korean-American?"

"Those weren't his exact words—"

"But all I said was that almost no one ever mentions the 100,000 Iraqis who died. Most of them didn't want to be there either."

"I know what you said. It's just that—"

"Forget it. I don't want to know what Aiello said."

Robert was absolutely sure that Italians had more Mediterranean ancestors in common with the Arabs than any Asian could have, but he also knew that even the most rational observation could easily be destroyed in the current whirlwind of race-tainted patriotism. But Robert's anger subsided quickly. He comforted himself with the thought that time heals all stupidity before calculating that Mark did not have enough years left in his lifetime to effect a cure. That made him laugh.

"I wish I could take such nonsense so lightly," Barbara said.

"Practice makes perfect," Robert commented, to change the subject, "and here's something I want you to practice." Robert handed Barbara a small sheet of paper with one word written on it.

"Nishizaki?" she asked.

"Say it a few more times," Robert said.

"Is this a game?"

"No. It's very serious. I want you to call a restaurant in Atlanta and make a lunch reservation for tomorrow. And I want to listen in on your conversation."

"But I'm not in Atlanta."

"That's clear. But don't worry. If my hunch is correct, you won't even get a reservation." Robert explained to Barbara exactly what he expected to happen and then called the same unlisted number he had let ring the night before.

Over Robert's speaker phone they could hear two clicks after the third ring and then two more rings before the phone was answered.

"Nishizaki," a woman said curtly.

"I'd like reservations at Nishizaki for lunch for tomorrow at one," Barbara said.

"I'm sorry, but the restaurant has been reserved tomorrow for a private party," the woman said. Robert recognized her voice, but he was not surprised.

"Then how about on Monday?"

"We're fully reserved right through the end of April. Please try again then."

"You have nothing until May?"

"That's right. We do a lot of private parties. Call back then."

The woman hung up rather abruptly.

"What kind of restaurant—"

"I can't tell you now, Barbara, but you have helped solve a mystery for me. Thanks a lot."

"What?"

"That woman was Samantha Michaels, Sydney Brewster's secretary. And I'll bet she makes circles over her i's too."

"What?"

"It appears that Samantha likes to play games. But I've caught on to her."

"What's going on here, Robert?"

"Not much. Got to tell you later, Barbara. But thanks. That was very helpful."

Barbara Sexton left Robert's office intrigued by his obliqueness. But Robert was already thinking about how he was going to prove his suspicions to Stuart. It was clear he would have to hit him over the head hard or he wouldn't believe it.

Robert formulated his plan, deciding to call Tim Craxton that evening. Then he remembered the closing scheduled for tomorrow morning and thought that it was very fortunate that Stuart had personally checked out the food factories Mohadi Sukemi would be buying.

MM

Chapter Twenty Four

Two hours later Robert took the second copy of the Nishizaki Management Company documents and charts out of the old Prudential transaction file in which he had hidden them and walked over to the elevators to keep his appointment with Ted Swaine.

Robert had to wait 15 minutes outside ETS's office before he was available, but Ted greeted him when he walked in as if he were his long lost brother.

"Robert, I'm glad you're here," Ted began, "as I've never discussed with you that little conversation we had at the October reception for new associates. Do you remember what I'm talking about?"

"Sure, Ted."

"Who was that associate?"

"I don't remember his name. But he's a new tax lawyer—"

"Branford or Bradford or something like that," Ted Swaine said. "It doesn't really matter. But I always meant to ask you if you thought I came down too hard on him."

"No, Ted. I thought he deserved it. Asking you a confidential question about whether the partners' pension fund was fully funded was a little rich for someone just one month into his tenure here. So your telling him that his excessive optimism was wholly unwarranted was not out of line. He might not have liked it, but I thought it was funny."

"As I recall you supplemented the story by mentioning that fully funding the pension plan was one of my first acts as Managing Partner—"

"I also mentioned your foresight in doing so during the '80s boom years—"

"And during my own 50s, as you pointed out—"

"Was I that indiscreet?"

"I'm afraid so, Robert. But I didn't mind your mentioning that coincidence. It's no worse than that mixup when you were a summer intern back in—"

"1982."

"Right. Wasn't it you that that Haitian receptionist left a message for saying that I was looking for you?"

"That was me," Robert said, embarrassed that Ted Swaine still remembered. Robert had been told Ted Swaine was looking for him and had had a confusing five-minute meeting with him before realizing that the message had probably been left by Francis Lopez, a semi-retired partner whom Robert had been helping with a Pro Bono project. The Haitian receptionist had eventually accepted responsibility for the mixup, claiming that all the partners looked alike to her.

Ted Swaine laughed at the recollection. At the time he had not thought it so funny that as a 55-year-old he could be mistaken for a 66-year-old Hispanic aristocrat by a young Haitian woman leaving messages for an Asian-American intern, but Ted had gotten more accustomed to such diversity at Tilden & Hayes in the last nine years. Now it seemed funny.

Robert was relieved. "Mr. Lopez always got a kick out of that mix-up, too. But I also remember how startled he was by one intern when he asked her what her father did for a living, and she told him he was a fireman."

"I'm sure Francis was startled. He is old school all the way," Ted Swaine said.

"Then I was probably right to suspect he was about to ask me whether my father owned a fresh fruit market. But I'll never know because before he could ask I let it slip that my father is an aerospace engineer."

"As you know, Robert, the '80's changed a lot of traditions for us here. And it's been good for us. But we haven't changed everything. At least we were not stupid enough to expand willy nilly like Skelly Adams with their 18 floors at Chase Plaza!"

"T&H is just the right size," Robert dutifully agreed, but Ted Swaine had gotten excited. Any reminder of Skelly Adams always got him going.

"Prestige sought in sheer bulk! And in expensive, unproductive European offices! I'm sure you've already read about the layoffs over at Skelly, but mark my words, that's just the start there. And a lot of other firms are going to have to follow suit. They all thought the '80s would last forever, no doubt. Where did their historical perspective go?"

"Did they ever have any?"

"Maybe not! Fortunately, Tilden & Hayes does not have that problem. I personally saw to that."

Robert wondered if Ted would mention that he personally saw to the partners' profits, too, since Tilden & Hayes still outdid most of the other Manhattan law firms in that even more crucial element of professional prestige, but Ted didn't mention that. He never discussed profits in front of associates.

"Here we know that booms don't last forever," Ted continued, "so we made sure, during the boom, that all our debts were paid off."

"What debts?" Robert had not heard of firm debts before.

"Mostly those unfunded pension liabilities," Ted said quickly. "I figured that the future would probably not run on good will, that cold cash set aside was a lot better. Don't you agree?"

"Absolutely. I hate to think of how dependent on good will social security will be when I'm ready to retire."

"Mr. Kim, how old are you?"

"34."

"Well what the hell are you thinking about retirement for?" Ted asked emphatically. "I never gave it a single thought until I was over 50—but I take it for granted that your concern about the social security system is not the problem you came here to discuss, is it?"

"I don't really have a problem," Robert began, "but I do have a delicate topic to discuss."

"I'm listening," Ted said.

"I assume that you and the other T&H partners know all about Stuart's investment in the Nishizaki restaurants half-owned by Stuart's client, Mohadi Sukemi," Robert began, hoping to see in Ted's eyes whether that assumption was correct. But he could not read those eyes.

"My problem is that I did not know about his investment until yesterday, when I received a package of documents by mistake." Robert paused again, looking for reassurement that he was doing the right thing.

"Go on," Ted said amiably.

"Those documents show that Stuart earned over $2 million last year—"

Robert stopped in mid-sentence. He thought he had noticed surprise in Ted's eyes, but it had disappeared so quickly that he couldn't be sure.

"Yes?" was all that Ted said.

"—as an owner of Nishizaki Management Company. I did help form that owner, a Panamanian corporation called A.T. Accident, Inc., four years ago, but I thought it was owned by Stuart's client. The documents I received make it clear that A.T. Accident, Inc. is owned by Stuart—and earns 50 percent of the profits in excess of a 20 percent return on Sukemi's investment in 30 Nishizaki restaurants."

"I hadn't heard those exact terms before," Ted said calmly. "Are the restaurants really that profitable?"

"The return on capital was 29.5 percent last year."

This time Ted Swaine reacted. "29.5 percent? That's incredible."

"I think so too," Robert said ironically, but he decided on the spur of the moment not to discuss with Ted Swaine his concerns about the Atlanta restaurant.

"No wonder Stuart made that investment."

"I'm glad to hear you know about it," Robert said. "I assumed that you did, but since I had not heard about it and had worked on this deal from the start, I felt it was my duty—"

"Indeed," Ted Swaine said, suddenly understanding Robert's visit. "It was your duty, Robert. And I appreciate the difficulty of your position. But you should be assured that Stuart discussed this with us at length and we are very pleased that his investment is doing so well."

"It's very good to hear that, sir," Robert said, without realizing he had become so formal. "As in that case I have nothing more to discuss."

"And that file you have? Those are the documents you received?"

"That's right."

"Do they include the latest financial reports?"

"Yes they do."

"Well, since Stuart hasn't sent them over to me yet, do you mind if I keep a copy?"

"Not at all," Robert said, "I made this copy for you."

"Great," Ted said, as he opened the file and started looking through it. As he read Robert inched his way toward the door. When Ted looked up again, he saw the concern on Robert's face.

"Don't worry, Robert, I will keep your doubts confidential. You have performed your professional duty to the firm admirably. But let me explain. Stuart wanted this investment kept confidential, and the firm approved that request, which is why you have never been informed. If I had been in your shoes, I would have had the same doubts, and done my duty just as you have. So carry on as usual. You work for a remarkable man."

"I appreciate that, sir."

"I know that you do."

Robert Kim left Ted Swaine's office and walked back to the elevator. He could not pinpoint what left him feeling so uncomfortable, but he felt that somehow he had just made a serious mistake.

After Robert had left, Ted Swaine told his secretary to reschedule his next hour's appointments. He spent that hour reading the documents and financial reports Robert had given him. Then he unlocked the file drawer built into his desk and opened it.

There was one slot inside for each of his partners. Many of those slots were filled with information that Ted Swaine had no intention of ever using. In fact, he had never consciously used any of the secrets that desk drawer contained. But those secrets supplied Ted Swaine with the illusion of personal power over his unsuspecting victims, and that illusion was almost always powerful enough to create an aura of polite but effective intimidation.

Ted Swaine flipped quickly through his secret files and then slipped the Nishizaki Management Company documents into the until then empty slot reserved for Stuart Emerson Craxton III.

Chapter Twenty Five

Shortly after Stuart left the office to catch the 6:35 Express that same evening, Robert Kim called Stuart's home in Scarsdale. Catherine answered the phone.

"Is Tim there?" Robert asked.

"Yes he is. I'll go get him," she said. Robert was sure she hadn't recognized his voice.

A minute later Tim answered the phone. "Hi," was all he said.

"Tim, this is Robert Kim."

"Hello, Mr. Kim," Tim said, eager to talk, "did you ever get the scoop on Sydney?"

"I did. And I'm sorry I didn't get back to you, Tim. It's been a very long month."

"You don't have to convince me my Dad is a slave driver. Just look at the job he got me."

"How's it going?"

"Nowhere."

"Have you heard anything else about Sydney?"

"Nope. So how about you? What'd you find out?"

"That Radcliffe rumor you heard was correct—except she never graduated."

"She never finished college?"

"That's right."

"Then how'd she get into law—"

"Tim, you've got to keep this a secret, OK?"

"OK."

"She never went to law school."

"No way."

"I'm afraid so. She lies about being a lawyer."

"My Dad must be mighty pissed."

"You would think so, wouldn't you?"

"Yeh."

"Well, he said it doesn't matter if she's not a lawyer."

"I can't believe it."

"Neither can I. That's why I'm calling. I was wondering if you'd like to go fishing with me on Sunday."

"What?"

"We could talk—privately."

"Sorry. Got to work."

"Sydney's making you come in on Easter?"

"Yup. Some contractors are redoing the accounting department on Saturday and I've got to clean up after them."

"Sorry to hear that," Robert said, but he was delighted.

"It's OK," Tim said ironically. "Besides, I don't fish anyway. Don't like to kill things much—"

Tim was momentarily flustered because he suddenly figured that Robert Kim probably ate a lot of fish, so he quickly added, "of course, the cold-blooded bastards deserve to be eaten, don't they? They're not all dolphins."

Robert laughed. "I don't want to go fishing for tuna," he explained. "I was thinking more of an expedition to Sydney's office."

"Angling for tropical fish?"

"Something far more exotic—in her file cabinets."

"Oh."

"Interested?"

"Does my Dad know?"

"No. I need to convince your Dad of something and it's got to be a slam dunk or he won't even notice."

"I hear you. You think Sydney's a fraud, right?"

"Right."

"And a crook?"

"Could be."

"And my Dad won't listen to reality?"

"You've got it."

"That's my Dad. I'll help anyway I can."

"Good. What time are you supposed to be there on Sunday?"

"7:00."

"That's great," Robert said, thinking that he probably wouldn't run into any of the Skadden Arps attorneys he knew if he arrived that early on Easter Sunday.

"I don't think it's great," Tim said. He hated to wake up that early.

"Great for our purposes, I meant."

"Oh."

"Say, Tim, is there anyway I can get into the Nishizaki offices without going through security?"

"Sure. I can let you in through the freight entrance."

"Fantastic. So, if all goes well, we'll be waiting at the freight entrance for you at about 7:15."

"We?"

"I'm going to ask Christine to help me."

"OK."

"We'll be waiting for you."

"Cool."

Chapter Twenty Six

Early on Good Friday morning Robert walked quickly to his office. It was rainy and cold, in sharp contrast to Thursday's sunny, warm and windy afternoon. Robert Kim was not usually superstitious, but he did not like the abrupt change in weather. He was very worried that his decision to investigate the Atlanta restaurant, and to look for more details on Nishizaki Management Company, would create a storm of reactions whose most likely victim would be himself. And the cold rain soaking him felt like a preview of what he could expect.

But he felt he had no choice. Unless he simply walked away from the whole situation, he had to know. And he knew if he walked away he would worry about it for years, so he did not regret his decision. He just regretted having to make it.

Christine Lava was already at her desk when Robert walked in. He hung his wet raincoat up on the back of his office door and walked over to her desk.

"Christine, I have a favor to ask of you."

"A big favor?"

"A very big favor."

"It better not be too big—"

"I want you to come in on Sunday morning."

"On Easter?"

"That's right."

"You're acting more like a partner every day."

"Just this once, Christine. Let me explain."

Robert did. He emphasized the need for secrecy, especially from Stuart, and explained that he had uncovered a lead which could expose Sydney's entire operations, but that he needed more proof. But Robert never mentioned Stuart's own role in his concerns. Instead he discussed with Christine the bizarre Atlanta restaurant, hinting that it might be a cover for an unsavory business.

Christine's interest was stirred by Robert's proposed clandestine investigation, but she was also interested in protecting Stuart from his own excessive reliance on Sydney Brewster. Although Christine liked Sydney, she felt that Stuart was beginning to praise her too highly for his own good. Robert's worries, which she was hearing for the first time, increased her own developing concerns.

When Christine agreed to help, Robert felt better and worse, since he hadn't told Christine he was also concerned about Stuart's role. If their investigation proved damaging to Stuart, Christine would look extremely disloyal.

For that matter, so would he, he thought.

Just as they were agreeing to meet outside 919 Third Avenue's freight entrance at 7:05, JayDee, one of the messengers, dropped off the mail and the faxes which had arrived since last night. Robert stopped talking and JayDee smiled his fathomless smile. As usual, he didn't say a word in response to their greetings, but just smiled again and continued making his rounds.

About half an hour later JayDee filled Robert's office doorway. He had played college football for two years before an injury to his knee had crippled both his athletic abilities and his scholarship money. Ten years of calm had healed his knee, but he remained reserved with his speech.

Robert was surprised, then, to see JayDee standing there, and asked him to come in and sit down. Robert had only been able to draw JayDee out of his silence three times in the last five years, but for JayDee that had been enough to consider Robert a good friend.

"Sounds like you're in trouble," JayDee began.

Robert got up and closed his office door so they could talk privately. Stuart's arrival was expected any minute.

"What did you hear?" Robert asked, but he was not worried. By his very nature JayDee kept everything secret.

"That you and Christine are going to rifle someone's office—"

"That's not what—"

JayDee's laugh rumbled through the room. "I can help."

"You want to help us?"

"Man, you needs help. You Kams just ain't big enough." To JayDee, Robert's slim five-foot-six-inch body looked nearly helpless.

"Kams?"

"Korean-Ams."

"Oh."

"You need an AAm, and ahm yo' man," JayDee said, intentionally exaggerating his pronunciation. Then he smiled his mysterious smile.

"Well—"

"Course, if you think Lava is strong enough to protect both of yous—"

"But JayDee, there's no danger."

"If you say so."

"Well, maybe—"

JayDee stood up. "Great. See you Sunday at 7:05."

As JayDee left, Robert wondered just how much JayDee had heard around the office over the years, and whether the rumor was true that JayDee had grown wealthy from a variety of astute investments in the stock of takeover targets.

As JayDee walked away from Robert's office, whistling quietly to himself, Stuart Craxton arrived at 101 Park and quickly made his way to his power office. He greeted Christine cheerfully, reminding her that she would be rewarded with an early start on the weekend if all went well with the wire transfer.

When Stuart had gone into his office, Christine checked her watch. It was 8:41. That was not early enough to be the sole cause of Stuart's good humor.

Stuart was very happy, in spite of the cold, wet weather. He had calculated the night before how the addition of the Japanese food factories could increase the Nishizaki Management Company fees. And then had projected the results if Japanese food stores were gradually added in all the major metropolitan areas. He was feeling exceedingly wealthy and benevolent.

Stuart called Robert Kim into his office at 9:30 for the conference call with Mohadi Sukemi's Zurich banker and Sydney's banker at the Republic National Bank of New York, where Nishizaki International USA, Inc. had several accounts. Since Stuart had given instructions for the wire transfer on Thursday to the Zurich banker, they only needed to confirm that the $5 million transfer had taken place.

The call only took three minutes, as the money had already arrived at Republic National, causing Robert to hope that his other worries would soon prove to be as baseless as his worries about possible wire complications on the last business day of the quarter.

After the wire transfer confirmation, Stuart was in a mood to celebrate. He invited Robert to join him for lunch at the Nishizaki restaurant on the ground floor of 101 Park and then broke precedent and invited Christine Lava to join them.

When they were prepared to leave for lunch a few hours later, the office was already clearing out for the weekend. But Stuart had yet another surprise for them. Yoshio Mori, a Japanese lawyer who had started working for Tilden & Hayes a month earlier, had been invited to join them for lunch.

Stuart surprised the small closing lunch party by praising Robert's excellent work on the documentation and Christine's unequaled speed in preparing them accurately. He painted a rosy, but not exaggerated, picture of the efficiency of his team for Yoshio Mori's benefit. The surprise came not because the praise was undeserved, but because Stuart rarely made such statements publicly.

As the coffee and desserts were being served, Stuart showed everyone a copy of the letter to Takahiro Nishizaki which Yoshio had hand-written in Japanese.

"It's my usual congratulations on our latest joint venture project, but this time I'm sending it in Japanese, thanks to Yoshio," Stuart explained.

Stuart then read the different Japanese words that he recognized, pronouncing them well enough for Yoshio Mori to understand. Stuart had accelerated the efforts he was putting into his Japanese language studies after he had returned from Japan. Robert and Christine were duly impressed.

But a few minutes later, as he was finishing his dessert, Robert's thoughts wandered to his plan to search Sydney's offices on Sunday. He blanched as he watched Stuart's unwavering enthusiasm, realizing all too clearly that his illegal search could lead to huge problems for his boss.

Chapter Twenty Seven

Tim Craxton opened the side door of the freight entrance of 919 Third Avenue at 7:10 on Sunday morning, March 31st, having guessed that Robert would arrive early. Still, he was surprised to find three people waiting for him. But Tim understood the purpose of JayDee's presence immediately.

Tim directed Christine, JayDee and Robert to the freight elevator, which they rode up to the 37th floor after Robert had set his heavy pile of photocopy paper on the elevator floor. No one felt like talking.

Silence continued to reign as they walked down the 37th floor hallway to the entrance of Nishizaki International USA's offices. It was only broken after they were all standing inside Sydney's private office. JayDee had been immediately distracted by the two pink jade statues of the cheerful, corpulent buddha of future prosperity, which were resting comfortably on a thick Persian rug just outside the entrance to Sydney's private bathroom.

"I'll bet Ms. Brewster sure feels safe in there protected by these gods," JayDee joked, helping everyone relax somewhat.

Robert and Tim, already familiar with the luxuries of Sydney's office, immediately began testing the file cabinets. But Christine followed JayDee around the office, feeling the plush luxury of the Persian carpets under her feet and being fascinated by the bonsai tree alcove and the ten- foot long aquarium. The exotic tropical fish did not look like vegetarian piranhas to her.

Robert and Tim soon discovered that four of the seven file cabinets were locked. Within 15 more minutes it became clear that the three unlocked cabinets contained irrelevant records.

Frustrated, Robert wondered out loud how he could break into the locked file cabinets. Christine heard his complaint, letting him know that that would probably not be necessary. She walked out to Samantha Michaels's desk near the entrance to Sydney's office and returned with a key in just three minutes.

"There are only so many places for secretaries to hide keys," she explained, having found this one taped under Samantha's rolodex.

Although the key Christine had found did not unlock any of the file cabinets, it did open Sydney's locked desk drawer. And inside that drawer were more keys, including those which opened each of the four locked file cabinets.

Now that he had gained access to the locked files, Robert's worries increased. He sent JayDee out to watch the front door before assigning one file cabinet to Tim, and one to Christine, so they could help him search for any records connected to the Nishizaki restaurants or Nishizaki Management Company.

Robert was still looking through his first locked file cabinet when Christine shouted out that she'd found some records for the Nishizaki restaurants. A moment later Tim found more restaurant records in the locked file cabinet assigned to him.

Robert was surprised by the separate locations of the records, but that was only the start of their differences. The files Christine had found contained the records of 12 of the restaurants, the six in New York, Chicago and Los Angeles and another six in Seattle, San Francisco, San Diego, Boston, Washington D.C. and Miami. The documents were well-organized and included up-to-date detailed financial records.

The files Tim had found on the other 18 restaurants had been thrown haphazardly into the file drawer. Most of the usual documents were missing from the files, and there were no detailed financial records, just annual summaries. The file on the Atlanta restaurant was particularly sloppy.

Robert helped bring the files on the 12 restaurants over to the office photocopiers and then gave Christine and Tim the reams of photocopy paper he had brought with him. While they made copies of those records, Robert sat on the floor in Sydney's office and studied the documents Tim had found.

Fifteen minutes later Robert suddenly jumped up, with the annual financial summary of the 30 Nishizaki restaurants in hand, and ran out to the photocopiers, where he quickly looked through the detailed financial records of the 12 restaurants. As he had just guessed, the numbers did not match.

He returned to Sydney's office and tested his new hypothesis. Then he chose various documents that proved his points and brought them out to be copied. When he returned to Sydney's office he thoroughly searched the other drawers of the same file cabinet. In them he found several of the missing partnership agreements, apparently thrown into the wrong file drawer without much interest in retrieval.

Among the documents stored in the last of the four locked file cabinets, Robert found the files on Nishizaki Management Company, but since they were identical with the documents he had seen by mistake, he did not have them copied.

Instead he began to feel the need to get out of Sydney's office. He walked over to JayDee and asked if he'd seen or heard anything. "Nothing" was JayDee's soothing reply, but Robert's concerns returned a minute later when he found out that one of the two photocopiers had run out of toner. There were still several hundred pages of documents to copy, and only one photocopier to do it, and that made Robert nervous. Recognizing there was nothing to be done about the delay, Robert decided to use Tim, and his janitorial keys, to make a more thorough search of Nishizaki International USA's offices.

After finding nothing of consequence in the other offices, Robert and Tim returned to Sydney's corner office. But Robert's suspicions had grown so quickly in the meantime that he even knocked lightly on the walls supporting the aquarium, trying to determine if anything was being stored under the huge tank. The hollow sounds should have reassured him, but there was a slight crack between the outside wall and the top of the aquarium which he wanted to look down, so he moved Sydney's desk chair over and stood on it. When he peered down into the crack he couldn't see how it could possibly be used to hide anything important, but as he was getting off the chair, he did notice something else that was amiss.

"Do you think that alcove is as deep as the entranceway?" he asked Tim.

Sydney's private bathroom jutted out from the middle of the wall opposite the aquarium, splitting the originally rectangular office space into two unequal sections. Robert's viewpoint from the far end of the aquarium made it clear that not only was the entranceway section wider, but also that the bonsai tree alcove on the window side of the bathroom had four or five feet less depth.

"The alcove's not nearly as deep," Tim said, already on his way there. He was followed quickly by Robert. But the wall behind the three levels of bonsai trees seemed solid, so they left Sydney's office and checked out the wall in the reception area and in the accountant's office behind reception. Both were directly on the other side of the unusual wall in Sydney's office, but the reception and accountant's office walls formed a straight line.

Robert and Tim went back into Sydney's office to check again. There was no mistaking the depth difference. Tim mentioned that a support pillar was probably responsible, but Robert found that hard to believe and decided to search Sydney's bathroom.

Surprisingly, the bathroom door was locked. After testing several of the keys they had taken from Sydney's desk, they found the right key and unlocked the door. Inside, at the far left end of the bathroom, was their answer. A large shower had been built behind the alcove wall.

Robert went back to the bonsai alcove, measured its width and returned. There was still a discrepancy of six to eight feet. He slid open the glass shower door and stared at the white plastic wall in front of him. Tim noticed the notch in the wall at the same time Robert did, and they both stepped into the shower to investigate.

"I can just imagine what she keeps in here," Robert said as he slid back the white plastic wall to reveal a huge walk-in safe.

"So can I—gold bars," Tim said dramatically.

"Gold?"

"Yeh. Sydney carries one around with her sometimes just to show off. Anyway, that's what the secretaries say."

"Are you kidding?"

"Nope. That's what I've heard."

"If you ever hear any other rumors about gold bars, call me right away, OK?"

"You or my Dad?"

"You've told your Dad about the gold?"

"Sure."

"Wasn't he just a little surprised?"

"Nah. He says she's loaded."

"Then make it me. Please."

From that moment on all Robert could think about was getting out of Nishizaki's offices as soon as possible. He knew he had already acquired more than enough information to sink Sydney's ship, but he had decided to keep that conclusion to himself until he had had a chance to put all the details together from the documents being too slowly copied.

Even after he had slid the white plastic wall back into place, Robert's anxiety did not subside. And it would have risen to intolerable levels if he had heard the quiet whirring sound, which had begun the moment he had stepped onto the shower floor, or had seen the shower head pivoting slowly as it followed each new movement of his feet.

Chapter Twenty Eight

Late on Monday night in Kyoto, Takahiro Nishizaki took his son Kaoru out for a drive. They left the city and drove for almost an hour before stopping at a small inn. Takahiro ordered a glass of sake and then squeezed into the public telephone booth with Kaoru.

"Remember what I told you to say," Takahiro reminded Kaoru sharply in Japanese as the telephone in New York began to ring. Takahiro Nishizaki had been upset ever since he had noticed the letter from New York sitting in his fax machine early that morning.

"Stuart Craxton's office," Christine said when she picked up the phone.

"I am Takahiro Nishizaki's son. Call from Japan," Kaoru said slowly in English. "Please talk with Mr. Craxton."

"Just one minute, please." Christine let Stuart know that Nishizaki's son was on the line. Stuart asked her to invite Robert Kim and Yoshio Mori to join him as soon as they could.

"Hello, this is Stuart Craxton."

"My name is Kaoru Nishizaki."

"I am pleased to hear your voice," Stuart said too quickly for Kaoru to follow. "Has your father received my letter?"

"Letter? Yes. Father has letter from you. Father ask me to say letter is all wrong."

Robert Kim walked into the office as Kaoru struggled with his English.

"The letter is wrong? Have I offended your father? I did not mean to do that," Stuart said.

"No. Father say he has small business. 50 million yen each year, not more." Kaoru said. "Has no American business. No factories in Japan. Just sell food."

"What do you mean, just sells food?"

"Buy from farmers, sell to others. No factories. No American business. Father not talk English."

"But he signed a contract, he signed many contracts," Stuart protested.

There was a short pause as Kaoru asked his father a question in Japanese before answering.

"Father say he sign one English paper this month, but must sign. Father in danger. Watch out Mr. Minoru Yoshida."

"Yoshida?"

"Father say watch out Mr. Minoru Yoshida."

"But—"

"Father say must go now. Danger to talk."

Kaoru hung up the phone. He saw his father's bowed head and his right hand grasping the empty glass tightly, but he was proud that his father had had the courage to warn the Americans of the danger.

When Christine saw the red light disappear, indicating that the call from Japan was finished, she stepped over to Stuart's office door and told him that Yoshio Mori had not yet arrived at the office. It was just after 9:30 on Monday morning in New York.

Stuart looked at her, not quite comprehending her comment. He was still stunned.

"Just leave a message for Mr. Mori that we received a response to his letter to Mr. Nishizaki, that Stuart is pleased with that response and that he appreciates Mr. Mori's help in this matter very much," Robert said.

Christine looked at Stuart for confirmation of that message and received it. As she stepped back to her desk, Robert walked over to Stuart's office door and closed it, letting Christine know with a look that their work on Sunday was about to bear bitter fruit.

Robert sat down in the chair on the right in front of Stuart's desk while Stuart continued to stare at him. But Robert Kim was quietly elated. The shock on Stuart's face during the phone call had eliminated his fear that Stuart had been involved in the fraud. And his job as a bearer of bad news had just been made much easier.

"You don't seem surprised," Stuart said bluntly. "How long have you known?"

"Only since yesterday. I did some research over the weekend that helped me put several pieces of the puzzle together," Robert said. "Want to hear about it?"

"Certainly," Stuart said without enthusiasm. He felt extremely reluctant to know any more details.

"The news is worse than I thought," Robert began.

"Get on with it," Stuart said impatiently.

"First, there is an unusual pattern in the finances of the restaurants. In 1987 the four original restaurants were open for an average of 6 months each, and they earned a 26 percent return on capital of $10 million. In 1988 the six new restaurants were open for an average of 8 months each, and there was a 25 percent return on total capital of $24 million. In 1989 the eight new restaurants were open for an average of 4 months each, and there was a 28 percent return on total capital of $56 million. In 1990 the 12 new restaurants were open for an average of 10 months each, and there was a 29.5 percent return on total capital of $98 million.

"Since the management contract specifies that Nishizaki Management Company receive 50 percent of any return on capital in excess of a 20 percent annual return, I calculate that—" Robert handed Stuart a sheet of paper on which he had written down his calculations.

	Total Return	*20% Return*	*50% of Difference*
1987	$1,300,000	$1,000,000	$150,000
1988	4,833,333	3,866,667	483,333
1989	9,706,667	6,933,333	1,386,667
1990	26,845,000	18,200,000	4,322,500
Totals	$42,685,000	$30,000,000	$6,342,500

"That total payout of $42,685,000 over the four years was

probably split as follows," Robert continued, handing Stuart a second sheet of calculations.

	Nishizaki USA	AJ Restaurants	Nishizaki Mgt.
1987	$575,000	$575,000	$150,000
1988	2,175,000	2,175,000	483,333
1989	4,160,000	4,160,000	1,386,667
1990	11,261,250	11,261,150	4,322,500
Totals	$18,171,250	$18,171,250	$6,342,500

Stuart reviewed the numbers carefully. He noticed that Robert's estimate of Nishizaki Management Company's share was only off by about $100,000. The current balance in his A.T. Accident, Inc. Swiss bank account was just over $3.3 million, including accrued interest.

"And what do you conclude from these numbers?" Stuart asked coldly.

"I was confused about them before Nishizaki's phone call, but it all makes sense to me now."

"Then enlighten me too," Stuart said sarcastically.

"Well, let's take Nishizaki at his word. Let's assume that he has never invested any money in any American business," Robert said, ignoring Stuart's tone. He had expected a worse reaction.

"For the sake of your argument," Stuart said.

"Right. Because that helps explain why the Atlanta restaurant does not exist."

"What do you mean?"

"Just that. There is no actual restaurant."

"And the profits? I suppose they're also fictional?"

"I assume that is true."

"Why?"

"This is how I see it, Stuart. Working backwards, of the 12 Nishizaki restaurants supposedly opened by Sydney last year, only one was real—the one right here in 101 Park Avenue. The first four opened in 1987 were all real, and Atlanta was the first complete fraud in 1988, but judging by my research I am now assuming that only 12 Nishizaki restaurants actually exist."

"And the other 18?"

"Complete frauds."

"And their profits?"

"Ditto. That's my assumption, anyway. Ironically, the 12 real restaurants appear to be well-run. But they probably only cost about $11 to $12 million to construct and their annual earnings aren't anywhere near the $25 million her 30 cash cows were supposedly producing. The detailed records show the real annual profits are about $1.5 million."

"But that means—"

"They're worth only $15 to $20 million."

"And the rest of the money? Where do you think that is?"

"My calculations suggest that of the $49 million Mohadi Sukemi invested in these restaurants, $11 million went to the cost of the 12 real restaurants, $18.2 million was returned to him in pretend profits and $6 million went to Nishizaki Management Company. That means $13.8 million is still missing—plus the $5 million wired on Friday, plus maybe another $2 to $4 million in real profits from the 12 existing restaurants."

"And where is all that money?"

"Until Nishizaki's call I was guessing that $20 million would be found in Nishizaki's pockets. But now I assume that he never sent any money over here. And that Sydney never sent Nishizaki his $18.2 million in profits either."

"But—"

"Sydney's been handling all the finances, hasn't she?"

"Uh—yes."

"Well I heard a disturbing rumor over the weekend that she buys gold—lots of gold. Which explains why Nishizaki International USA banks at Republic National."

"She's just showing off."

"With whose money?"

"We don't know that, do we?"

MM

"Not yet," Robert said, becoming distressed that Stuart still wasn't listening, "but I'm willing to bet that almost half of the $6 million in management fees covered Sydney's overhead, her staff—and her office artwork."

Stuart didn't even notice the personal jab about half the management fees. Robert's numerical conclusions were making him numb.

"So, if my assumptions are correct," Robert continued, "Sydney Brewster has made Sukemi's money disappear in a classic Ponzi scheme—one that can't last much longer.

"Of course, Sukemi hasn't lost all $54 million. The 12 restaurants may be worth $15 million, the $5 million sent on Friday probably hasn't disappeared yet and he has unknowingly transferred $18.2 million from one of his pockets to another, but he has lost the time value of his money and almost $20 million of his capital has probably disappeared."

"You are dreaming, Robert. This can't be true."

"I have the proof in my office."

"I'm sure you do—"

"Sorry, Stuart, but I do. Anyway, I figure Sydney started slowly, and mostly legitimately. Well, half-legitimately, since I assume Nishizaki International never put any money into the deals right from the start. But I don't see how Sydney can keep this up much longer. The need for cash is voracious. She could only manage one real restaurant out of 12 last year and only two out of eight the year before."

Robert paused. He could see his scenario was finally taking hold in Stuart's mind. He let him think a minute longer and then reminded him, "of course, the $5 million wired on Friday should help—"

"Good God!" Stuart groaned quietly.

"—but Sydney's hand is almost played out, because even a miserly 20 percent return to Sukemi for this year, which she could blame on the slow economy, will cost her over $10 million. And I don't see how she can manage that. That is, unless—"

"Unless what?"

"Unless this is all worth it to someone. Someone who has a lot of dirty laundry to do."

"What?"

"That is just a guess, Stuart, but I can't think of any other reason why that nonexistent Atlanta restaurant has also consistently been the highest producer of cash flow."

Chapter Twenty Nine

"Robert, I hate to interrupt, but you have a very important call," Christine Lava said as she opened Stuart's office door and looked in.

"Can't take it now," Robert said abruptly. Stuart was still silently absorbing Robert's arguments.

"But it's very important, please take it out here," Christine said.

"Is it Lily?" Robert asked, suddenly worried.

"No. But he said it was absolutely crucial."

Robert jumped out of the chair and ran out to take the call, closing Stuart's office door behind him. "Absolutely crucial" was the signal he had arranged with Tim Craxton for when something was seriously wrong at Sydney's office.

Robert took the phone from Christine, who looked very worried.

"What's up?" he asked Tim.

"Sydney is taking me with her to buy gold," Tim said anxiously.

"What?"

"She said she needed help carrying it back. Three others are also going."

"Any sign she knows?"

"No. But I don't like this."

"Can you hang on? I want to ask your Dad—"

"No. I hear—"

Tim hung up the phone without finishing his sentence. Robert walked right back into Stuart's office.

"Stuart, that was your son, Tim. I asked him to call me if he had any news. It seems Sydney is going to buy some more gold. And she's bringing four people with her to help carry it—including Tim."

"That's a lot of showing off," Stuart said wryly. His shock was wearing off and his anger was rising quickly.

"I'm not so sure she's just showing—"

"Where's the Republic National Bank?"

"At Fifth and 39th. The gold desk is on the 12th floor."

"We have to stop her," Stuart insisted.

"On what grounds?"

"I thought you were the one who's so sure—"

"She can't go far with that much gold, can she? And if we have her arrested right at the bank there might be complications—for your client. Publicity. Scandal."

"You're right," Stuart said and immediately pushed the button on his phone that called Sydney directly.

Samantha Michaels answered.

"Is Sydney there?" Stuart asked politely.

"She's on her way out the door, Mr. Craxton," Samantha said, but Sydney heard and came back to answer his call.

"Something important has come up, Sydney, and I was wondering if I could come over to chat."

"Not now. I have to run an errand."

"Then how about lunch?"

"Great."

"At the 101 Park Nishizaki restaurant?"

"I'll be there at 1:00. Got to go now, Stuart."

Stuart leaned back in his chair and stared out the window. He could see clearly enough to decide which office building must be on the corner of 39th and Fifth, and he imagined seeing inside to the 12th floor. He wondered how much of his client's money the Republic National Bank of New York had turned into gold.

Robert Kim sat silently too, ignored by Stuart for more than ten minutes. Robert's imagination was also busy, picturing Sydney's employees stacking $5 million in gold bars in the safe hidden behind her shower.

Finally, still staring out the window, and without looking at Robert, Stuart asked, "are you sure about all this?"

"No, Stuart, I'm not completely sure. I have evidence for my conclusions, but I haven't flown to all the cities where Nishizaki restaurants do not exist. Still, I'm quite sure there is some kind of major fraud involved. If you think about it, Sydney says that in 1990 there was a $26,845,000 profit. Even if they could make $10 per person per meal profit, each of the 30 restaurants would have had to feed almost 90,000 people to create that much profit in one year. That's 250 patrons each and every day in each and every restaurant."

"Sounds highly unlikely, doesn't it," Stuart conceded.

"Quite," Robert agreed.

Stuart was silent for another minute, still staring at the blurred Manhattan skyline. Finally he said, "I appreciate it that you dug your fingers in here and never gave up, Robert. And I'm sorrier than you are that I gave you such a hard time about it. But I still want to know what made you so suspicious of Sydney Brewster."

"In a nutshell?"

"OK."

"I got that from you. Ever since the day I found out Sydney was the daughter of Senator Brewster I've been watching her carefully. I mean, what did you expect? He's a Democrat."

Stuart wished he felt like laughing.

Chapter Thirty

"Please shut the door on your way out," Stuart said to Robert a few minutes later, and Robert did just that. He was happy to leave Stuart alone.

For the next few hours Stuart Craxton refused all calls. He sat in his chair, swiveling it every 15 minutes to change the view, and stared at the Manhattan skyline. He made several attempts to bring it into better focus, but they were all unsuccessful.

As he stared Stuart alternated between formulating a plan to rescue what was left of his client's money and imagining Sydney Brewster's convincing and coherent explanations that destroyed all of Robert's suspicions and continued the stream of generous wire transfers to his client's Swiss bank accounts.

Somewhere in his mind Stuart realized that he should check the evidence Robert said existed, but he did not do it. He wanted to hear Sydney's explanation first.

At 1:00 Stuart stepped into the Nishizaki restaurant 43 floors below his own office and walked to the private room he had reserved to wait for Sydney. She arrived about ten minutes later in a whirlwind of energy and enthusiasm.

"Sorry I'm late, but I have a very tight schedule today," she explained. "In fact, I really don't have time for lunch, so I'd like to get right down to business—if that's all right."

"Sure," Stuart said, but he did not know how to get right down to this business.

"So what is this thing you're so eager to chat about?"

"I'm not really that eager—"

"You sounded like it this morning."

"Well, I wish that I could say this more gently, but there seem to be some mistakes in the restaurant records."

"What is it this time? Another signature Robert Kim doesn't like?" Sydney said as she sat down in a chair, looking tired and very impatient. She did not have time today for trifles.

"No. But something doesn't quite add up right to us. It's a larger mistake, actually. Quite a bit larger—"

"Oh, that reminds me," Sydney interrupted, recovering her energy, "how is Ashley the Mistake doing?"

"She couldn't be better," Stuart said, annoyed at her interruption.

"That's great for a mistake," Sydney said pleasantly.

"Actually, we call her Ashley the Accident. Not to her face, of course. But she wasn't a mistake, just an accident," Stuart explained once more.

"Well, accident or mistake, Ashley must feel safe having so successful and powerful a father—so, what is this problem with the restaurant records you wanted to ask me about?"

Stuart did not want to attempt another explanation, so he just laid Robert's two charts in front of Sydney and added his own hand-written summary of where Mohadi Sukemi's $54 million might have gone.

Sydney Brewster took the three pages and studied them silently for a few minutes. She noticed that the code at the bottom of first two sheets was TH8307, which she recognized as Robert Kim's computer identification number. It had been explained to her once as indicating that Robert was the seventh attorney hired by Tilden & Hayes in 1983.

Stuart was forced to speak first by Sydney's continued silence. "Does this place really average 250 people a day, 365 days a year?" he asked skeptically.

"You know this isn't our most successful restaurant."

"But if not here in New York, how do we do it in Atlanta?"

Sydney looked down at the charts. She didn't answer.

"And what about the gold you bought this morning? Whose money did you use?"

Sydney ignored the question. Instead she whispered very quietly, pointing to the charts, "it seems to me that the two owners of Nishizaki Management are doing very well."

When she looked up she saw that Stuart was staring at her in shock.

"But Sydney, this is impossible," he stammered.

"Not impossible, but perhaps a mistake." Sydney paused for effect before continuing. "Ah yes, that's right. It was all a mistake, Mr. Craxton. Please forget all about it."

Stuart wanted to scream. He grabbed the legs of the table and held on tight. For some reason that prevented his scream from escaping as he concentrated on the naked cunning he saw in Sydney's eyes. An emotional vise gripped his insides so intensely that he felt nauseous.

Sydney stared at Stuart calmly, coldly. "Be here on Friday at noon. There's someone who wants to talk to you," she commanded.

"Who?"

"Never mind. You'll find out soon enough—and don't bother asking Mr. Kim to find out for you."

"What?"

"Just tell your little spy that I understand now why Jackie Messer is on the short list and he isn't. And tell him he really should have gone to detective school before he broke into my offices. Even the fish knew he'd been there."

"I didn't," Stuart said quietly.

Sydney was standing up to leave and didn't hear Stuart clearly, so she ignored his comment. But as she left the private room she added, "oh yes. I knew there was something else I've been forgetting to tell you—please remind Ashley not to play with clowns."

Chapter Thirty One

That evening Robert Kim stepped onto the elevators to leave the office earlier than usual. Lily was waiting in the lobby, having left Columbia University right after Robert called. As they walked home together, Robert explained what had happened, how surprised Stuart had been in the morning, and how devastated he had been when he had returned from his lunch with Sydney.

Robert told Lily that after meeting with Sydney, Stuart had returned to the office and had asked him to review the evidence for his assumption that Sydney's operation was a Ponzi scheme: a pyramid scheme which uses new money to make old money look profitable.

"Stuart concluded our meeting by scolding me for not telling him about my Sunday morning escapade—"

"Ungrateful bas—"

"He didn't mean it, Lily. He was trying to thank me."

Lily caught Robert's arm as he tripped on an uneven block of sidewalk. "Rather clumsy with praise, isn't he?" Lily said.

"Stuart wasn't in the mood for praising anything."

"I can understand that."

"I really feel sorry for him. He's been fooled so badly. That's what hurt him the worst."

"It's a bad day to find out you've been a fool."

"Unless it all disappears tomorrow."

"Fat chance of that happening."

"True. But even I can't believe Stuart got himself into this jam. I just can't explain it."

"Let me try," Lily said. "Maybe Stuart is an idealist, of sorts, who has lost faith in humanity but keeps his pursuit of perfection alive by making economic efficiency the goal. Sydney dazzled him in that area. And so did Japan."

"And now both his gods have fallen," Robert said, although he didn't agree with Lily's analysis. He saw Stuart as motivated more by the avoidance of pain, economic and emotional, than by any ideals. But Robert liked Lily's analysis for what it told him about her. And he had never tried to dissuade her from thinking that everyone was underneath, sometimes deep underneath, just another idealist at heart.

Robert and Lily relaxed at home that evening, having dinner together and then reading on the couch. The tension Robert had been under for months had broken, and even though the news was worse than he had expected, knowing the facts had relaxed him.

The hours drifted by pleasantly until something Robert read reminded him of Bounteous Love.

"Lily, sorry to interrupt," Robert said, "but I got a strange call from Bounty today."

Lily put her book down and gave Robert a look that let him know this had better be important. "I thought you told me Stuart had all her calls cut off."

"That's to him. She called me directly."

"Oh. So what was strange about it?"

"She told me that while she was doing her Clarification work on Saturday—"

"What is this Clarification work she's always talking about?"

"She's just being dramatic. I think what she does is sit back in a chair and imagine how the Universe could be better for a few hours every Saturday afternoon."

"Is that all?"

"I think so. But after being so successful when she was a child, I suppose she needs a very dramatic encore."

"I've seen the reruns. Bounty was adorable. So what ever happened to her acting career?"

"I guess she never got big enough or something."

"It's a cruel world."

"That's just what she called to tell me. It didn't sound like Bounty and her usual optimism at all. She said that while she was doing her Clarification work she saw an image of SEC with his head shrouded in thunderstorm clouds. And I was standing nearby. But I was the one who got wet when it rained."

"Sounds like the usual life of an associate."

"Except Stuart *is* in the midst of a real storm."

"Then maybe it was an April Fool's joke."

"Not from Bounty. She really believes in her Clarification work."

"Well all her talk about Clarification sounds harmless enough at first glance," Lily said, "but I must confess I don't like the part about eliminating sin. That could be expensive."

"Like having to pay for another ark big enough to hold all those animals?"

"No. Like having to pay all those flood insurance premiums."

"That's a great capitalist solution," Robert laughed, "but still, Lily, you've got to admit Bounty has a point. Things are a mess."

"I don't really buy that," Lily said seriously. "The world has been much, much more corrupt and survived quite easily."

"Well you know that. And I know that. But Bounty? Without the special protection and intervention of Mother Nature she believes all the good people would have perished long ago."

"That reminds me, Bobby. Mother Nature wants me to discuss forbidden topic number one."

"Did you go to the doctor already?"

"No. No need. I was just late again."

Robert looked at her mischievously. "We can see to it that that doesn't happen again next month."

"Not much use right now. It's Bloody Monday."

"No harm in trying."

"That's true. From what I hear, there are plenty of teenage girls who get pregnant from just kissing—even when it's supposed to be safe."

Robert stood up and stretched lazily. Their recent decision to give making babies a chance had taken its toll on his spontaneity, but the effort seemed worthwhile. Robert knew that he would soon have more time on his hands to help out. And he also knew that Lily's mind was thoroughly made up.

As they walked slowly to the bedroom together, Lily said, "why don't we try something exotic for a change?"

"What do you have in mind?"

"The missionary position."

"What?"

"I'd like to try being dull and unresponsive once. You take advantage of me. I do my marital duty. That kind of thing."

"I doubt you'll ever experience that, dear."

"Can't we just try it?"

"Why?"

"I want to be passive in the face of unyielding male passion—just once."

"But you know I'm not interested in borderline necrophilia. What's come over you?"

"It makes a lot of girls pregnant, Bobby."

"Women, Lily, women," Robert laughed. "How many times do I have to tell you?"

"I can say girls if I want to. But you can't."

"You don't sound too passive, dear. Maybe you aren't in the mood for this."

Lily proved he was wrong, and Robert had a difficult time with her passivity. He abruptly lost interest after five minutes of real work. He was starting to feel old, to feel that a sense of duty could destroy any kind of fun, when Lily whispered encouraging words and he recovered.

But he was exhausted without being relaxed afterwards.

As Robert lay next to her, Lily slipped a slim book out from under the mattress and glanced at a diagram. She propped herself up on pillows and then didn't move again.

Robert noticed and said, "that won't do any good, not today."

"A lot of schoolgirls get pregnant during their period, don't they?"

"I don't know," Robert said, exasperated.

"Say, do you think Stuart and his wife always make love this way?" Lily asked.

"I've never asked him."

"Why not?"

"What a question!"

"No. I mean it. Why haven't you asked him?"

"Because men just don't discuss that kind of thing."

"They don't?"

"No. They don't."

"Then I'll call Catherine and ask her."

"Don't you dare."

"But I'd like to know."

"Just forget it. Besides, at his age I find it hard to imagine Stuart ever making love."

"He's not *that* old. But I'd bet he still pretends he's a missionary every time."

"That's not why it's called the missionary position, dear."

"Tell that to our great-grandmothers!"

Chapter Thirty Two

Stuart kissed Catherine tenderly, holding her in his arms as she lay quietly by his side. They listened for the sounds of their children, but the house seemed empty. Ashley was asleep in the next room and Tim was probably reading in the basement. Stuart was relaxed, but more from having told Catherine all his secrets than from having made love.

Stuart had called Catherine right after Sydney had left the Nishizaki restaurant, telling her to pick Ashley up from school immediately. Then, after making sure that Robert's evidence supported his assumptions about the extent of the financial fraud, Stuart had gone home.

He had spent the entire afternoon playing with Ashley. Until it began to rain they had played soccer in the backyard. Then Ashley had initiated Stuart into Nintendo's video game world. And after dinner he had helped her with her math homework for more than an hour.

Catherine had waited patiently through all those hours, knowing that Stuart was reluctant to talk with her, but once Ashley was in bed, Stuart had told her everything.

He had explained why he had not told her that he had thought a crazy woman, Bounty, had been Ashley's kidnapper and he let her know that Bounty had once seen a wire confirmation for a Nishizaki Management Company transfer to his Swiss Bank Corporation account in Geneva. Stuart had explained the existence of that account as his attempt to build a legacy for their accidental daughter. Even the corporate name, A.T. Accident, Inc., made that clear.

Stuart had conceded that he had lied to Catherine, that he had never called Mohadi Sukemi to arrange a loan, and that they did have over a million dollars in a Swiss bank account that she did not know about, but he argued that he had had a good reason for those lies. He had been hoping to surprise her on Ashley's 10th birthday with a doubling of the value of their investments.

But mostly he had asked her to stick by him. Against his own better judgment, he told her, he had played at being an investment banker and had been completely duped. He worried that his investment in Nishizaki Management Company, if discovered, would put an end to his legal career, and he promised to do whatever was necessary to avoid that problem. Whatever was necessary, that is, without lying. He did not want to lie again, even as part of a pleasant surprise.

He had a plan, he told her. Unfortunately, he was not certain it would work without revealing his own investment, and once his investment was revealed it would be nearly impossible to make anyone believe he had not been involved in the fraud. If that happened, he felt especially bad about how it would affect their boys. He hoped that his disgrace would not cloud their future careers. But he had to try his plan anyway. He would not give in to Sydney's threats.

Catherine supported him. She even secretly hoped that they might be poor in the future, assuming that would solve so many of their personal problems. But her concern about the distance that had been growing between them dissolved within another hour of tender talk.

Catherine had long ago stopped trying to explain to her friends that Stuart was actually very tender with her. They could only see his arrogance, coldness and efficiency, and had often told her that with her beauty, brains and wealth she could have had anyone.

But Catherine had never felt that confident. As a child she had been pampered, and as a young woman she had been courted by many men, but Stuart's tenderness, when they were alone, was the most persuasively genuine affection she had ever known. The depth of Stuart's tenderness had surprised her, winning her affection then just as it had tonight.

Although Stuart had always been a little awkward as a lover, a little stiff in places where it wasn't useful, and persistently unimaginative, he was an attentive lover, never making love unless he desired to express his tenderness for her.

For Catherine such continually affectionate treatment had effectively disarmed all her friends' protests. She simply assumed that they would never understand unless they had experienced such affection themselves. And, knowing their husbands and lovers, she doubted that they had.

It had also been impossible for her to explain that this part of their life together had never suffered, not seriously, during the 23 years they had been married. She had always felt she was the woman in Stuart's life, the only woman, and she had good reason for feeling that way. Partially it was because she knew that Stuart considered extramarital affairs to be incomprehensible follies engaged in by men of lesser intelligence, usually with women who were less interesting and beautiful than their own wives. But mainly it was because she knew that Stuart had been raised to be a gentleman by his mother.

Stuart's initial success with Catherine was the result of a rule he had devised when he had first decided to try to make her his wife. His rule was that he would never kiss her unless he felt tender toward her at that moment. After they were married, he had expanded the rule and then kept it religiously through the years.

Catherine was unaware of this rule. She was aware that there had been times when Stuart hadn't kissed her for ten or twelve days in a row, but always when the next kiss came it was a tender one, and so Catherine had never complained.

Stuart's rule had worked well for him, too, first by winning Catherine's affection and then by giving him an excuse to be tender, an excuse to indulge someone in ways he would never indulge himself. And so, without realizing it, he had carefully protected Catherine's sensitivity over the years so that it would always be there to arouse his deeply submerged desire to be tender.

On this rainy April afternoon, though, Stuart's desire had surfaced as quickly as if Sydney's threats had been depth charges. And it had remained on the surface ever since.

"Today is Monday, the First," he said to Catherine as they lay in bed together, "and I have no idea how long it will take to get my plan to work. And it might not work at all if I'm worried about you—and Ashley."

"We'll take care of ourselves."

"I know you will. But there's just too much danger. I don't want to come home and find—"

"What should we do?" Catherine asked after Stuart had left his fears hanging in the air, wordless but clear.

"Go someplace. Get away. Sydney doesn't have a big operation. She won't be able to track you down if we are careful."

"Where should we go?"

"Someplace unusual."

"Japan?"

"Are you trying to be funny? I'd even prefer Massachusetts."

"Then how about Stockholm?"

"That's good. You won't stick out there—but better yet, take Icelandair's flight to Luxembourg, but get off in Reykjavik and stay there at a spa. OK?"

"You're not just being frugal?"

"Not this time."

"Should I take Tim?"

"No. Just Ashley. I need Tim here. And I'll let Stu know what's up."

"If anything happens to—"

"I'm sorry. I was really trying to make it safer for all of us."

"I know you were, dear."

"Let me help you pack," Stuart offered, getting out of bed in an effort to avoid discussing the danger Tim was in.

As they packed Stuart tried to explain his thoughts, his decisions, over the last four years, and how they were supposed to have helped the family. Catherine listened, but mostly just heard an uncertainty she wasn't used to in Stuart, an uncertainty that magnified her own fears.

"And if you see any clowns, run," Stuart was saying as Catherine's mental image of being snow-bound and stranded in Iceland melted away.

"We will."

"What was that clown's name again?"

"Roo."

"Haven't I heard that name before?" Stuart asked.

"I'm sure you have," Catherine said, her memory having been triggered by Stuart's question. "It's the name of the baby kangaroo who gets kidnapped in *Winnie the Pooh*."

Chapter Thirty Three

Minoru Yoshida paced back and forth across the length of the small private dining room in the 101 Park Nishizaki restaurant on Friday afternoon, April 5th. He stared at Stuart Craxton, not believing what he had just heard him say.

"You don't know what you are saying. And you don't know who you are dealing with," Minoru Yoshida nearly shouted.

"With whom am I dealing?" Stuart asked, intentionally precise in his wording.

"Well it's not Sydney Brew—"

"Roo, I've got to talk you," Sydney interrupted, using the nickname she had devised for Minoru shortly after they had met.

"Not now," Minoru said.

"Now," Sydney insisted.

Minoru was angry, but they left, leaving Stuart sitting alone in the room. He changed his seat so that he faced the entrance.

When Minoru and Sydney returned, Stuart watched them carefully. It was clear that something Sydney had said had calmed Minoru down.

"Mr. Craxton, let me put it this way," Minoru began. "We cannot maintain the profitability of the Nishizaki International USA investments without a fresh and sizeable input of capital and—"

"I said no."

"We know that. But you must reconsider. The stakes for you, and for us, are just too high. Sydney has suggested to me, and I have agreed, that we revise our offer. Instead of requiring a continuing commitment on your part, we will be satisfied if you induce your client to make one final capital contribution, of $25 million, to build a chain of Japanese food stores—"

"Will you build them? Will you build any?"

"I'm afraid that won't be possible before bankruptcy proceedings have—"

"No. I won't cooperate," Stuart insisted.

"But your money in Geneva will be very hard to explain."

"I will accept the consequences of disclosure."

"But what you don't seem to understand are just what those consequences might be."

"That doesn't matter."

"But we want you to think about it. There are a lot of other financial advisors out there getting real rich real fast, too. And some even dabble in gold bars. You could be one of them."

"I'm a lawyer, not an investment banker."

"You might not be a lawyer much longer."

"I can live with that."

"That's what we're not so sure about," Minoru said, putting his hand into his jacket pocket.

Stuart stood up to face him. "Certain people know I am here. And who else is here." The calmness of his voice surprised even Stuart.

"The same can be said for us, right Sydney?"

"I am not threatening you," Stuart said.

"You certainly are. We have been counting on your client's money."

"I can't help that."

"Well think about it. Just think about our latest offer. One last deal. $5 million more in your Swiss bank account. And your client will never know what hit him—and he'll never miss a dime either. He's got way too much money anyway."

"No."

"Just think about it. And be here next Wednesday."

"Make it Friday."

"Wednesday."

"Friday. I have to talk to a few people."

"The police?"

"Certainly not. You've already made sure of that, haven't you?"

"OK, if you're going to think about it, we'll make it next Friday. At noon," Sydney said.

"I'll be here."

"We know you will, Mr. Craxton," Minoru Yoshida said.

Stuart decided to gamble. He stood up and walked toward the door, and then turned around and addressed Minoru Yoshida personally.

"By the way, Roo, my daughter told me you are very good at Concentration."

"Yes I am," Minoru said immediately. "It is always important to remember what's been turned over and what hasn't. And you can't be too anxious or you'll forget the facts. It's a good game."

"And are you a good clown?" Stuart asked more directly, his anger obvious.

"That was just business," Minoru Yoshida said. "Just business."

"No. That wasn't just business. That was my daughter."

"It was just business," Minoru repeated. "I have two daughters myself."

Stuart visibly relaxed. This was just about money, just about business, and that he could handle. Then he remembered the fight with Catherine about getting Ashley examined by a doctor. He was very happy she had won.

"I wish every man had a daughter," Stuart blurted out.

"I would have slept easier too," Minoru agreed.

"For no good reason," Sydney said harshly, "that never stopped my father."

Minoru laid his hand over Sydney's for just a moment.

"But then why?" Stuart asked, still standing in the doorway.

"We only needed to know one thing. Would you go to the police or would you pay."

"You certainly have a peculiar way of doing business, Mr. Yoshida."

"So have you, Mr. Craxton. That is why we are doing business together."

"Because now you know I will pay?"

"Certainly. You see, our game was nearing its end—and we didn't want you to be left with all those pairs, now did we, Sydney?"

"Certainly not," she said.

"And our new game is about to be laid out. We want you to keep playing. We want you to concentrate. And it helped you concentrate, didn't it Mr. Craxton?"

Stuart's silence made his answer perfectly clear.

Chapter Thirty Four

That same Friday afternoon Stuart left his office ten minutes earlier than usual to catch the 6:35 Express back to Scarsdale. He stopped in the main concourse of Grand Central Station and used a public phone to call Catherine in her Reykjavik hotel.

Catherine was still awake when he called, relieved to hear that his negotiations were proceeding smoothly. But they only talked for a few minutes, Stuart insisting on being careful. In the three days Catherine and Ashley had been gone, Stuart had not called them from a phone that could be traced to him.

At home, after tossing a casserole Catherine had prepared into the microwave oven, Stuart sat down with Tim for dinner.

"Tim, I'm sure you realize you are in danger—"

"That doesn't bother me."

"And I owe you an explanation."

"You don't owe me anything."

"Maybe. But I want to explain anyway. I know I can confide in you. And what I am about to tell you I don't want your mother ever to know—or Ashley or Stu either."

"I can keep a secret."

"I know that. And I also know that if my plan doesn't work, we will both be in serious danger."

"What's your plan?"

"I don't have all the details worked out yet. There are several options and they depend on how others play their roles. But none of the options includes a happy ending."

"That's OK by me. I'm a pessimist."

"I wish you weren't, Tim. But it won't hurt right now because what you've got to do above all is take care of your mother and Ashley if anything happens to me. They will need you."

"I can do that."

"I know you can. But if you hear anything has happened to me, I want you to jump on the first plane to Europe, make your way to Reykjavik slowly and carefully, and then move them around every week. And don't come back to New York for at least six months. Your mother will know how to get to our funds."

"OK."

"So let me explain," Stuart said, and told Tim everything he had told Catherine on Monday night. And then he explained in more detail his Swiss bank account.

"No matter what else happens, I want you to go to Geneva sometime in the next six months and make sure Swiss Bank Corporation transfers all $3.3 million into one of Mohadi Sukemi's accounts."

"$3.3 million?"

"It's not our money, son. I thought it was, but it's not."

"How did—"

Stuart interrupted Tim's question, but then decided to explain in detail what he had thought and what had really been happening. He told Tim about the original $100,000 investment he had made in Nishizaki Management Company, and the easy money he thought he had been earning giving excellent investment advice to his client.

He also explained that Mohadi Sukemi had approved of the arrangement, but that he had never disclosed it to his partners at Tilden & Hayes. He had considered that unnecessary because the profits were from an investment he had made, and were based on investment, not legal, advice he had given to his client. But he admitted to Tim that he did not want his partners to find out. He was concerned that they would want to divide the profits among themselves, and he had no intention of keeping the money.

Stuart also explained that one of the tax partners, Frank DeSocio, did know some of the details of his investment in A.T. Accident,

Inc., in case Tim ever needed his help. Stuart had discussed with Frank the income tax effects of the enormous earnings that had been deposited in his Swiss bank account during 1990 and in March of 1991. But since Stuart had not yet filed his tax returns for 1990, Frank was redoing them based on the new assumption that the money accumulating in the Swiss bank account had never been earned by Stuart.

Stuart also explained to Tim that he had decided not to file amended returns for 1988 and 1989 in order to receive a refund from the IRS of the almost $225,000 in extra income taxes Stuart had paid on the investment income he had received from A.T. Accident, Inc. during those years, because avoiding IRS scrutiny of the transactions seemed worth even more than that. And Frank DeSocio had agreed with Stuart's conclusion that he had no legal obligation to pay taxes on the money now accumulating in the Swiss bank account if it could be treated as having been held by A.T. Accident, Inc., as trustee, on Mohadi Sukemi's behalf. All of which explained why it was so important to transfer the money back to Mohadi Sukemi.

Stuart wanted Tim to feel that obligation strongly. And that was how Tim felt, even before he knew all the tax consequences and in spite of his dislike of his father's client.

Then Stuart told Tim several of the details from his meeting with Minoru Yoshida and Sydney Brewster, including the not-so-veiled threats and their clear responsibility for Ashley's kidnapping. Stuart's elaborate speculations as to how they would react to his absolute refusal to cooperate frightened his son more than Stuart realized.

"Of course, this is my problem, son, not yours. But I wanted you to know how I want these matters settled if—"

"Man, you're really up shit creek without a paddle," Tim said in amazement.

"No. I have a paddle."

"What's that?"

"Minimize the pain. And if not for yourself, at least for others."

"That's very paternalistic, Dad."

"I got it from my father. What do you expect?"

"I expect you to paddle furiously."

"That's exactly what I intend to do."

Chapter Thirty Five

On Monday morning, April 8th, Stuart walked into Ted Swaine's office on the 47th floor of 101 Park Avenue. Ted had been standing by the window, waiting for him to come in.

"How are you doing, Stuart? Beautiful day, isn't it?"

"Gorgeous," Stuart agreed.

"Say, have you heard that Tom Carnahan has landed a billion dollar project?"

"No, I haven't," Stuart said, somewhat surprised that Carnie hadn't told him.

"It'll be in the paper tomorrow. Apparently the Coal Miners Union Pension Fund he represents is investing in a joint venture to build Niagara Malls. From what I hear it's going to be the world's largest double mall, just about a mile away from the Falls. It's being designed to outdraw them as a tourist attraction."

"That's great for Carnie."

"Great for us too. There's more than a million in legal fees in a project that size."

"No doubt about that."

"So I guess it was worth it after all to let Carnie take on that union as a client, don't you think? Still, I'm not quite used to us representing coal miners."

"I know what you mean," Stuart said, remembering his fight years ago with Ted about allowing Carnahan to take on a union as a client.

"Your father would certainly never have allowed it."

"Probably not."

"But we have to adapt to the times."

"I guess so," Stuart reluctantly agreed.

"As long as we're speaking about the problems of not adapting," Ted said, "I received your latest request about getting Robert Kim onto the short list in time for the Anniversary Dinner. It's a non-starter, Stuart. Can't do it."

"You'd better look at his billings again, Ted. I'm sure you can see your way to—"

"He's just not partner material," Ted Swaine said.

"I don't agree."

"Of course you don't. You work with him. But I've talked to him a few times myself, too, and I just don't think he has it."

"What's it?"

"Adaptability," Ted answered, having concluded that that was the legal virtue missing from Robert's character due to his excessive honesty.

"But he's even more adaptable than I am!" Stuart said, not understanding what Ted Swaine had meant.

"That may very well be. But that just shows it's a damn good thing you aren't still an associate."

"But—"

"Look, Stuart, it's impossible. The short list has been final for months. You've done your duty by Mr. Kim. Now forget it."

"But, Ted, think how good it would look to have a minority on the short list."

"Nice try, Stuart, but I said forget it. Besides, I know you don't even buy that argument yourself. And I sure hope this isn't what you thought we needed to discuss so urgently."

"It's not."

"So what's up?"

"I need to have your authority to negotiate with our insurance company."

"Which one?"

"Liability."

"AFPIC?"

"That's right."

"You'd better tell me all about it, Stuart."

Stuart did, but without revealing his indirect ownership of half the shares of Nishizaki Management Company. To Ted Swaine's secret satisfaction, that information was already locked away in his desk in the slot reserved for Stuart Emerson Craxton III.

Chapter Thirty Six

At noon on Friday, April 12th, Stuart walked into the Nishizaki restaurant and was shown to the private room where Sydney Brewster and Minoru Yoshida were waiting for him. They stood up when he entered.

"Have you made up your mind?" Sydney asked.

"Absolutely," Stuart said.

"Then we have no time to lose. Robert should get started on the new joint venture agreement—"

"There won't be any more new joint ventures. I've made up my mind," Stuart said firmly.

"You don't seem to understand," Minoru Yoshida said. "I'm not giving you a choice."

"You have to. I am indispensable."

"No you aren't. I can make you completely irrelevant in just one second," Minoru said.

"But I am highly relevant—if you want to walk away from this fiasco."

Minoru Yoshida went to the door and looked out. No one was there.

"Are you bluffing?"

"No."

"Have you told the police?"

"No—but I have left instructions that will give the police all the information they need if anything happens to me."

"But our last proposal—"

"I cannot knowingly cheat my client. I cannot do it. And I won't do it. But I do have a counter-proposal for you."

"I am not here to bargain with you, Mr. Craxton," Minoru

Yoshida said.

"Then I may as well leave—and call the police."

"Let's hear your proposal," Sydney said.

"Since the joint ventures were frauds, the first thing to do is to acknowledge that Mr. Sukemi's contributions to them are actually debts incurred by Nishizaki International USA, Inc. And then Nishizaki USA must declare bankruptcy. And I mean now, not later."

"I will not listen to—"

"Go on, Stuart," Sydney said, cutting off Minoru's objections.

"We have calculated that you have used only $11 million of my client's $54 million dollar investment to buy the 12 restaurants which actually exist. $18.2 million was returned to him in profits. $6.3 million went to Nishizaki Management Company in fees. And $5 million was wired to you just two weeks ago—which we assume is still sitting in Republic National. Or in a gold vault nearby. That adds up to $40.5 million. Which means that $13.5 million of my client's money is still missing.

"However, my client is prepared to drop all charges against both of you if the $6.3 million in fees, the $5 million recently wired to you and that missing $13.5 million is returned to him within one month."

"You're—"

"I'm not done, Mr. Yoshida. My client is aware that the time value of his money will be lost, and that several million dollars might remain in your pockets, but he is willing to allow that injustice to occur as long as you both disappear discreetly and the ownership and management of the restaurants is transferred to his own chosen assignee."

"You can't be serious," Sydney said.

"I am perfectly serious," Stuart replied.

"But the $6.3 million in fees—"

"I have already arranged for the entire $3.3 million in A.T. Accident, Inc.'s account to be transferred to my client's account. And he expects you to do the same with your share of the fraudulently earned fees."

"That's impossible."

"Let's talk about it."

"No, Mr. Craxton, we won't discuss this any further," Minoru said. "Since your client knows all about—"

"I didn't say that," Stuart said calmly.

"But—"

"I am authorized to negotiate on my client's behalf. And I know exactly what he will find acceptable."

"You arrogant fool," Minoru Yoshida said angrily, taking an automatic pistol out of his jacket pocket.

Stuart stared at the pistol for a moment and then played his trump card, having anticipated the possibility of Minoru's deadly threat.

"I can't be any blunter than this," Stuart said. "You can kill me if you wish, but then your fraud will never pay off. I have made sure of that. You have only one choice if you don't want to go to prison. And that is to accept my proposal."

"Impossible," Minoru shouted.

"Not at all," Stuart replied.

"Let's talk about it," Sydney said.

"No," Minoru insisted.

"Privately," she answered and Minoru saw he had to agree. He warned Stuart to remain where he was until they returned.

"I have no intention of going anywhere," Stuart replied. He knew he was winning.

As they left the private dining room Minoru motioned to one of the waiters to keep an eye on Stuart. Then Sydney and Minoru left the restaurant to discuss their options in the privacy of the crowded streets of New York.

"He is a fool," Minoru said.

"A stubborn fool," Sydney agreed, "but I've seen him like this. He will not change his mind."

"He has to."

"He won't. He means it. I'll bet he's already made a new will since last Friday."

"Is he really that stubborn?"

"Yes, Roo. You haven't been working with him. So trust me. We aren't going to get any more money out of our Indonesian sieve. But I'll bet Stuart will let us keep what we already have."

"But they are expecting more gold in Kyoto. We have promised."

"How much of the first $2 million in shipments has already arrived?"

"About $1.5 million, I think. The rest is still in transit."

"Then we've just got to explain that this source has dried up. We have no control over—"

"That argument won't fly."

"Then it's time for us to retire," Sydney said.

"But we were so close to our goal. One last killing and—"

"Roo, we have between eight and nine million, right?"

"Maybe a little more."

"That's more than enough. Let's get out now while we have a chance."

Sydney and Minoru discussed their options, and their negotiation and escape strategies, at length before returning to the Nishizaki restaurant. Stuart was sitting there patiently, waiting for them to return.

"We have discussed your offer," Sydney began, "and are willing to accept the bankruptcy of Nishizaki USA and your client's assumption of the ownership and management of the restaurants. But it is impossible to return 100 cents on the dollar to your client."

"What is possible?" Stuart asked.

"First, the value of the restaurants is far in excess of the $11 million paid for them," Sydney argued. "Their actual cash flow is over $1.5 million—"

"Can that be independently verified?"

"Not on the tight time schedule you are demanding."

"So how much do you calculate they are worth?

"$25 million," Sydney said.

"To whom?"

"To your client."

"I am certain they are not worth more than $15 million to him."

"Twenty."

"Sixteen."

"Eighteen."

"Sixteen."

"It doesn't matter. He will not get 100 cents on the dollar anyway. So let's say the restaurants are worth $16 million. And the rest of the business, the office here in New York, the computers—"

"The art," Stuart said.

"Yes, that's another $5 million."

"I included all that in the $16 million figure."

"That's ridiculous."

"Was the office overhead deducted from the restaurant's cash flow?"

"Of course."

"Then it's all part of the same package."

"Have it your way, Stuart, it'll just look worse."

"Not worse. Accurate. I want it to look accurate—for a change."

"OK. OK. So there's $16 million. And he has received $18.2 million, which is worth $25 million by now—"

"We are not going to count the time value of that money. He lost that by putting it back into your operations anyway."

"OK. So there's $16 million and $18.2 million—$34.2 million out of $54 million. That's more than 60 cents on the dollar. What more can he expect from a bankruptcy?"

"My $3.3 million—"

"We have no objection to that," Minoru said.

"And your $3.3 million, plus the $5 million just wired—"

"I'm afraid that $5 million has already been spoken for," Minoru said.

"You'll have to cancel the contracts."

"Impossible."

"Nothing is—"

"Absolutely impossible."

"Not a single penny?"

"Maybe $500,000 is left," Sydney said.

"And your $3.3 million?"

"It's all long gone."

"That is unfortunate. I am not authorized to accept less than 75 cents on the dollar."

"Then perhaps the restaurants should be valued at $25 million after all—"

"Seventy-five real cents."

"Then perhaps you will have to dip into your own funds," Minoru said.

To Minoru's surprise, Stuart agreed. "I will do that as long as you are willing to match my contribution."

"Let's figure that out," Sydney said, taking out a calculator. "16 and 18.2 and your 3.3 is 37.5. And we need $40.5 million to get your client 75 cents on the dollar."

"You are forgetting the $500,000 left from the last wire transfer."

"Right. So we need $2.5 million more. Are you saying you will contribute $1.25 million of your own money if we can arrange to transfer $1.25 million to your client?"

"If you put in $1.25 million, plus the $500,000, and transfer ownership of the restaurants—we have a deal."

"And you will not press charges?"

"That's right. My client will not press charges, provided that his privacy is permanently maintained."

"Then have Robert draw up the notes, and the bankruptcy papers—"

"We will take possession by a deed in lieu of bankruptcy."

"However," Sydney said.

"Then the papers will all be finished and available for your signature as soon as several other minor details are worked out."

"Are you setting more conditions?"

"No. Just more details. They will take me a little time to arrange, but I am confident our deal will be acceptable."

"We have a few details to attend to as well, Mr. Craxton," Minoru Yoshida said.

"Do you wish to reopen the negotiations?"

"No. But I am curious. You are, after all, allowing us to walk away. And you are paying a high price to make us do that."

"But you already knew I'd rather pay than go to the police, didn't you Mr. Yoshida?"

"You are a very clever man, Mr. Craxton—but I am not yet convinced that the price you are paying is high enough to cover all the costs of your cleverness."

"What do you mean?"

"I mean we must placate the anger of those whose expectations of future profits are being eliminated by your proposal."

"I can understand that," Stuart said.

"I'm not sure you can," Minoru countered.

"Well, then, to show my good faith, I am willing, if you transfer that $1.75 million into a Tilden & Hayes escrow account by Monday afternoon, to have $500,000 retransferred to whatever bank account you specify, as long as that second transfer can be made by early Tuesday afternoon."

Minoru Yoshida sighed. "That is not what I had in mind, Mr. Craxton, but it may suffice."

Chapter Thirty Seven

At 4:25 on Wednesday afternoon, April 17th, Stuart reentered the large conference room on the 47th floor of 101 Park Avenue. Five executives of the Attorney Fraud Protection Insurance Company and four of its in-house attorneys were seated at the mahogany table, along with E. Theodore Swaine and Robert Kim. During Stuart's absence they had discussed for almost an hour the potential legal problems, and their effect on AFPIC's coverage of Tilden & Hayes, that would arise if Mohadi Sukemi decided to sue Tilden & Hayes for legal malpractice.

Robert Kim had had the uncomfortable job of discussing at length the various problems he had uncovered, including the forgeries, the lies Sydney Brewster had told about her own qualifications and the peculiarly notarized deed for the Atlanta restaurant. And Robert also explained that, while recently reviewing all the Nishizaki files, he had discovered that only unrecorded deeds were found in the files for each of the fraudulent restaurants, while copies of recorded deeds existed for each of the real restaurants. It was that fact that had caused the most distress to the AFPIC executives.

Stuart had cooperated with the discussion, and had encouraged Robert to explain that the trail of clues he had uncovered should have caused more scrutiny and caution. And Stuart had accepted full responsibility for minimizing the significance of the damaging clues. Stuart's explanation of his behavior was that the profitable returns of the Nishizaki restaurants had so pleased his client that he had given Sydney Brewster's operations the benefit of the doubt. And he mentioned that he felt she deserved that benefit, being the daughter of Senator Anthony Brewster.

Stuart had suggested to each of them that, under the same

circumstances, they would also have considered those problems minor indiscretions, not the tip of an iceberg. But he had admitted that his eagerness to believe was unprofessional. And then he had left the room at their request.

Upon his return Stuart could see that the AFPIC executives were very unhappy.

"We have decided to retain representation in this matter," AFPIC's general counsel, Dianne Hirshfield, said. "And we expect that Tilden & Hayes will do the same."

"We certainly will," Ted Swaine said. It was clear that he was very angry.

"Before you both do that," Stuart said, "I arranged for this meeting to be held without outside representation because I think I have a plan that will take care of our mutual problem."

"Mutual?" Joseph Agosta, an AFPIC vice president, asked skeptically.

"I have been assuming that the millions of dollars we have paid you in insurance premiums make this a mutual problem," Stuart replied, "but you can decide that later. First I want you to consider an alternative solution to a protracted battle with us over your coverage and the enormous expense of a probably successful suit by my client."

"We are listening," Dianne said.

"I propose that AFPIC cut a certified check for $35.8 million, made out to Mohadi Sukemi."

"Perhaps you didn't understand, Mr. Craxton," Dianne began, but Stuart interrupted her.

"And this is what AFPIC will get in return for cutting that check: the ownership of the 12 Nishizaki restaurants, currently earning, we think, about $1.5 million a year. Isn't that right, Robert?"

"That appears to be the real cash flow. About $1.579 million in 1990, if I remember correctly," Robert said.

"Those restaurants are worth at least $16 million, including the New York office, and maybe even $20 million if you find the right buyer."

"And how would you arrange to obtain the ownership for us?" Dianne asked.

"We have already prepared deeds in lieu of bankruptcy for each of the properties. Isn't that correct, Robert?"

"That's correct," Robert agreed.

"And I have already negotiated their signing by Sydney Brewster. If you agree with my plan, we can get them signed tomorrow."

"But that's only half of the check amount. We are not persuaded," Ken Dwyer, the AFPIC executive vice president in charge of their negotiating team, said.

"In addition, I have $1.25 million sitting in an escrow account waiting to be transferred to you," Stuart said.

"Where did that come from?" Dianne asked.

"Sydney Brewster. She claims that is what remains of the last $5 million transfer. And we know for a fact that she returned that much in gold to Republic National last Friday afternoon to cover Monday's wire transfer to our escrow account."

"And the other $3.75 million?"

"Ms. Brewster claims that other creditors had to be satisfied first."

"And she was convincing about that, too?" Dianne asked sarcastically.

"Yes. Very convincing. But I understand my responsibility in this matter. We found out about the fraud on the Monday after that $5 million was wired. But I decided it was in my client's best interests to negotiate with Sydney rather than provoke a confrontation with her at Republic National. And that proved to be an expensive decision. As a result, I have decided to transfer $3.3 million of my personal funds to AFPIC to cover the bulk of that loss."

The AFPIC executives and attorneys were stunned. "That is extremely generous," Ken Dwyer said.

"But I insist," Stuart replied. "I would find it impossible to contribute any less—under the circumstances. In fact, that $3.3 million is already sitting in the same escrow account waiting for your decision."

Ted Swaine and Robert Kim shared a glance. Robert could not help smiling.

"We appreciate your contribution," Ken Dwyer said.

"Hopefully it won't cost me any more than that."

"We wouldn't think of asking you for more."

"I didn't mean that," Stuart said cryptically, and then unexpectedly lost his temper. "I meant the Japanese are—", he said furiously, before cutting himself off in an effort to retain control. But almost immediately he added angrily, "I'm damn glad they got taken on the Rockefeller Cen—"

"Stuart, the Japanese race is not responsible for Sydney's fraud," Robert Kim interrupted forcefully, in an attempt to give his boss time to recover before saying anything damaging to his cause. "Of course, there are a few who do commit crimes. But they are, after all, only human."

"Unfortunately!" Stuart agreed, still angry, but back under control.

No one was surprised at Stuart's outburst. It only made all the more amazing the detached objectivity he had shown during the lengthy discussions.

"So, that is your settlement offer?" Dianne asked, ignoring Stuart's outburst.

"Yes. And I think my client will accept it," Stuart answered, calm again. "I will explain to him that he has already received $18.2 million of his own money back, and that the $35.8 million check makes up the difference. My guess is he will be pleased to get all his money back, even though he will have lost the time value of it."

"Maybe you can talk him down even lower," Bob Wallace, another AFPIC vice president, suggested.

"Perhaps. But I think if I tell him he's going to have every cent of his $54 million back in his pocket, he'll buy it. Otherwise he'll start thinking of his losses, and then his lost profits, and I don't know how expensive that could get. Remember, he thought he was earning more than 25 percent on that money."

"Do you think Mr. Sukemi will listen to you?" Joseph Agosta asked.

"I will convince him. He will understand that it was simply too good to be true."

"It's about time you noticed that," Dianne said.

"I just hope I never feel that way about our AFPIC policy," Ted Swaine interjected angrily.

"Let's not fight," Stuart said, but he was extremely pleased with Ted Swaine's support. "What I am trying to convey to you is that you should feel confident I can obtain Mr. Sukemi's agreement to this settlement offer. He trusts me."

"That is clear," Dianne said ironically.

"Just think it over," Stuart said, ignoring her disbelief. "Tilden & Hayes has a $50 million policy. It is my considered opinion that my client will be satisfied with $35.8 million. And AFPIC will get the restaurants and $4.55 million in cash. That means your loss will be between $10 million and $15 million."

"That's a lot of money," Ken Dwyer said.

"True. But it's only 20 to 30 percent of our policy coverage. And if you hesitate, I suspect our thieves, and their cooperation, will disappear. The longer we wait, the less value I know we're going to find when we take over those restaurants."

"We have to think about it."

"Of course. But remember the legal fees, yours and ours, that you'll be saving if we settle."

"We certainly will," Dianne Hirshfield said. It always annoyed her that AFPIC, if found liable for coverage, had to pay the legal costs of both parties.

To give the AFPIC executives time to make their decision, Stuart Craxton, Robert Kim and Ted Swaine left the conference room. They only had to wait in Ted's office for 15 minutes before AFPIC's general counsel called them back to the meeting and agreed to allow Stuart to attempt to settle with his client, the Indonesian oil billionaire, Mohadi Sukemi.

Chapter Thirty Eight

Two days later, on Friday, April 19th, Stuart was met at the Zurich airport by Mohadi Sukemi's limousine. He was brought to the financial district and escorted to the 12th floor of a modern office building, where the Indonesian Oil Refinery Company had a modest-sized office.

There was nothing modest, though, about the room where Mohadi Sukemi and three aides were waiting for Stuart's arrival. The walls were decorated either with elaborately carved Javanese-style wood panels or with built-in bookcases on whose shelves ancient stone statues and antique Javanese puppets shared space with leather-bound volumes of Western literature.

Mohadi Sukemi sat at the head of a conference table which could seat twelve people. Two of his aides sat on either side of him and the third stood a few feet behind him. When Stuart entered the room, he was invited to sit at the other end of the table.

"Mr. Sukemi, as I told you by phone, we have discovered a serious problem with the Nishizaki restaurant investments," Stuart began.

"I warned you about your excessive enthusiasm for Japanese joint ventures," the 49-year-old executive said quietly but firmly. It was clear from his manner that Mohadi Sukemi was accustomed to being obeyed without ever having to raise his voice or issue commands.

"That is true. You did. And I should have listened. But—"

"Get to the point, please, Mr. Craxton. What is this problem you mentioned, and how serious is it? And I assume it must be very serious indeed for you to have insisted on coming all the way to Zurich to discuss it in person."

"It certainly is serious," Stuart agreed, and then told his client all the details of the fraud perpetrated by Sydney Brewster and Minoru Yoshida.

"And what remains of my investment?" Mr. Sukemi asked when Stuart was done.

"There are some tax benefits from the losses, sir. We transformed your investment into debt, so that as the only creditor, your Delaware holding company, AJ Restaurants, Inc., could force Nishizaki International USA into bankruptcy. On your general authorization I arranged for that to take place last week."

"What are the tax benefits?"

"The losses can be used to offset other income."

"And what are the losses?"

"$18.2 million."

"I don't understand. My investment was over $50 million."

"Exactly $54 million," one of his aides said.

"Yes, but the profits you have already received from the Nishizaki restaurants total $18.2 million."

"$18,171,250," the same aide said.

"I rounded," Stuart said, slightly defensively.

"Continue," Mohadi Sukemi said, "$18.2 million is close enough. But why are the losses not higher?"

"$35.8 million is the value of the sale of Nishizaki International USA's assets to AFPIC, an insurance company with whom I arranged the transfer in lieu of bankruptcy proceedings."

"AFPIC?"

"Attorney Fraud Protection Insurance Company."

"I see," Mohadi Sukemi said, the start of a smile turning up the corners of his mouth. "And now AFPIC owns all the Nishizaki restaurants?"

"The 12 that exist."

"And they are worth $35.8 million?"

"No. Closer to $15.8 million," Stuart said.

"And you negotiated a $20 million premium with this, uh, insurance company?"

"No. We also arranged for AFPIC to obtain $4.55 million in cash."

Mohadi Sukemi laughed. "Did $3 million of that cash come from Geneva?"

"$3.3 million," Stuart said, smiling. This was going to be easier than he had thought.

"And the rest?"

"It was the minuscule residue of honor among the thieves."

"But that still leaves—"

"Ten to 15 million dollars—which just happens to be the exact value of your signature upon this release absolving Tilden & Hayes, and its insurer, AFPIC, of any liability concerning your investments in the Nishizaki restaurants."

"Let me see the release," Mohadi Sukemi said, but handed it to an aide without glancing at it.

"So I need only accept an $18.2 million loss? Is that what you came here to ask me to do?"

"No. I don't see it that way, Mr. Sukemi," Stuart said. "The $18.2 million returned to you in profits was just your own money coming back to you—"

"After tax," an aide mentioned.

"That's correct. And you could amend all your returns for the last four years—"

"But we didn't pay any taxes," the same aide said.

"Also correct. The investments are structured so that the income is all earned outside the United States. So there is no reason to attract attention by adjusting those old returns. But the loss of $18.2 million can be used to shelter the next $18.2 million of income in the United States that might otherwise be difficult to shelter."

"But—"

"In any case, you have your $18.2 million in your pocket already, and here is a certified check for $35.8 million from AFPIC that will make you whole."

"Mr. Craxton," one of the aides said accusingly, "you are ignoring the time value of that money."

"I am not ignoring it. But there are the possible tax benefits and—"

"You needn't explain," Mohadi Sukemi interrupted Stuart. "My aide means well—but he doesn't know about your Geneva source. I accept your solution to this problem, Stuart. It is more than satisfactory, provided that I can sign the release." He looked at the aide on his left, who was still reviewing the contract.

"This release is written in standard legal language and is definitely limited to the Nishizaki restaurant investments," the aide concluded cautiously.

"Then please allow me the privilege of signing it." Mohadi Sukemi took the release from the aide, who reluctantly gave it up without reading it a second time. Stuart held his breath a moment while Mr. Sukemi signed it.

Stuart stood up and started to walk over to Mohadi Sukemi's end of the table. Mr. Sukemi also stood up, and handed Stuart the signed release at the same time he received a certified check drawn on the Union Bank of Switzerland for $35.8 million.

"Sir, I know I am not worthy of continuing to handle the legal work on your other U.S. investments, but I am willing to do so if you think it is appropriate."

"I will think about it, Mr. Craxton," Mohadi Sukemi said, feeling mischievous, "but I don't need to think about asking you to stay and join us for dinner tonight."

"I would love to," Stuart replied, "but I have a weekend date to catch in Reykjavik, and the last plane leaves at 6:00."

"I am surprised," Mohadi Sukemi said. "I have always thought of you as—"

"The date is with my wife and daughter," Stuart explained.

"In Reykjavik?"

"Yes."

"Have you had a very hard time of it?" Mohadi Sukemi asked, having just penetrated Stuart's personal defenses.

"Very hard," Stuart had to say.

"I am sorry to hear that. I will have to think of some way to make it up to you."

"You already have, Mohadi. You already have."

Stuart shook the hand his client offered him, and then rushed back to the airport in his limousine. Stuart's hope that he would get there in time to catch an even earlier flight to Reykjavik was not frustrated.

After Stuart Craxton had left Mohadi Sukemi's office, one of the aides asked to see the certified check. He stared at it for a while and then laughed. He was soon joined in his laughter by the other three Indonesians.

"These American lawyers are too good to be true," the aide said.

"Yes," Mohadi Sukemi agreed, "it is quite incomprehensible how they arrange insurance for everything. After all, there was a theft. A total fraud. And they didn't do it. But they paid for it anyway."

"Well, sir," the same aide said, still laughing, "we could all certainly sleep a lot easier at night if you could just persuade the Indonesian government to purchase some of that same insurance."

Chapter Thirty Nine

Just before noon on Wednesday, April 24th, Ted Swaine swung past Christine Lava and through Stuart's open door. He looked like he was in a very light-hearted mood.

Stuart heard a noise and looked up from the first draft of an acquisition agreement Robert had prepared for the potential purchase by Prudential of a Dallas apartment complex. He was surprised to see Ted Swaine standing there in front of his desk, whistling softly.

"So what's this message I got from you about Sydney Brewster disappearing?" Ted asked.

"Apparently she has," Stuart said. "It happened sometime over the weekend. Samantha Michaels, Sydney's secretary, called me just after I got back on Monday afternoon to ask if I knew where she was. That's when we called the police."

"How do they know she isn't just on vacation?"

"It seems clear enough. She didn't tell anyone she was going. She hadn't even told any of the employees that she sold the entire business to AFPIC last Thursday. And the police told me both Sydney's apartment and her office look like they were hastily cleared out."

"Anything of consequence missing?"

"To AFPIC? Yes. Sydney's office safe was cleaned out and some of the art from her office is missing, including two pink jade buddhas she adored. Those buddhas alone are probably worth half a million. And they belong to AFPIC, wherever they are."

"So what are we doing about this?"

"I've let the AFPIC lawyers know. They weren't surprised. Someone from AFPIC had already moved into the Nishizaki offices on Friday to take control of the operations. But apparently Sydney just told her employees he was an auditor."

"But they know now?"

"Sure. But everyone wants to stay. It's amazing what a struggling economy can do for employee loyalty. Only Samantha Michaels didn't come back, and she probably figured AFPIC has no need for someone who makes little circles over her i's."

"Are the police on to her?"

"No. AFPIC decided to let her go. She couldn't have been that important. After all, Sydney didn't even tell her the game was over."

"And our involvement is?"

"Minimal. I just told the police that I was aware that last Thursday AFPIC had bought the entire operations of Nishizaki International USA, Inc. in lieu of bankruptcy. And that Sydney must be reacting to that reversal in her fortunes."

"Well how are you reacting to the reversal in yours?"

"Coping."

"Is that all?"

"No. I was planning on talking to you next Monday about it, but I guess now is as good a time as any. I will be tendering my resignation as soon as I've cleared up a few outstanding issues—"

"When?" Ted Swaine asked harshly, but he could not completely hide his smile.

"As soon as I can, Ted. I'm sorry about what happened. But I still find it hard to believe that I was fooled so badly. This is not the kind of thing that's supposed to happen to us. I'm one of the Initials, for Christ's sake." Stuart did find it hard to understand why his status had not protected him from this embarrassment.

"It was an expensive mistake," Ted said, this time successfully imitating anger.

"It certainly was," Stuart agreed. "And I understand your position. All I ask is a few weeks to get my affairs organized—"

"Get off it, Craxton. You're so organized you could probably walk out this door tomorrow and be in operation someplace else on Friday."

MM

"If that's what you want, Ted."

"No, that's not what I want, Stuart. That's what I came down to tell you. I just talked it over with Jack Kendall and he's very unhappy, but he agrees with me it's for the best. It's a shame, but we'll just have to pass over another Harvard grad."

"What? JWK isn't going to be the next Managing Partner?"

"No. He's not. And I'm not going to stay past my 65th birthday in October either."

"You're withdrawing your request to amend the partnership agreement?"

"That's right."

"And you've discussed my situation with the new Managing Partner and he wants me out by Friday?"

"That's wrong. I haven't discussed anything with him yet. But he knows all about your situation and I suspect he'll agree we need another NYU grad as Managing Partner of Tilden & Hayes."

"Then you've chosen Paul Morgan after all?"

"No."

"Then who is it? Baker or McCoy?" This was a complete surprise to Stuart and he was curious which of the two younger Initials who were NYU grads had gotten the nod.

"Sometimes you can be pretty dense, Craxton. Let me make it simpler. I haven't chosen PJM, MFB or MMcC."

Stuart was confused. "But—"

"I've chosen you! I want *you* to take my job. I'm tired of it. I want to spend more time in Hilton Head. And some day I want to shoot less than 100. So I'm heading out the door on my 65th birthday in October. And I want you to move into my office on that same day and take over these operations."

"I was not expecting this, Ted." Stuart was floored.

"That's obvious."

"I've been preoccupied."

"That's a Craxton understatement if I've ever heard one. But you must have realized I've been watching you. And I couldn't be more impressed—especially with your adaptability."

"I hadn't thought of it that way."

"You wouldn't, I'm sure."

"I take it, then, that you don't need my resignation."

"You take it correctly. I'd kill you if you resigned now. I want out."

"And I'm in?" Stuart was finding this hard to believe. He had steeled himself for the possibility that Ted Swaine would accept his resignation, though he hadn't thought it likely, but he had never imagined he would become the heir apparent.

"Don't sound so thrilled," Ted said. "Tilden & Hayes may be a professional partnership, but you have to run it like a business. You have to take in more money, much more money, than you spend. And if you don't, all the unhappiness of the other partners will be laid at your doorstep."

"You make it sound like an enormous burden."

"It is. But it has its compensations," Ted said, thinking of the $1.5 million annual draw he had set for himself several years ago. "And I've found that if you just think of all these men as your dependent sons, it all works out fine."

As Stuart listened to this advice he understood better what had irritated him most over the years about Ted Swaine. But his irritations were dissolving quickly.

"Well, wouldn't my father be surprised!"

"I don't think so," Ted said. "I knew your old man and I'll bet he calculated that the future of his legacies at the firm would live the longest if he retired early, so that you could eventually step into his shoes."

"No one thinks that far ahead."

"Maybe. Maybe not," Ted Swaine said, "but before you decide, I'd like you to read this." Ted Swaine handed Stuart a few pages stapled together. "It's required reading for each new Managing Partner as preparation for the job."

Stuart looked at the memo and began to read. He was soon thoroughly absorbed.

Memorandum to: Future Managing Partners
From: SEC
Date: July 21, 1963

For the Firm to continue to prosper, keep these few precepts in mind.

A) Resist these temptations:

1) To nickel and dime clients to death.
If you do, clients will see through to your mercenary character. No one who discovers that each paper clip you used on his behalf has cost him a penny will ever trust you with multimillion dollar decisions.

2) To bill the training time of new attorneys.
Give their thoughts no cost. They are often not in proportion to the task given.

3) To employ relatives.
They may be familiar, but hiring them is vulgar. And always breeds ill will. If a son or nephew is that important to someone, he should retire early. I am the example.

4) To expand to other offices.
Do not deplete resources entertaining each new-hatched, unfledged idea other firms have. New York will yield sufficient wealth all by itself.

5) To decorate imperially.
Our offices should proclaim our great value, and reflect the depth of our purse, but not expressed in gaudy baubles. Crystal and gold chandeliers will make our cli-

ents doubt, but mahogany will make them comfortable with our success.

B) Insist on these Firm traditions:

1) Neither a borrower nor a lender be.
Be a law firm. Borrowing to fund partners' draws is a disaster-in-the-making. And we will lose clients who can't pay cash anyway.

2) Charge the highest, or nearly the highest, hourly rate in the Manhattan market for attorney time.
But this above all, to our clients be true: make sure every minute charged was valuable to him. Discipline inefficient partners by requiring them to record less than the actual time spent.

3) Appoint the best man available to be the next Managing Partner.
Over the years you will probably have antagonized each of your partners at least once, even if you have never been false to any man. Ignore your personal feelings. You will be gone anyway. Pick the man most likely to resist these temptations and to insist on these Firm traditions.

4) Never create more than 40 partnership slots.
Forty is already too many, but still manageable. You must know each of your partners well. Aim to be the best, not the biggest.

5) Turn away work.
And our success must follow, as the night the day. It is imperative that even our best clients find us too busy for an assignment sometimes, though rarely, because

every time our clients are forced to go elsewhere, they will find less efficiency, higher bills and sloppier work. That will remind them why they come to us, why our higher hourly rates still yield lower bills for superior service. Only a coward, who has not insisted strongly enough on the Firm's traditions, will fail to perceive this secret's preeminent value to our continued success.

Five temptations. Five traditions. If you resist the former and insist on the latter, Tilden & Hayes will continue to thrive, your partners will continue to possess what they want most, whether they realize it or not: professional respect and reasonable wealth, and the Managing Partner of Tilden & Hayes will continue to be the most lucrative respectable legal position in New York.

As I take my leave of Tilden & Hayes, I am humbled by my good fortune in having worked here. Fare thee well, as I have fared.

Stuart Emerson Craxton, Jr.

Afterthought: If this advice strikes no familiar chords, stop donating to your undergraduate Alumni Fund.

Ted Swaine watched patiently while Stuart read the memo. He was fascinated by the emotions playing across Stuart's usually immobile face. When Stuart looked up after reading the last page, Ted asked, "finished?"

"Yes," Stuart said quietly. He was returning from deep in his memories.

"Your father's memo always reminds me of a joke. Who's the most overrated author in literary history?"

"Who?" Stuart asked, playing along.

"Shakespeare. He just strung together famous quotations."

Stuart had heard Ted Swaine tell that joke several times before. He laughed with him a while, but then tried to explain his father's memo personally.

"My father always liked Polonius's advice to Laertes. We used to read *Hamlet* out loud at home when I was a boy. I read Hamlet's part, my mother read all the female parts and my father read all the others."

"Well, how did it feel just now to read advice your own paternal Polonius wrote almost 30 years ago?"

"What is this, Ted, the Oprah Winfrey show?"

"No, no. It's just that I saw on your face—"

"Well, it did feel very odd to see my own initials on the memo, that's true. Of course, I knew right away it had been written by someone else, but it took me a few seconds to realize that that someone else was my own father. As I read it I suddenly felt that only 12 years now separate my father, as the writer of this memo, and me, rather than the 40 years I am used to. I could even hear my father's voice as I read."

"I'm not surprised. His voice speaks clearly, but from a different era."

"Sometimes I think I am also from that same era."

"You're not alone in that judgment, Stuart. And I must admit I've had my own doubts about you. But now I am convinced you have updated your father's skills. That's why my choice is clear."

"And Kendall? He's been your heir apparent for years."

"I like Jack. That hasn't changed. But he would have just been a caretaker for the next five years. And I don't know who he would have picked after that. So I took your father's advice and forgot about our clashes."

"Seems like he's still watching out for me after all these years."

"It's just good solid advice, Stuart, that's all. Strong wills clash at times. But a strong will is needed to run Tilden & Hayes. Besides, the size of my pension will be dependent for the next 30 years on just how profitable T&H is."

"I see," Stuart said as they both laughed. Ted was always clear about where his own interests lay.

"Anything else?" Ted asked Stuart.

"I do have one question about my father's advice. Have you really ever had to discipline partners who became inefficient?"

Ted Swaine looked surprised. "Often. Since you are Mr. Efficiency himself you'd better be prepared for a lower standard for others, but even with a lower standard some will slip below it. I haven't ever had to discipline one of the Initials. Usually they stay on top of things until they're at least 62 or 63, and I have never bothered to discipline anyone that old."

"63 is not *that* old," Stuart said.

"It certainly isn't," Ted agreed, from his viewpoint at 64, "but whenever ambitions start to wane, you have to beware. And there are two common times that occur well before retirement rears its bald and ugly head. Sometimes new partners get a little lazy, feel they've made it and can relax, and you have to let them feel the crack of your father's whip. But even more often there is a slump around 54 for those who don't become Initials. It starts the day they realize they will never have a power office. But they get over it. With a little discipline."

"I would never have guessed."

"That's a nice compliment for me," Ted Swaine said, "and for your father's method of restoring their pride by reminding them graphically just how much money their advice is worth per hour. When they work efficiently. But I'll fill you in with more details later."

"I'd appreciate it."

"Anytime. But now I have question. Is there anything you want changed in the arrangements so that the Anniversary Dinner can be an unqualified success for you?"

Stuart thought a moment. The request had already occurred to him, but it was complicated politically. Being reticent, however, was clearly not going to be perceived by Ted Swaine as a virtue in a future Managing Partner.

"I have only one request, Ted, but it is very important to me. I want Robert Kim to be one of the five associates invited to the dinner."

"Now, really, Stuart, we discussed that last week. He doesn't have any chance at all to get my partnership slot, and you know it. I mean, he's not even a real American."

Stuart understood what Ted meant but ignored it. "I know that either Thompson or Fenwick will get your slot, Ted. That is clear to everyone. But how will it look if my senior associate, who has just helped me through a crisis, is not even on the short list?"

"Not good. I can see that."

"And there is someone on that list now who doesn't really deserve to be there. She might as well know that sooner than later."

"Jackie Messer?"

"Yes. Ms. Messer. I know we have worked her hard, but that is par for the course, isn't it? She has already lost her spark, if you ask me."

"Burnt out even," Ted Swaine agreed.

"I'm afraid so. But I should've guessed six or seven years ago that she would burn out too soon. She fell asleep once, exhausted, right in my office, and slept for over an hour. I must say I was more than a little surprised. Slipped right off her chair about 3:00 in the morning, as I recall."

Ted Swaine looked at Stuart curiously, but didn't find what he was looking for. He had heard this concern for Jackie's exhaustion several times before, but in a different context, and with more than a paternal passion aroused.

"You are right, Stuart. As long as you realize that Robert has no chance for my slot, I see your point. It will help you if the boys notice. And I can assure you they will if Jackie Messer slips off the short list. She has worked for quite a few partners over the years and has a lot of backers—at least for the honor of the invitation to the dinner. But you are right. Difficult, but I can arrange it. And I'll even put Kim at the head table with us. From what I've heard, he deserves it."

"I think so."

"Of course, no one else knows about Robert's role in untangling the Nishizaki investments, but I've heard people talking about the settlement of the Garuda Oil fight, about how last Sunday, while you were still in Europe, he rounded up that signature—"

"R.P. Krishnanda's."

"I thought it was someone called Ralph."

"That's just a joke."

"Oh. Well, anyway, what I heard is that this fellow Ralph was off on Mauritius, but no one knew where. Even his own staff in Rome, the ones who could be tracked down on a Sunday, didn't know where he was. But Kim claims finding him was easy. He just went up to Travel and looked up the top resorts in Mauritius. Then he started his search by calling the only five star hotel in the biggest town, Port Louis, and he found this Ralph fellow right away, vacationing with his trophy wife, I'd bet, if not a mistress."

"That's right. All anyone knew was that R.P. Krishnanda was out in the middle of the Indian Ocean, but Robert found him, faxed him the settlement agreement, got his signature back by return fax, and the fight was over."

"And everyone at Garuda Oil was back at work again on Monday. Right?"

"Right. And the settlement came none too soon, I might add. Today was the deadline. Garuda Oil could have been forced to liquidate."

"Now that's what I call playing heads-up ball. So what was in the settlement agreement?"

"Not much. Sukemi and the Krishnandas agreed to disagree for now."

"No real change?"

"Just one. They've kicked J.P.'s astrologer off the unofficial Board of Directors."

"And how much did that cost Garuda Oil?"

"We estimate about $12 million, including the $45,000 we'll get for our time." Stuart didn't mention to Ted that the settlement also included an agreement that Garuda Oil would pay the Krishnandas'

Skelly Adams legal bill, which had weighed in at well over $100,000 for indefinable services.

"$45,000? Is that all?" Ted asked.

"It was just Robert and I. And mostly hand-holding. We only billed 155 hours altogether."

"Can't you charge a premium?"

"I really didn't think it would be wise to charge Mohadi Sukemi a premium under the circumst—"

"I can see your point. But don't let Kim get a big head over all this."

"I wouldn't dare."

"And don't you promise him my slot."

"Wouldn't think of it, Ted."

"Then it's done."

"I appreciate it."

"Don't mention it—more than twice," Ted laughed and then turned to leave, already thinking about how the new seating arrangement at the dinner would throw both Sally Thompson and John Fenwick off balance, always a particularly good position to observe someone in. Jackie Messer had already disappeared from his mental list of eventual problems.

Chapter Forty

Early on Thursday afternoon, April 25th, a tall Japanese man, about 30 years old, wearing an expensive, British-tailored pin-striped blue wool suit and black Gucci loafers, watched from the Bermuda airport's flight deck as an American Airlines freight crew loaded two large crates onto a plane headed for New York.

The crates had been handled very carefully, as ordered. The cargo truck which had carried them to the plane had moved at one-tenth its usual speed, and extra men stood close by just in case. Five pairs of eyes watched each slight jiggle of those two crates.

Inside each crate was a large pink jade buddha.

Chapter Forty One

When Stuart arrived at the office at 8:42 on Friday morning, April 26th, Robert Kim was waiting for him, but Christine Lava was not at her desk. Robert explained that, at his suggestion, she had already gone home for the weekend. Stuart stepped into his office confused. Robert followed him in and shut the door.

"Don't get settled, Stuart. We have to go to the Nishizaki offices."

"What's up?" Stuart asked.

"Christine got a call from the police a half an hour ago. They want us to come over as soon as possible. I told them we'd be there just before 9:00."

"The police?"

"They found two bodies they want us to ID."

"What?"

"Sydney Brewster is no longer missing. And no one can identify the other body. They want us to come right over."

"Sydney's dead?"

"That's what the police told Christine."

"God," Stuart sighed, "I was hoping this was all over."

"So was I—"

"And?"

"Ron Kassner also called."

"AFPIC's man?"

"Yup. He insists on seeing you when we're there."

Stuart and Robert went directly to the elevators and then down to the 101 Park lobby. Waiting on Park Avenue at 40th was a White Shoe cab Robert had ordered. During their slow trip up Third Avenue during rush hour, Robert wondered whether it would have been quicker to walk. Stuart did not say a word during the entire trip.

They arrived at 919 Third Avenue shortly before 9:00 and got on an elevator, relieved that they had not seen any of their Skadden Arps acquaintances. When the elevator doors opened onto the 37th floor, the police were everywhere. Stuart identified himself and Robert. They were quickly escorted to the officer in charge.

"I hate to have to ask you two to do this, but we want a positive ID before we move the bodies—if that's possible."

"OK," is all Stuart said and Robert just nodded. The officer led them into Sydney's former office.

Two naked bodies were submerged in her large aquarium, tied together face-to-face at the neck, the waist and the ankles. Dangling from each neck was a small fishnet, weighted down by a bar of gold. One large pink jade buddha also had been submerged in the aquarium. The other was still standing in an opened air freight crate three times larger than necessary for transporting it. Two dark green body bags lay on the floor next to the crate.

Stuart noticed that the tropical fish were nibbling at the bodies. He turned away, pale.

"Like I said, I'm sorry I have to ask you to—". The officer's voice trailed off.

Stuart looked around the office, away from the aquarium, and noticed the professional lighting set up to surround it. At first he thought it was police equipment. But when he glanced again at the aquarium he noticed the sign in Japanese still dangling from the hand of the male body.

"What does the sign say?" Stuart asked the officer.

"In polite English?"

"Please."

"It says, 'you can screw each other, but you can't screw us'. They must have wanted that sign prominent in the pictures they took. It's big enough."

"They?" Stuart asked.

"We think it was a yakuza killing," the officer said bluntly.

"Oh," Stuart said. Robert had just guessed that himself. It explained the gold bars perfectly.

Stuart walked up closer to the aquarium and stared at what he could see of Sydney's face. Although it was scrubbed clean of make-up, there was no mistaking her profile. Then he looked at the male face which, judging from its unnatural position, must have been the focus of the pictures. Stuart was very surprised.

"This is definitely Sydney Brewster," Stuart said to the officer, "and I recognize the man, too. His name was Minoru Yoshida. His close friends knew him as Roo."

"Did he have any friends closer than her?" the officer asked irreverently.

"Yes," Stuart answered, ignoring the officer's sarcasm. "Mr. Yoshida has an invalid wife and two adult daughters in Japan, from what I've heard."

"They'll be surprised," the officer said.

"I certainly was," Stuart admitted.

After hearing that Sydney Brewster had disappeared, Stuart had wondered whether he would ever see her alive again. But he had assumed that Minoru Yoshida was the source of her potential danger. Minoru's own death hinted at complications Stuart had never allowed himself to imagine.

"I'd love to get my hands on the distribution list for those pictures," the officer said. He assumed correctly that that would be the quickest way to find out who were all the New York policy holders of yakuza protection insurance.

"Is it possible for the newspapers to be kept off that list?" Stuart asked obliquely. "I assume you know Sydney is Senator Brewster's daughter."

"Yeh. We heard that."

"At his age I don't really think he deserves—"

"We've already gotten the word from the top to keep this one to a minimum."

"Good," Stuart said. He could see the officer's resentment that the media game was played differently for the powerful, so he asked politely, "is that all you need from me?"

"Yeh. That's it," the officer said, "unless we decide to call on you next week to verify the IDs."

"I'll be happy to cooperate," Stuart said, and started to leave. Robert followed him out the door. When he saw Stuart was heading for the elevators, he reminded him of Ron Kassner's request.

They found Ron in his office, very upset. He protested vigorously that AFPIC had had no idea that the yakuza had been involved in the Nishizaki restaurants when they had agreed to buy them. Stuart convincingly insisted that he had had no idea either. And then Stuart mentioned that about half a million dollars in AFPIC assets, which they had all thought had disappeared for good, had just showed up again.

During most of the ride back to the office Stuart was silent, but just as they turned off Lexington onto 40th Street, Stuart asked Robert why he had sent Christine home.

"First of all, she was very upset about Sydney Brewster's death."

"And second of all?"

"I assumed it would be nearly impossible for her not to talk about it, no matter how hard she tried not to."

"That was a safe assumption, Robert. Now, do you think you should also go home for the weekend?"

"Only if you think you need to go home too."

"Then let's pretend we're getting some work done. It'll make tomorrow night's dinner a lot easier on both of us."

"As long as the papers cooperate."

"Let's hope they do."

While Stuart and Robert were discussing the best way to minimize uncomfortable gossip at the 150th Anniversary Dinner, Ron Kassner was in Sydney Brewster's former office, making sure that AFPIC's claim on the pink jade buddhas was perfectly clear to the police. While there, Ron also had the presence of mind to push AFPIC's claim to the two gold bars dangling in the fishnets in the aquarium.

Chapter Forty Two

On Friday evening, April 26th, Jackie Messer sat at her desk in her office on the 45th floor of 101 Park Avenue and stared out the window. Her door was closed and her lights were off. She watched the sun setting over New Jersey. A deep orange sheen tinted the Pan Am Building and dozens of midtown skyscrapers behind it.

The seating chart for the 150th Anniversary Dinner lay crumpled on her desk. She had obtained a copy of the seating chart, for $100, from a messenger she had done many favors for over the years. Archie had insisted on the high payment because he had been specifically warned by Ellen Mackin, the Managing Partner's secretary, that the seating chart was secret and that only one copy was to be made. But Jackie Messer had gotten to Archie first.

The seating chart had confirmed the obvious: that Jackie had been uninvited to the party. But it also had revealed that a new heir apparent had been chosen. Jackie assumed there could be no other meaning to Stuart Craxton and his family being seated at the center table with Ted Swaine and his family. Stuart's new influence was driven home by the fact that Robert and Lily Kim were also seated at the same table.

Stuart's unexpected ascendance was undoubtedly part of the surprise yesterday's rumors hinted at. Jackie knew she was also part of the surprise. The part left out.

As she stared out the window Jackie wondered if the seating chart also meant that Robert would be given ETS's partnership slot. But she doubted it. She considered Stuart far too WASPy to insist on a Korean-American against formidable opposition. Besides, Tilden & Hayes really needed another female partner to shore up their image at the eight law schools they hired from. Having only two female partners stuck out like a sore thumb on the firm's résumé and female students far outnumbered Asian-Americans. Of course, if Robert's wife Lily had been the Kim who had survived eight years of hard work, she would have been a shoo-in.

Jackie Messer had hoped against hope for years that she would be the third female partner at Tilden & Hayes. She had worked hard to make it possible. She had done everything she could to line up votes. But she was a gracious loser. She had always considered Sally Thompson to be her stiffest competition. And now she wanted Sally to get the slot.

Jackie Messer was very tired. She tried to laugh about her fate, but found it difficult. The one thing she had never counted on was Stuart Craxton gaining power at just the wrong moment. Stuart had always been impervious to, even unaware of, her quite successful method.

She had patiently collected over the years a dozen very valuable chips, including the one ETS himself had given her late one night five years ago. But now that she had failed in her attempt to cash them in, she decided to forget all about them. It had all been absurd, she realized, and would probably only have gotten her one free dinner anyway. Her résumé didn't need that dinner, she thought, and started to imagine how to condense nine years of work onto one sheet of paper.

The thought made her very thirsty. And suddenly Jackie couldn't think of a single reason why she was still in the office. She stood up and stretched, smoothed out the crumpled seating chart, folded it and slid it into her purse. She intended to decorate her refrigerator with it for a week or two.

As she got off the elevator in the 101 Park lobby a minute later, Sean Murray, the night watchman for the 43rd floor, was getting on. He winked at her mischievously. She was too tired to respond until he pretended to frown. Then she laughed. And he laughed.

"I'm mighty sorry you aren't working late tonight, lassie," Sean said.

"I might be back," Jackie teased as the elevator doors were

closing.

She felt a lot better as she signed out at reception on the firm's special register. She looked at her watch and recorded her departure time as 8:07.

When she looked at her watch again it was 11:12. She was sitting in the dark at the far end of the Conduit Bar, just a block away from her Upper East Side condo. Her strong preference for the Conduit Bar had become nearly an obsession in the last year. She had discovered that whenever she had to make her way home alone, getting there from the Conduit Bar could always be managed.

In the dark Jackie often attracted attention. But even in the dark the few men who had glanced at her face this evening, after seeing her shapely legs dangling off the stool, decided against approaching her. To one she had looked exhausted. To another she looked as if she had been crying for a year. And to a third she looked as if she were 41 and had just found out her husband was leaving her for a 28-year-old. The men had each concluded that Jackie would be more trouble than she was worth.

Only one checked back at 2:00 in the morning to see if she was still there. But Jackie was never still at the Conduit Bar at 2:00 in the morning. She always stuck to her rule that no one you meet after 12:30 is worth it.

When Jackie finally glanced at her watch again, at 11:47, to see how much longer she should wait before giving up, she noticed a young Japanese businessman was watching her. He was about 30 years old and taller than Jackie. He was wearing a very expensive, British-tailored gray herringbone suit and maroon Gucci loafers. He looked exceedingly young and handsome to Jackie. She had been in the Conduit Bar for more than three hours.

When she noticed he was watching her, the businessman walked over to her end of the bar. "I no try to stare," he said very politely, struggling somewhat with his English, "but I see you before. At Tilden & Hayes?"

"Maybe. I used to work there," Jackie said sullenly.

"So quick you quit? I see you last week I think," the businessmen said as he ordered a new round for both of them and sat down on the stool next to Jackie's.

"I still work there. Just a joke."

"Oh. I see," he said. "I know your Mista Stuart Craxton there."

"Goddamn it's a small world," Jackie swore.

"No like Mista Craxton?"

"Oh, no, I like Mr. Craxton," Jackie said angrily. "If you ask me, he's the perfect Stoic."

"The perfect what?"

"The—never mind. They are out of fashion now anyway."

"But you no happy when I mention Mista Craxton."

"It's just that—well, his good fortune is my bad luck."

"Good fortune?"

"He's going to be the next Managing Partner of Tilden & Hayes."

"Managing Partner?"

"Dictator is more like it. It means he gets to make all the important firm decisions. And the first one he made is that I am expendable."

"Sorry to hear that," the businessman said, but Jackie was too deep in her own woes to notice that her news about Stuart had a strong impact on her new drinking companion.

After letting Jackie sip her drink silently for a while, he continued, "I also know Mista Craxton's client, Ms. Sydney Brewster."

"I've heard of her," Jackie said. "She was profiled in *International Investor* a year or two ago. Stuart sent copies of the article around to everyone at the firm. Something about her brilliant management of some Japanese-American joint ventures, if I remember correctly."

"You a very smart woman. Remember well."

"I try."

"You success."

"Sure," she said.

The Japanese businessman winked at Jackie conspiratorially.

"Do you hear rumor Ms. Brewster and Mista Craxton are lovers?"

"Not bloody likely," Jackie laughed.

"No?"

"No way!"

"Why so sure?"

"'Cause Craxton is, well, Craxton. It's just not likely. He doesn't go in for that sort of thing."

"He a homo?" the businessman asked straightforwardly.

"No fucking way!" Jackie exploded.

The Japanese businessman joined in her laughter. The idea of Stuart Craxton being gay had never occurred to her before. But she dismissed the idea immediately.

"How you know?"

"I know. I know. I'd be sitting pretty today if Mr. Craxton was in the least bit—"

"You look pretty sitting today to me."

"Well, thanks," Jackie said, "but that's not what I meant. Stuart Craxton is just hopeless. He's a thoroughly married man, if you know what I mean."

"He no play around? Not at all?"

"I've never heard a single rumor to that effect. Not one. And let me tell you, if I ever heard one I wouldn't believe it. Because if he didn't go for me when I was 27, he wouldn't go for anyone."

"You fall for Mista Craxton last year some time and he no respond?"

"Not last year. Nice of you to lie like that, though."

"No lie. You very pretty girl. No understand Mista Craxton."

"Well, I fell for him all right. But not like you mean. Want to hear the story? It's a long one."

"Sure. Very much like to hear."

"OK. The fact is, I was a hotshot at NYU Law School, and I thought, after I'd landed a coveted spot at T&H nine years ago, that I was all set for life. I was so damn confident. But about a year after I was there I noticed how several of the partners were paying more attention to my legs than to my work. So, as a lark, I made an experiment once when I was working late with a tax partner. He was about 46, married, three kids, the usual. So, as I was saying, I made a little experiment. Just a real little one. I pretended to fall asleep at the table where I was working in his office. I just lay my head down and was quiet, very quiet.

"In about ten minutes he came over and stood over me, I think, trying to look down my blouse. Anyway, I could hear his breathing getting louder. So I turned my head to the side away from him and he scurried back to his desk. A little later I pretended to wake up and yawn. He looked at me funnily, but I went right back to work.

"Three days later, as I was walking past his office, I suddenly realized how damn easy it would be to compromise that man, to make him owe me one, and I decided to set a trap for him. The next time we worked late together I rearranged my clothes to be more revealing, and then, whenever I had to ask questions, I stood close to him—and I had to ask lots of questions. Finally, when it was very late, I pretended to fall asleep. A few minutes later I slid off the chair onto the floor, making sure that my blouse opened up and my skirt got hiked up a bit.

"I only had to wait ten minutes before he touched me. I responded, but as if I were still asleep. Then he really got excited. And I 'woke up' only when it was too late, and in a storm of passion of my own.

"Afterwards *I* apologized. I told him that it must have been all my fault and that I hated the idea of damaging another woman's marriage. And I told him I'd been dreaming about my fiancé. I begged him to forgive me and not tell anyone."

Jackie paused as she remembered her triumphs before adding, "and they were always so grateful I wanted it kept secret that they were quite willing to do me favors in return."

"They?"

"Over several years my little trap caught a dozen partners like that."

"Nice little trap you got, lady," the businessman said in a tone of sincere admiration.

"Well, to tell you the truth, I also rather enjoyed the only time my trap didn't work, the time I tried it on Mr. Craxton. It was dumb of me, because I had gotten so cocky that I hadn't even bothered to test the waters first, if you know what I mean. But I never really minded all that much because I figured his one vote would never make any difference. Besides, I always kind of liked what he did."

"What he did?"

"He saw me lying on the floor like that, exposed, if you know what I mean, and he took his overcoat right out of his closet and laid it over me and went back to work. About an hour later he called a cab to take me home. And when I pretended to wake up after he made that call, he was very kind. Said I should go home right away and get some sleep. I mean, what can you do with a guy like that? It's just my luck that of all the partners in the firm, the hardest one for me to compromise had to become Managing Partner at just the wrong time."

"He not fall for your fall, right?" the Japanese businessman said, laughing at the little joke he had made in a very difficult language.

"He certainly didn't. And that was seven years ago. In my prime. My little trap actually hasn't been working that well with anyone lately."

"It work with me," the businessman said. He smiled politely, but eagerly. An intense interest shone in his eyes.

Jackie Messer looked carefully at his face, and then noticed the maroon Gucci loafers again. "You're rather tall for a Japanese man, aren't you?" she asked.

"My father an American," he replied. She could see that now that he mentioned it, but it was not obvious other than in his height.

"Did you grow up here or in Japan?" Jackie always asked a few personal questions before making her decision.

"Japan."

"So your father speaks fluent Japanese?"

"I don't know," he said abruptly.

"Oh," Jackie said quietly. She had noticed a flicker of pain in the hard but eager eyes. She felt sorry for him as she swallowed the last drops of her drink.

When she looked at him again the pain had disappeared, but the eagerness remained. She smiled mischievously at him, closed her eyes, swayed a little on her bar stool, and then slid off it onto the floor. Her skirt had inverted so that her long slim legs and hips were covered only by pantyhose and bright red lacy bikini briefs. Her blouse had opened wide, spilling her left breast nearly out of the matching red lacy bra.

The Japanese businessman took off his expensive suit jacket and leaned over, placing it over her exposed body. Then he slipped off her black high-heeled shoes and put them on top of the suit jacket.

He lifted Jackie Messer up in his strong arms and carried her out the front door of the Conduit Bar.

Chapter Forty Three

Late on Saturday afternoon, April 27th, Robert and Lily Kim were in their bedroom preparing for the 150th Anniversary Dinner. Lily already had her dark rose evening gown on, but as she applied her makeup she kept threatening to switch to a tuxedo she had in the closet. Robert had already convinced her five times that her dress was more suitable for the black tie event. So when she suggested the tuxedo might look nice for a sixth time he reminded her she was a woman.

"You know I am trying very hard to forget that fact," she teased, "and it isn't nice of you, Bobby, to remind me so bluntly."

"Well, look on the bright side," he said. "You don't ever have to struggle with bowties." Robert had been attempting to get his tied properly for the last ten minutes.

"Do you remember the time it took you over an hour to get it right?"

"Sure. That was before the party at the Met."

"You are stubborn about it, you know. You could just buy a falsie—one already tied."

"We've discussed this at length before, Lily. I want it to be a real one. Besides, I just use this tux once or twice a year. A man can give an hour of his time here and there in support of integrity in clothing."

"What a cause!"

"You could raise a lot of money for it if you tried."

"Speaking of raising a lot of money," Lily said, "I'm still dazed at how AFPIC laid out over $10 million to get Stuart out of trouble."

"There was a very good chance it could cost them three or four times that much. They would have been dumb to pass up Stuart's offer. I mean, he did personally kick in $3.3 million. Of course, I have a feeling Stuart would probably have burned that money if he couldn't have gotten it back into Sukemi's pocket without Sukemi knowing what happened. And I admire Stuart for that."

"But?"

"But I can't admire everything—about anyone."

"Not even me?"

"Exceptions prove the rule."

"But you didn't say if the rule had just been proved."

"Got me again."

"You lawyer!" Lily shouted.

"Did you want me to lie?"

"Is there a difference?"

"I sure hope so."

"Well, Mr. Honesty, you don't have to admire everything about me as long as you admire my—"

"Wit?"

"Good enough."

"For government work?"

"Don't tell me you have a new job lined up."

"No. Not yet. But after seeing Sydney submerged in her own aquarium yesterday I'd rather forget I ever heard of Nishizaki International."

"Then shall we make that forbidden topic number two?" Lily asked.

"Absolutely—as long as that means we don't discuss it as often as we discuss forbidden topic number one."

"It's a deal."

"So what are we going to talk about while you finish putting your face on?"

"And you finish tying that bowtie."

"I'll get it right this time, I know—"

"What I know is that at your current pace you're well on your way to breaking your Met party record."

"It's all for a good cause."

"Well you wasted your noble efforts on that Met party," Lily said. "That was the worst one ever."

"What do you mean? I didn't think it went so badly. The Temple of Dendur made a great backdrop for a party."

"It was splendid," Lily agreed, "but it sure left me feeling empty."

"I know what you mean. The cast of thousands, the noise, but no warmth?"

"Not exactly that," she said. "It was just that once, while you were off getting our drinks, I watched the crowd in their glittering formal clothes and one second it seemed all so bright and fun and elegant, and the next it seemed all so—"

"Meaningless?"

"Right. It reminded me of staring at wallpaper."

"What?"

"Didn't you ever stare at wallpaper when you were a kid?"

"Not that I remember."

"I did," Lily said, "especially the kind you could never keep in focus. You keep staring at it and one second the dots in the center of the flowers are concave and the next second they are convex. And you can never tell what they really are. The party at the Met reminded me of that."

"I didn't realize you'd had a bad time."

"It's not that I had such a bad time," Lily said, "it's just that it was confusing. Like that one partner, I don't remember his name, who looked so proud and so embarrassed at the same time. The one who brought the model."

"I don't remember a model."

"Well she looked like one. I suppose he was embarrassed because everyone might think she was a bimbo."

"You're talking about Jonathan Beck, right, the partner who looks like he used to be a quarterback?"

"That's him. The one with that peculiar smile that looks so nice, but disappears so quickly you wonder if it was for real."

"That's Beck. The rumor is he's gay. He was probably embarrassed about breaking faith with his lover by coming with a woman."

"That's really sad," Lily said. "I wish they would just enjoy the lives they've chosen. Why do things always have to be so complicated?"

"Maybe they don't have to be, Lily. But they certainly are."

"Well pretty soon things might get more complicated for us too, Bobby. I'm late again."

"Lily, your 28th day is not late. Maybe your 35th, but not your 28th. With your luck your period will come full force tonight, right in the middle of the dinner."

"The next thing you'll say is make sure you bring your stuff with you."

"I was just going to say that."

"I can handle this myself, dear."

"I know you can."

"But?"

"It's just that I remember that dinner at The Tavern on the Green—"

"When I met Barbara Sexton. She was very helpful. Didn't mind leaving the party at all."

"Barbara is great."

"And she had everything, in abundance. She told me she doesn't take the pill, so—"

"So?"

"So I guess that's why I wonder if she's a lesbian. They don't need to take the pill."

"Maybe she's just Catholic."

"I wonder if they'll be healthier because they don't take the pill."

"The Catholics or the lesbians?"

"The lesbians, silly."

"Hey, Lily, what's up? Do you want me to get you an application?"

"No, dear. I can handle that myself too."

It's so easy to get men riled up, Lily thought, as Robert doubled up in simulated abdominal pain.

"Oh, Lily—darling—you always hurt the ones you love," he protested melodramatically.

"That's just because the others don't stick around long enough," Lily said matter-of-factly, "otherwise I'd get to them too."

Robert stayed doubled over, but this time with laughter. Lily ran over and made things worse by tickling him.

"I'm sorry to have to cause you all this pain, Bobby, it's just the way I am. I can't help it," Lily said. She kept tickling him, ignoring his protests, until she reached just the right point. Then she stopped. And unzipped his tuxedo pants, pulled the studs out of his formal shirt, and, in general, caused havoc in their preparations for the dinner.

A half an hour later they had to start the whole process of dressing all over again. But neither one minded missing the first half of the cocktail hour.

Chapter Forty Four

The cocktail hour for the 150th Anniversary Dinner of Tilden & Hayes began at 6:30 on Saturday evening, April 27, 1991, in the Celeste Bartos Forum of the New York Public Library. The entrance on 42nd Street, just off Fifth Avenue, had been specially decorated for the occasion with a flowering-vine-covered canopy leading all the way out to the street.

Tilden & Hayes spent over $50,000 to celebrate its anniversary. The dinner was attended by all 40 partners, the five senior associates on the short list, the eight retired partners who still maintained more than just a financial connection with their old colleagues, and almost 100 family members.

Tilden & Hayes never advertised, but it was preferred that its 150th Anniversary attract some attention in the press, so three guests from the media had also been invited to the dinner. Only one, the social editor of *The New York Times*, attended. He was an old family friend of the Swaines. The other two lived to regret their decision.

As the guests began to arrive shortly after 6:30, it appeared to strollers in the area that everyone was arriving in the same car, a white 1991 Lincoln Continental, but after 20 minutes had passed, and the guests began to arrive more frequently, it became clear that at least five identical cars were involved. In reality, nearly the entire fleet of 60 cars of the private cab company, White Shoe, was engaged in ferrying the T&H partners, and their families, to the dinner. Most were arriving from New Jersey, Long Island, Westchester or Connecticut, but a few had only a short trip to make from Fifth Avenue residences. Those White Shoe drivers who were unlucky enough to have been assigned such a short trip had been promised one of the longer return trips by their dispatcher.

The cocktail hour was livelier than a usual gathering of T&H lawyers due to the presence of six children under the age of ten. Ashley Craxton, in a white dress with blue trim which Catherine had bought in Iceland, led the small gang on an exploration of the Celeste Bartos Forum, but never passed outside the range of her mother's attention.

The glass and metal ceiling fascinated the children, with its oval inside a circle inside a convex square of thick dull white glass. Four large gray metal columns held up the square ceiling, providing a focus for running around, or hiding behind and spying on others, until they were forced to take their seats for the dinner.

Other than the children, everyone was on their best behavior. Even Patrick Davis, the only current Initial who had graduated from Yale Law School, behaved himself. PHD, a notorious womanizer and unsocial drinker who had begun to slow down only after turning 50 two years earlier, usually made the rounds during cocktail hours by greeting each group with a more or less felicitously chosen insult. And, as a T&H party wore on, they usually became less felicitous.

But tonight PHD had discovered too many children, and teenagers, scattered among the groups. Having been able to unfurl only three mild insults in 15 minutes, PHD had retreated to the northeast corner of the Celeste Bartos Forum, near the unofficial Yale table, to chat with Herbert Anthony Goodman, a 74-year-old retired Yalie Initial who had always encouraged PHD in his misbehavior. Since Mr. Goodman had never approved of the practice of addressing the Initials by their initials, he always called PHD Patrick. Patrick Davis returned the favor by never addressing Herb Goodman as HAG, at least not when Mrs. Goodman was present.

When the cocktail hour officially ended at 8:00, the caterers demonstrated their eagerness to begin serving the first course by removing all the hors d'oeuvres. This led to the slow process of waiters politely nudging each of the conversing groups closer to their tables until eventually someone had the courage to be the first one to sit down.

Twenty minutes later, as the salad plates were being removed from all the tables, Ted Swaine surveyed the scene over which he presided from the center table. He decided that the decorations had been generally well-chosen, although the table centerpieces were slightly too large for facilitating cross-table conversations. But all had gone well at his table.

He had not realized before that Robert Kim's wife, Lily, who was sitting directly across the table between her husband and Tim Craxton, had quite a sharp and funny wit. Catherine Craxton was also quite charming and the young Craxton girl had fortunately not spilled anything yet. He still expected that to happen, but it wouldn't affect him. She was sitting between her parents.

Stuart had also been funnier than Ted had expected. Stuart had told a few stories about the Krishnanda brothers that had had Ted's wife in tears. And his adult sons Eddie and John had been quiet, but respectable. He was especially pleased that Eddie had worn only one small earring. Ted assumed that turning 40 had finally subdued his long lost, but loved, black sheep. And he was grateful to Catherine Craxton for having quickly dispersed, with her warm reception of his oldest son, the awkwardness caused by Stuart's slight hesitation before shaking Eddie's hand.

All in all, judging by the satisfied look on his wife Beverly's face, the dinner was already a success. He just hoped he could pull off his prepared speech well enough to avoid spoiling her mood before the main course was served.

As the last of the salad plates disappeared out the southeast corner entrance, Ted Swaine stood up and glanced around at the 15 circular tables that surrounded the center table. The hum of activity gradually diminished until Ted used his spoon to strike the side of his water glass, bringing the hum as close to silence as it would ever get.

"Ladies and Gentlemen," Ted Swaine began, "I have the pleasure—oh yes, and Children, as Miss Ashley Craxton is reminding me—"

A quiet wave of polite laughter circled the room.

"—of hosting this dinner celebrating the 150th Anniversary of Tilden & Hayes. There are some in this room, I know, who have technical objections to calling this a 150th Anniversary, but since Samuel Jones Tilden was the prime mover of our firm, and the addition of John Lord Hayes in 1877 was of minor importance to everything except the firm name, we have traditionally dated the beginning of Tilden & Hayes to the Spring of 1841, when the illustrious Mr. Tilden graduated from the Law School of the University of the City of New York, now known as New York University.

"And if Tilden & Hayes can be proven guilty of showing a preference for NYU, my own alma mater, over the years, our history certainly has justified that preference."

"Guilty!" someone shouted out from the vicinity of the Yale table. Ted Swaine ignored the comment.

"Of course, our history is well known—"

"By whom?" someone asked. Ted Swaine glanced quickly at the Yale table and realized that HAG had asked the question. Ted had little power over retired Initials, so he played along.

"Mr. Herbert Goodman has asked an appropriate question. Perhaps among our younger guests, and even among some of our inattentive partners, there are important parts of our history that remain unknown. I can sketch it for you quickly."

"Very quickly," someone shouted, but it came from the other side of the room. Ted couldn't blame that comment on the Yalies.

"I am sure that Mr. Goodman would like me to remind everyone that Samuel Tilden graduated from Yale University in 1834 at the age of 20."

"Hear, hear!" Four Yalies were slapping their table top in unison. Carolyn Trent, the female tax partner, and Tom Carnahan had joined PHD and HAG in the raucous approval of their alma mater. When they had quieted down, Ted Swaine continued.

"Soon after graduating from NYU Law School seven years later,

Mr. Tilden became corporate counsel to the City of New York—and an ever more ardent Democrat. In time he became a shining light of those who supported the Union cause during the Civil War but still advised 'loyal opposition' to the Republican President, Abraham Lincoln. And although his political career was momentarily becalmed by that principled position, it was reinvigorated in 1872 when Mr. Tilden proved instrumental in destroying the corrupt Tweed Ring that used to run New York City. On the strength of the popularity of his reforms, he was elected Governor of New York in 1875 and President of the United States of America in 1876."

Muttered protests arose from several tables at once.

"Elected, I said. Samuel Jones Tilden did not serve as our 19th President, of course, but he was elected. The popular vote was heavily in his favor, and Mr. Tilden even won the electoral vote 184 to 165, due to contested results in four states. But, through the corrupt maneuvers of Republicans in Congress, and in Louisiana, South Carolina, Florida and Oregon, all the contested electoral votes were deemed to be Republican, giving Rutherford B. Hayes a 185 to 184 stolen electoral college victory. And our noble Mr. Tilden, concerned about the strong possibility of a renewal of bloody civil strife, set aside his personal ambitions and agreed not to contest the Presidential election.

"So, in 1877, Mr. Tilden returned quietly to New York and continued his legal career. Among other things, he helped found the Bar of the City of New York. And he left a legacy of over $6 million to the Free Public Library of New York. Which is one reason why the Trustees of the library graciously allowed us to use these facilities to celebrate here tonight—"

"Recent donations carried a little weight too," PHD let fly from the Yale table. Ted gave Patrick Davis a glance reminding him that he was not yet retired like HAG, but it was a mild one. Ted had relaxed sufficiently to enjoy the interruptions. They too were a Tilden & Hayes tradition, carefully nurtured by each succeeding generation of Yalies.

"Samuel Jones Tilden—yes, he was quite a man, and a quiet hero. But he was not so quiet that his name has been lost in the mists of time. It is still our firm's greatest pride. And it is etched in stone above the main entrance of this magnificent library, on his statue at 112th and Riverside and outside the wonderful ruins of his Roman-style gardens which overlook the Hudson River at Greystone, in Yonkers, where he died on August 4th, 1886.

"Now, there are those who say that the 1876 election fraud embittered Mr. Tilden's life. But our firm stands as incontrovertible authority that he withdrew gracefully from the political fray without having been beaten.

"And it was characteristic of our man that he chose John Lord Hayes to be his partner in 1877, shortly after the election fraud had been perpetrated. He must have searched everywhere for a man with the appropriate character—and name."

The partners who knew the story all laughed.

"Actually, according to reliable accounts, it took him only half an hour. That was because he wanted, above all, a man named Hayes to be his subordinate partner. And not Rutherford Birchard either. He found what he was looking for in a directory of semi-illustrious Washington D.C. lawyers: John Lord Hayes.

"Mr. Hayes had graduated from Dartmouth in 1831 at the age of 19. He went on to graduate from Harvard Law in 1834, but due to the deficient education he received there—"

"What's this?" someone shouted, but everyone else was laughing.

"—he didn't qualify for the New Hampshire bar until 1835. Mr. Hayes worked in Washington D.C. for decades, advancing to such glorious posts as chief clerk of the U.S. Patent Office and secretary of the National Association of Wool Manufacturers. He wrote treatises on tariff taxation, for God's sake. He was, in a word, boring. But he had gray hair and a Name.

"And thus Tilden & Hayes came into being."

"That didn't take as long as I expected," HAG shouted from the Yale table. Ted ignored him.

"Of course, our history makes clear the reasons for our traditional reliance on NYU and Harvard law schools, with a few rumpled Yalies thrown in for good measure—"

"We're not all rumpled!" PHD shouted.

"You sure are!" Chris Manzano, a Harvard man, yelled from across the room, and everyone laughed. Whenever they thought of rumpled Yalies, PHD was exactly whom they had in mind.

Ted Swaine laughed along with the others at PHD's expense. He felt it was always good to freshen the rumor that Yalies were hired by T&H simply to give the Harvard men someone to dump on whenever they felt abused by the ruling NYU elite.

"But even more important than our history," Ted Swaine continued, picking up the threads of his prepared speech, "is our tradition at Tilden & Hayes that we practice law as a profession, not as a business. We adhere to the principles of the past in ways most of our legal brethren have unfortunately forgotten.

"Of course, it must be admitted that there are a few other Manhattan firms who keep one eye on their traditions, who maintain ties with their glorious pasts, such as our brethren at Cravath, Simpson Thacher and Dewey Ballantine, but who among even them showed the traditional restraint during the 1980's?"

"No one!" shouted John Fenwick a little too loudly. There was an extremely brief moment of embarrassing silence before Ted Swaine continued. Sally Thompson felt confident that John Fenwick had once again seriously misjudged ETS's mood, that his habitual overeagerness would soon seal his fate as the probable loser in their contest for Ted Swaine's slot.

"Well," Ted Swaine said, "other firms have shown *some* restraint, but certainly none so well as Tilden & Hayes! And that is why we stand alone today, at the pinnacle of our profession, while even white shoe firms must trim their sails in unbecoming ways, not to mention the wholesale slaughter that has taken place during these last few months at behemoths like Skelly Adams & Neff."

A loud chorus of hisses and boos, started at the Yale table, circled the room.

"And how have we accomplished this miracle? By a once traditional but now considered outmoded practice: we turn clients away. We don't represent just anybody. And we rely on our strength: a Manhattan corporate practice second to none, supported by the best tax lawyers in the City."

Cheers and even a few whistles supported Ted Swaine's assessment.

"We practice law the old-fashioned way, by adhering to the values of honesty and hard work. Our clients must have a robust confidence in us, not a thin veneer of it. And under no circumstances can it be thin enough to shatter under the pressure of an increase in our billing rates!"

The approvals and laughter which filled the room this time inspired Ted Swaine to fly a little higher.

"And now I'd like to get personal for a moment, if I may."

"Not too personal," was Carolyn Trent's almost unnoticed comment. But the Yalies at her table all smiled in appreciation.

"As you all know, I am sitting next to our partner Stuart Emerson Craxton III. But what some of you don't know is that in 1963, when Stuart's father retired so that his son could compete for a position at the firm, SEC chose me to fill his partnership slot.

"You would expect, given what you all intimately know about how such partnership decisions are made, that I had worked many years for the elder Mr. Craxton. But that was not true. I had only worked for him once during my first year at T&H and, to be honest, I did not do such a good job.

"But he listened carefully to the advice of each of his partners, drew up the short list—we just called it The List back then—and then one morning in June he interviewed each of us on The List. He made his decision that very afternoon—"

"Haste makes waste!" HAG slipped into the speech. He was again ignored by Ted Swaine.

"—and told each of us within the hour what he had decided and why, talking to me last. I assumed, of course, being last, that I was a loser, but I was wrong. SEC just wanted to make sure that he was the first one to explain his decision to the other four. And then he told me why he had chosen me. He said I had the character to become an excellent Managing Partner—"

"What happened?" At some dinners HAG just couldn't keep his mouth shut. This was one of them. His last two comments had fallen flat.

"—and now, after nine years of being the Managing Partner, I'm not so sure any more that he meant that as a compliment."

Everyone laughed in relief. Ted had gotten too personal for most of the lawyers, but he had dug his way out of the hole with his joke.

"So, before his memory fades, I would like to express once more my admiration for the elder Mr. Craxton, who served Tilden & Hayes wisely for so many years."

The audience applauded politely, but without much enthusiasm. Only 15 of the T&H partners had ever met Stuart's father.

"Now perhaps I've already gone on too long," Ted continued, "and perhaps I haven't, but—"

"You have," HAG yelled loudly.

"Well, I guess I have, HAG," Ted said, finally showing his irritation by using Mr. Goodman's initials. "But I didn't want to forget anything important before stepping aside—"

The partners reacted with surprise. The rumors that had flown around the office on Thursday and Friday had mostly been ignored by them.

"—which I intend to do on my 65th birthday in October. So, now, one of you five youngsters on the short list will not have to wait as long as the rumors led you to believe, will you?"

Ted looked at each of them in turn for dramatic effect. He looked first at Robert Kim, who was sitting right across from him at the center table, and then at Sally Thompson, Frederick Hirsch and Mark Aiello. Finally he glanced briefly at John Fenwick. Everyone knew that meant he was dead meat, including John, who quickly reached for more wine.

"As for the four who will not get my slot—well, you could

always kill off one or another of these extra Yalies we have over here," he said, pointing to the Yale table where everyone was laughing at the joke, "or you could just rely on the laurels you have already won to coast all the way to retirement. We all know that having been chosen to attend this dinner is more valuable, in and of itself, than a partnership slot at any other law firm—and they know it, too!"

"Hear, hear!" HAG agreed somewhat meekly, but his comment met with a strong chorus of approval and he felt much better than he had seconds earlier.

"We at Tilden & Hayes have been so careful about who makes The List that there isn't a single person who has received that honor over the years who hasn't distinguished himself or herself before the New York Bar—that is, except one man, who shall remain nameless until hell freezes over, since he has seen fit to abuse his talents as a member of the Management Committee of Skelly Adams—"

"Danny Metzger!" the three male Yalies shouted in unison. Daniel Metzger had also attended Yale.

"I said nameless, gentlemen! Don't they teach vocabulary at Yale?" Ted was quite serious about this last rebuke and they all shut up.

"The only thing worse he could have done was to have been involved in that fiasco over at Finley Kumble!"

At this comment nearly all the lawyers laughed nervously, but the reference to the failed law firm escaped the understanding of most of their guests.

"So, as for the four of you who will not get my slot, let me assure you that the resources and connections of Tilden & Hayes are at your disposal. Never sell yourself short. You don't need to.

"And as for me, I've decided to start having fun again."

"Right!" PHD shouted sarcastically. He knew HAG had not yet recovered from Ted's rebuke, and he could not let such a ridiculous assertion pass without comment under the Yalie honor code.

Ted Swaine smiled confidently as his partners laughed and

applauded. He was proud of his reputation for always putting business first. And he was happy with how his speech had turned out. He was even feeling benevolent again toward the loud Yalies. He was completely aware that they had helped keep his speech entertaining. When the laughter had died down again, Ted continued.

"As for Tilden & Hayes, I would like to announce tonight my appointment of its next Managing Partner."

This time the partners' surprise was even audible. More than a dozen quickly glanced at Jack Kendall and found the information they were seeking there. JWK's face made it perfectly clear that yet another heir apparent Harvard grad had been passed over for an NYU upstart.

Ted paused only for a short breath while his partners' caught theirs. He loved being dramatic.

"And I have complete confidence that, as his father did before him, Stuart Emerson Craxton III will burnish the reputation of what we all know is the most lucrative respectable legal position in the whole world."

Stuart stood up to loud and continuous applause. As Stuart became the center of attention, Ted Swaine unconsciously took two steps to the side, but he did not sit down. He was just beginning to realize how unwilling he was to part with his power.

Stuart acknowledged the unexpectedly loud approvals. He glanced around the room and enjoyed the pleasure he saw on so many of the faces. But just as he noticed that even the Yalies seemed delighted by his appointment, he was startled by a crash of glass behind him. He turned suddenly, looking for a clumsy waiter, but saw instead a black form staring at him from a jagged gap in the southeast corner of the glass ceiling.

A moment later a single shot rang out, hitting Stuart in the right shoulder. In his shock, Stuart continued for another fraction of a second to stare at the blurred black form lying prone on the ceiling. Extended through the jagged hole were two hands gripping a weapon held in front of a black enshrouded face.

In that fraction of a second, silence abruptly descended on the dinner. Stuart, in a blur, saw the weapon move. His shock disappeared immediately. He dove to his left, knocking Ashley to the floor underneath him and dragging Catherine down under the table at the same time with his left hand. But before they had even hit the floor, the silence was broken by a burst of automatic gunfire and screams of panic.

The burst of gunfire seemed to go on forever, but it stopped nearly as quickly as it had started. Another two seconds passed and then another shot rang out, but this one originated near Stuart. While remaining crouched on top of Catherine and Ashley under the table, Stuart glanced at the source of the sound and saw Eddie Swaine, Ted Swaine's oldest son, kneeling behind the table. He had a gun in his hand. Then Eddie jumped up and ran out of the room.

Catherine and Ashley were both screaming beneath Stuart, but he held them down firmly, only moving enough to put his full body between the jagged hole in the ceiling and them. When he moved his left hand into a better position he realized there was a puddle on the floor. He glanced at the wound in his right shoulder, but his blood was dripping slowly onto Catherine's back, not onto the floor. He suddenly felt relieved Catherine and Ashley were both screaming.

Stuart didn't dare look to his left, so he glanced back at where Eddie had been kneeling and this time noticed Beverly Swaine holding Ted's head in her lap under the table next to them. Beyond them was a panicked exodus of legs leaving the Celeste Bartos Forum. Eddie had been the first one out the door, but he had been quickly followed.

Stuart's wet hand forced his attention back to his left side. He saw that only inches from his finger tips was Lily Kim's head. He looked further and saw Robert lying on the floor near her. Then he dared not look again. Stuart remained crouched over his family, eyes shut tight, for what seemed an endless amount of time.

Robert Kim's thoughts were struggling against confusion. He kept moving, but his body didn't move. He tried to run, but realized he was lying still. He heard loud noises, but they seemed miles away.

Slowly he realized why he was struggling. When Lily's face came into his mind clearly, he renewed his efforts and succeeded in opening his eyes. He could see her lying on the floor next to him, her face directly in front of his, framed by her deep black hair. Her face was pale but serenely beautiful, as it always had been in his thoughts, with a touch of mischief around her eyes.

In his confusion Robert thought that Lily looked like a high-caste Hindu princess. Then he recognized that the red spot in the middle of her forehead was not painted on.

Robert closed his eyes again and drifted miles away. With his last thoughts he wondered if Lily had already found them another place, hopefully an even better place, to play.

Eddie Swaine was also looking for a better place, one which would open onto the roof of the Celeste Bartos Forum. He had run up the stairs near the 42nd Street entrance and down the hallway that led to the library's main entrance on Fifth Avenue. He tried the doors to the Main Exhibit Hall, but they were locked. He swore because he knew the windows inside that hall looked out onto the courtyard above the old-fashioned glass ceiling.

Eddie calculated spatially in his mind and ran back down the hallway to the Gift Shop. The glass doors were locked but he could see that the window inside the shop overlooked the courtyard. And then he noticed the figure in black pulling himself up a rope.

Eddie ran back to just outside the Main Exhibit Hall and picked up a large bench used in the small video viewing area. He ran back to the Gift Shop and hurled the bench through the glass door. He cut his left hand as he reached through and yanked the door open. He tried the window but it also was shut tight. It probably had not been opened for years. As Eddie stepped back to use the bench again, he saw the figure in black fall heavily onto the top of the glass-domed ceiling.

Eddie quickly smashed the window with the bench and crawled through the large hole he had made, holding his gun in front of him, fixing his aim on the prone black form lying on the aluminum slats which protected the glass ceiling. The rope swung back and forth like a 50-foot pendulum, with ever narrower swings. It remained attached to the roof above the courtyard.

Eddie stepped over a small sledgehammer and around the jagged hole in the southeast corner of the glass ceiling, cautiously moving forward the 30 feet which separated him from the prone black form. It was difficult to walk on the aluminum slats. As he got closer he noticed the automatic pistol lying five feet away from the black form. He passed it, knelt down next to the body and checked its pulse. The wrist was still warm, but the assassin was clearly dead.

As Eddie knelt there, four policemen came rushing into the Gift Shop. One shouted for Eddie to put his hands up. Eddie did right away, and then asked to show his private detective's badge.

Eddie was soon suggesting that the police have the library surrounded and searched, just in case there were accomplices. But the assassin was lying next to him, he said, quite dead.

Two policemen came out onto the roof to join Eddie Swaine while the others set the search in motion. One policeman leaned over and lifted the black-gloved hand of the assassin to check the pulse again. Eddie noticed that the wrist looked strange. It was too thin and delicate. He looked at the prone, face-down body again.

Eddie suggested it was appropriate to take off the assassin's black head mask. The policemen agreed and removed it. Only Eddie wasn't surprised the assassin was a woman. But Eddie was surprised because he recognized her. It was Jackie Messer.

Stuart's seemingly endless protective crouching over his wife and daughter was finally interrupted by a gentle hand on his shoulder. "It's safe now," a female voice said quietly. Stuart opened his eyes and looked up. It was Sally Thompson.

"The police are already here," she added, "and the ambulances are on their way." Then she leaned over and whispered in Stuart's ear, "but I think we should get your wife and daughter out of here. Robert Kim is dead. His body is right behind you."

Stuart's thoughts raced. While crouched there he had thought that Robert might be dead, but he had not faced that thought. Now he hated himself for the other thought that entered his mind, the feeling that he was safer now that no one knew all the details. When he realized that his son Tim was also vaguely involved in that feeling he shuddered violently.

Sally Thompson put her arms around Stuart's shoulders. "I don't think you're hurt too badly," she said encouragingly. She had no idea what pain had caused his shudder.

"No, I'm all right," Stuart said. "But could you please take my wife and daughter home?" He talked to Sally as if they were not right underneath him.

"That was my idea too. You should stay here to look after Robert," she said, but she meant something else and Stuart thought he understood.

Stuart whispered to Catherine, trying to calm her down, saying everything would soon be all right. But between her sobs she kept insisting that no one could ever take Ashley away from her again. And she whispered something once about understanding how Jackie Kennedy must have felt watching her husband get shot.

When Stuart finally got through to Catherine, so that she could comprehend his actual words, he whispered, "Cath, you don't have to worry about me. I'm not hurt that badly. Really. And Tim will help. But you've—you've got to get Ashley out of here. Now. And don't let her look back. Robert Kim is dead."

Catherine groaned again but cooperated as Stuart helped her and Ashley to their feet. Catherine lifted Ashley in her arms and buried her sobbing face against her chest. Then Sally Thompson put her arms around Catherine and guided them both out of the room.

Sally led them right out the exit to 42nd Street. The crowd of T&H attorneys and their relatives who were standing on the wide sidewalk behind the police barricades stared silently as the blood-stained women walked past them, but one of the policemen interviewing witnesses to the shootings interrupted his conversation and motioned for the women to stop.

After talking briefly with that policeman, Sally led Catherine and Ashley to the first cab in the line of White Shoe cabs which waited nearby, alongside Bryant Park. She opened the cab door and helped Catherine and Ashley inside before getting in next to them.

The cab slowly pulled away from the curb, beginning its long, sad journey back to Scarsdale just as the first ambulance pulled up in front of the flowering-vine-covered canopy which lead all the way out to 42nd Street from the entrance to the Celeste Bartos Forum.

As Stuart watched Sally leading Catherine and Ashley out of the room, he had glanced to his left and saw that John Swaine was trying to help his mother Beverly lift his father up. Ted Swaine had a serious cut on his forehead which was already swelling, but otherwise he seemed unharmed. He had fallen head first against the edge of the table when the shooting had started. Beverly had had to drag him under it.

Stuart immediately suggested that they not try to lift Ted up. He assured them that emergency help would arrive any second and that the danger had passed. Beverly looked up at Stuart helplessly and then screamed when she noticed the blood soaking the right side of his tuxedo. Her son John gently held her.

Stuart slowly turned around. As he turned he noticed that his wife's departure had left the room almost empty. Two policemen stood guard at the entrance.

When he faced the southeast corner once again he stared momentarily at the jagged hole in the ceiling. It was still blurred. Then he looked down at the floor. He saw Robert and Lily Kim lying dead in a pool of their mingled blood. And then he finally dared to look to their left, to look directly down right in front of him.

At first he only saw Patrick Davis, the Yalie whose womanizing Stuart particularly abhorred. He was kneeling down. The next moment he realized Patrick was cradling Tim's head in his hands, whispering softly in Tim's ear over and over again, "hang in there kid, you're going to make it." Tears were streaming down PHD's rough-lined face. His tuxedo pants were already soaked by Tim's blood spreading on the floor around him.

Stuart quickly knelt down next to Tim and held his hand. Tim groaned quietly. It was the only sign that he was still alive.

Patrick looked up at Stuart. There, in PHD's eyes, Stuart saw a profound pain he had never been allowed to see before. And Stuart immediately knew that he would recognize that pain the next time he saw it—when he looked in a mirror.

Stuart and Patrick were still kneeling over Tim when Eddie Swaine ran back into the room. First Eddie made sure his father was all right and then he started to approach Stuart, Patrick and Tim.

When Stuart heard him coming, he turned around. He focused on the blood slowly dripping from Eddie's left hand. An intense fear entered Stuart's eyes.

"Stay away from my son," he commanded Eddie. Stuart was visibly shrinking away from the few drops of Eddie's blood which had fallen to the floor ten feet away from Tim.

Eddie Swaine went back to the table and securely wrapped his wounded hand with one of the cloth napkins. He picked up five more napkins and walked back to where the drops of his blood waited. As Eddie wiped up those drops of blood, he talked with Stuart calmly and Stuart's fear began to subside.

Eddie never bothered telling Stuart that he had had the same lover for the last 18 years. He had seen that fear of his blood before and he understood it. He too was afraid of AIDS. And judging from his observations during dinner, he wasn't completely sure that Tim Craxton's blood was safe.

But Eddie did not say that to Stuart. He had seen Stuart's left hand unconsciously clutch the wound in his right shoulder several times. He was certain their shed blood had already been mingled. So when Stuart's fears subsided, he just handed Stuart three clean napkins with his right hand. After Stuart saw that they were clean, he ripped open his formal shirt and pressed them against his wound. He listened to Eddie's suggestion that he'd better keep applying pressure.

Eddie continued to polish the floor where his blood had been while telling Stuart and Patrick that Jackie Messer had been the assassin.

"I don't believe it," Stuart said. Patrick Davis didn't believe it either.

"I saw her myself," Eddie insisted. "She fell during her attempted escape from about 40 or 50 feet up." Eddie looked up and they followed his eyes. Almost directly above them they could see the dark outline of her body through the glass ceiling. The sounds of police activity on the roof were starting to get louder.

"She's dead," Eddie added.

"But he stared right at me. I'd swear it was a man," Stuart said. He brought the frozen moment back before his eyes without releasing his grip on Tim's hand. The blurriness of the picture was infuriating.

"Eddie, you've got to tell the police I think the assassin is a man," Stuart said firmly. "If Jackie Messer was the assassin I would have seen, well, her breasts. The assassin was lying prone on the ceiling. The gun was pointed right at me. I have this picture in my mind and, I'm telling you, there are no breasts in that picture. It must have been a man."

"I'll tell them, Mr. Craxton. But there's Jackie Messer. And there's the gun." Eddie couldn't help glancing, while pointing to the dark outline of Jackie's body on the glass ceiling, at Stuart's half-glasses still sitting on the bridge of his nose. Stuart understood the glance and lost his confidence.

"Tell them it was a blur, though. It happened too fast for me to be sure. But I still think it was a man."

"I'll do that," Eddie said.

While they were talking the first ambulance crew had arrived and had wheeled a bed into place near Tim. Patrick Davis stepped back, out of the way, as the crew members lifted Tim onto the bed.

Stuart took Tim's hand into his again immediately. And all of them were running toward the door a second later.

The crowd of attorneys and their relatives were still standing on the wide sidewalk behind the police barricades, waiting for someone to explain the cause of their terror, when Stuart came out running next to his son Tim on the rolling bed. The crowd watched silently as Stuart jumped into the back of the ambulance. It left in a blare of lights and sirens. They only began talking again after four more ambulances had arrived and discharged their crews into the New York Public Library.

A few minutes later they saw Ted Swaine brought out on another bed. His wife Beverly climbed into the ambulance. His two sons jumped into the first White Shoe cab in line and followed the ambulance to the hospital.

The crowd did not even disperse when the bodies of Robert and Lily Kim, and Jackie Messer, each draped in white sheets, had all been wheeled out and taken to a hospital whose services could do them no good. The crowd had to talk first. The terror had to be rendered harmless.

That process took longer for some. For others a sudden pang in their stomachs reminded them that the main course of the dinner had never been served. They slowly drifted away from those who required more talking.

It was nearly 11:00 when the last of the White Shoe cabs finally left its post alongside Bryant Park on 42nd Street, and brought its passengers, still talking away the terror, back to their Long Island home.

Chapter Forty Five

The ambulance fought the Saturday night traffic on Fifth Avenue as it wailed its way to NYU Hospital. Inside Stuart was kneeling next to Tim, having overruled the emergency staff who had tried to get Stuart to have his shoulder bandaged first.

"That can wait," Stuart had insisted, "this is my son." The fact that they had acquiesced so quickly made Stuart even more afraid. He leaned over Tim's face and held his hands. Stuart's hopes had risen dramatically because Tim had been jolted back to consciousness by the run to the ambulance.

But Tim stared at his father for over a minute before he realized where he was. Then a light shone in his dulled eyes. Stuart was elated.

"Dad, do me a favor," Tim finally whispered.

"Anything."

"Quit this profession. Become a professor or something."

"I can't do that, Tim. You're always asking too much of me."

"Likewise," Tim whispered, but the pain in his father's voice haunted him, so he added, "it's just as well. I hear university politics are even worse."

"I've heard that too," Stuart agreed.

Tim lay there a moment, regaining some strength from his father's agreement, before saying softly, "Dad, I'm really impressed with how you stuck your hands right into shit creek and furiously whipped your boat around. I mean, not everyone can do that."

"A man's got to minimize the pain," Stuart said. It showed very briefly in his eyes that, in spite of his anguish, his son's compliment had pleased him deeply.

Tim couldn't see his father's eyes clearly, he couldn't see much more than a blur, but he had felt the pleasure in his father's voice. "And if not for himself, at least for others," Tim finished for his father and then drifted away once more into his overwhelmingly personal pain.

Stuart knelt there silently, squeezing his son's hands, not daring to pray to an unfamiliar God, but heard in the silence anyway. By his own son.

Tim opened his eyes slowly once again. "I just realized you're even more naive than Mom. Can you believe that, Dad?"

"Sure," Stuart said, not believing it for one second.

"Then I want to tell you about Sandy. Reach in my left jacket pocket."

Stuart did and pulled out a light blue piece of paper, soaked in Tim's blood. The paper had been neatly folded in quarters. Stuart could see that inside were the words of a short poem, but the soaked paper could not be unfolded.

"I can't read it, son," Stuart whispered.

"Then ask Stu. Tell him I want you and Mom to know all about Sandy."

"You can tell us later yourself," Stuart whispered desperately.

"I didn't want to go to college anyway," Tim answered, wanting to feel his father's smile again. But he did not feel it.

"You can't die, Tim. I order you not to. Why don't you ever listen to me?"

"Because you don't listen to reality, Dad," Tim said softly.

"Why, why do you always have to choose the harshest reality?"

"Oh, I don't. And Mom doesn't either."

"But she'll be harsh this time. She's going to kill you for this," Stuart said. Tim smiled weakly.

Hanging his desperate hopes on that weak smile, Stuart whispered defiantly in Tim's ear, "see, I knew this wasn't reality."

"But it is. And you'd better get used to it, Dad," Tim whispered tenderly in his father's ear, squeezing his father's hands one last time, "because Mom and Ashley still need you."

Chapter Forty Six

Very early on Sunday morning, April 28th, about two hours after he had heard the last footstep in the New York Public Library, a tall Japanese man, about 30 years old, unzipped from the inside a large black canvas duffel bag and crawled out. He was wearing black jeans, a black silk shirt, black gloves, black Gucci loafers and a black head mask.

He stretched his sore muscles before yanking open the huge old window of the Oriental Division reading room, located about 20 feet above the glass-domed ceiling of the Celeste Bartos Forum in the middle of the south wall of the internal courtyard above that ceiling. Then he reached behind himself into the duffel bag and picked up a coiled rope with hooks on one end. He sat down on the windowsill and leaned back out the window, with his legs pressed tightly against the inside wall.

He swung the rope back and forth below him, and then jerked it up. The hooks sailed up along the south wall of the courtyard and far over the top of the building. After he had pulled the hooks up against the edge of the building, and tested the tautness of the rope, he went back inside the reading room and turned on the light.

First he made sure that the other automatic pistol was still inside the duffel bag. The other rope, of course, was now gone, in police custody no doubt, along with the other previous contents of the duffel bag: the small sledgehammer, the used automatic pistol and the black-clad body of the woman.

He inspected the ragged spots of the duffel bag where, when full, it had scraped against the west wall of the library 23 hours earlier. The holes were not large enough for anything to slip out.

During those 23 hours, probably starting shortly after the

alcohol and drugs had worn off, the woman had permeated the duffel bag with the smells of her fear. He thought that his nose might eventually forget those smells, but he knew that his eyes would not forget hers, staring at him through the eye slits of her black head mask, wild with fear like any hog-tied animal.

That memory had been imprinted shortly after he had swung the dangling duffel bag, hanging from the first rope he had attached to the roof, through the large open window of the Oriental Division reading room. When he had unzipped the duffel bag he had found those wild eyes staring at him. He had felt momentarily sorry for her, convinced that fate had played a nasty trick on her. Then he had broken her neck, slipped off the gag, untied her arms and legs, placed her limp and still warm body on the reading room table near the open window, and slid down the rope to wait above the southeast corner of the glass ceiling of the Celeste Bartos Forum.

The second rope he had attached to the roof was now waiting for his departure as he studied the reading room carefully for traces of his visit. He noticed the floor was damp where the duffel bag had been, so he took the latest edition of *The South China Morning Post* off its rack and rubbed the floor dry.

He also found several drops of his blood on the floor behind the door to the reading room, which the newspaper soon absorbed. Several hours earlier he had sat there, the second automatic pistol near at hand, watching the entrance to the Oriental Division while he bandaged his right calf with his red and white print handkerchief. He had tied it over the deeply grazed skin after making sure the bullet had not entered his leg. Now he made sure that the handkerchief was still tightly tied.

After one last inspection of the reading room, he threw the soiled newspaper into the duffel bag, slung the bag over his shoulder and turned out the light. In the dark he stepped onto the windowsill, grabbed hold of the rope, shut the window firmly with his feet and quickly climbed up the rope to the roof.

There he detached the hooks, grabbed the rope, ran to the west edge of the library overlooking Bryant Park, firmly reattached the hooks, and slid down the rope to the ground. He glanced back at the dangling rope momentarily, but assumed correctly that it would not be noticed for weeks amid all the other construction scaffolding and equipment stored at the east end of Bryant Park, and that, when finally noticed, it would be assumed it had been left there by a young woman no later than just after dusk on Saturday evening, April 27th.

In the deep shadows of the construction scaffolding he slipped off his head mask, put it in the duffel bag, and then jumped over the park fence onto 40th Street. After walking a few blocks down Fifth Avenue he reached back inside the duffel bag, took out *The South China Morning Post*, and then tossed the rezipped duffel bag and its contents into a large green industrial waste collector filled with construction debris. Several blocks later he deposited the slightly bloodied, damp and crumpled newspaper in a litter basket.

He continued walking, pleased that no one had noticed the duffel bag sitting on top of the library all day Saturday. He would not have wanted to change his plan again, for good reason. His plan had gone so well. And the slight change in his plan he had received Saturday from Kyoto had been easy to accommodate. He had even agreed with them that Stuart Craxton, as the new Managing Partner of Tilden & Hayes, might eventually prove to be more valuable wounded than dead.

When he reached Washington Square he walked diagonally through it, and then down a block to Bleeker Street. He stopped just outside a bar, took off his gloves and slid them into the back pocket of his jeans. Then he disappeared inside.

Two drops of his blood still stained the windowsill outside the Oriental Division reading room. A light drizzle which started shortly after dawn washed them both away.

Chapter Forty Seven

On Tuesday afternoon, April 30th, Stuart Craxton stood in the carved mahogany pulpit of the Church of St. James the Less, his right arm held in a black sling to relieve the pressure on his wounded shoulder. The pastor of Scarsdale's Episcopal Church had just completed the first portion of Tim Craxton's funeral service, and had stepped aside to let Stuart speak.

From the pulpit Stuart surveyed the pews to his left, where he could clearly see the face of each of his 39 partners, including Ted Swaine's bandaged forehead, and the sea of Tilden & Hayes associates and staff members behind them, with even more in the church's left and right wings. Another dozen staff members were outside the dignified gray stone church, keeping the news media at a respectable distance down Church Lane.

Right in front of him Catherine sat in the first pew, her face pale, her anguish ineffectively hidden by a black veil. Stu sat next to her, holding Ashley's hand. Behind them, in the second pew, was his Aunt Lucy, almost 79 years old, the youngest and last of his father's siblings whom Stuart Junior had taken with him to New York from Massachusetts. Next to her were four of Stuart's seven cousins, and behind them were Catherine's brothers and their families.

About 30 of Tim's teenage friends, and several of the Craxtons' neighbors, had filled in the pews on the left side of the church, except for the last three pews, which Stuart could see had been taken over by Mohadi Sukemi and 11 of his aides.

As Stuart took several folded sheets of paper out of his suitcoat pocket with his left hand, many of the mourners noticed that he looked different. And it was not just the profound sadness in his serious blue eyes.

Frank DeSocio was the first to notice why. Stuart had caught his eye and held it for a second, and Frank suddenly realized that Stuart could see clearly at a distance. Frank looked again. Stuart was wearing new gold-rimmed full-frame glasses, not his usual half-glasses. When Stuart turned his head and the light from an altar candle glanced off the lenses, Frank could see that they were bifocals.

Stuart's thoughts raced quickly as he watched his family and his colleagues sit down in their pews. First he thought about Jackie Messer's funeral that morning, and how frustrated he had felt standing in the last pew, trying to think of something to say to comfort her parents. He had decided to tell them that he doubted that Jackie had killed his son, but his resolve had failed him after Mrs. Messer's angry glance darted directly at him as she left the service. Stuart had been afraid she would have screamed if he had so much as opened his mouth.

At first Stuart had assumed that Mrs. Messer blamed him for depriving her daughter of a place on the short list, thereby precipitating her crisis. But he had heard after the service, from one of the 22 associates who had attended, that Jackie's mother blamed the whole law firm for the long, slow but sure destruction of her bright and beautiful young daughter, and didn't care whether or not Jackie had actually been the assassin. Mrs. Messer had not even realized that he was Stuart Craxton, but since he was the only Tilden & Hayes partner to attend Jackie's funeral, she had fixed her fury on him.

Stuart understood her anger all too well, but was still relieved he hadn't spoken to her. He himself had momentarily wondered whether his decision to insist on Robert Kim being invited to the Anniversary Dinner had been responsible for all four deaths, but he had quickly decided that whether or not Jackie was the assassin, he was not responsible for her, or someone else's, unforeseeable reaction to that decision.

Stuart's memory of Jackie's funeral reminded him of the other rumors which had circulated there, those concerning his client, the Indonesian oil billionaire Mohadi Sukemi, who had flown from Zurich to attend Tim's funeral. The Sukemi rumors were winning the competition for the attention of the mourners, although the many rumors concerning the Anniversary Dinner tragedy came in a close second.

Some claimed Mohadi Sukemi had flown over from Zurich on Sunday night with 30 aides. Some said only 20. Others were certain that four of those aides were now in Los Angeles, having accompanied Robert Kim's father back there, carrying the ashes of Robert and Lily Kim in expensive antique Korean vases they had purchased on Madison Avenue.

And everyone at Tilden & Hayes had a story about being interviewed by at least one of these Indonesian men, who had asked questions about what Robert and Lily Kim had been like, about what they had liked and admired. Tim's friends were all discussing similar stories about questions asked about him.

But the rumors focused mainly on the money being distributed, the way old problems were being resolved overnight. Everyone had heard that, after one aide had spoken with Christine Lava, and then her mother, a long-outstanding, but slowly being reduced, hospital bill for her father's uninsured terminal illness had been fully paid. The rumors varied as to the amount, but none put it at less than $150,000.

And there was JayDee, the messenger, who had overcome his reluctance to talk and was telling anyone who would listen at Tim's funeral that he had been offered a full scholarship to NYU to complete college, including free rent at a condo near Union Square.

Chris Manzano was also kept busy before the service, verifying the rumor that Archie had called him a few hours earlier and had told him Mohadi Sukemi's aide had promised to buy him a photocopy shop in downtown Charleston.

That aide had tracked Archie down in South Carolina late on Monday night, where Archie had fled after quitting his messenger job at Tilden & Hayes. The aide had noticed Archie's $100 donation to the Robert Kim Scholarship Fund at Stanford, and had asked questions until Ellen Mackin had told him how bad Archie felt about the seating charts. It had been reported in the late edition of the Sunday *Times* that a copy of the Anniversary Dinner seating chart had been found on Jackie Messer's dead body.

Archie had despaired when he had read that. He had felt about the $100 Jackie Messer had given him as Stuart had felt about the millions in his Swiss bank account. He thought he had earned the money fairly.

Another similarity was that they had each given the money away as soon as they knew it was tainted. But there was a difference, besides the one of scale. Archie had believed the truth and then had been upset by a lie, while Stuart had believed a lie and then had been upset by the truth.

Ellen Mackin, Ted Swaine's secretary, was also kept busy before the funeral service vigorously dismissing the rumors that three copies of the seating chart had been made. She showed everyone her order for only one copy and the Duplicating Room copy that showed Archie had ordered two.

But the rumor that three copies of the seating chart had been made did not die. It was connected to Sean Murray's contention that one of SEC's Japanese clients had visited 101 Park late on Thursday night, asking for SEC and Robert Kim just ten minutes after Robert had left. Sean also insisted that the client had asked about Jackie Messer and about whether he could have a copy of the seating chart for the Anniversary Dinner. But few believed Sean because he seemed to have forgotten all those details until late on Monday night.

But even these rumors paled in their competition with the big three, that Mohadi Sukemi had pledged over $1 million to the Robert Kim Scholarship Fund, that he had pledged $3.3 million to endow three Tim Craxton chairs in Economics at NYU, whose research focus would be on redistributive economic policies, and that discussions apparently were already underway at a South Central

Los Angeles hospital to build a new Robert and Lily Kim maternity wing. Barbara Sexton had called Lily Kim's mother around noon to express her sympathy and had heard that one directly.

Although among Tim's friends the three endowed chairs gave rise to many ironic comments, they proved to be not nearly as absorbing a topic of conversation as a light blue piece of paper, stained with Tim's dried blood, which Stuart had arranged to be placed in Tim's cold hands during his wake on Monday evening. That had thoroughly altered their previously unfavorable opinion of Tim's father.

For most of the other mourners, though, the ever-expanding rumors of Mohadi Sukemi's largesse effectively replaced their earlier interest in repeating what had been mentioned in Robert Kim's two paragraph obituary in the *Times* on Monday: that Prudential Insurance had pledged $10,000 to the Robert Kim Scholarship Fund.

They also overshadowed the small talk about the Democratic political reaction to the publication in Monday's *New York Post* of a photo of the naked bodies of Sydney Brewster and Minoru Yoshida submerged in her aquarium, a photo which the other New York papers had still chosen not to run. There had been a short article in the *Times* on Sunday about the untimely but not unexpected death of the black sheep of Senator Brewster's clan, but none of the papers had connected the two stories.

The media had all accepted the Jackie Messer jealousy angle, playing up once more an exaggerated image of the intense pressures of the competition for partnership slots at Manhattan law firms. The dramatic murder-suicide of two brilliant but driven competitors had proved irresistible.

One story in *The Daily News* even featured a friend of Jackie's describing how Jackie had once threatened to nuke Tilden & Hayes if she didn't make partner. The friend was quoted as saying, "I guess she meant it."

But only the tabloid media added innuendo about Robert Kim and Jackie Messer having had an affair, one version claiming that her rage had been ignited by Robert's return to his wife Lily and another claiming that her rage had resulted from Robert's new-found preference for Tim Craxton.

It was also mentioned often, by proponents of gun control, that Jackie Messer had bought the automatic pistol used in the assassination on Saturday morning in New Jersey. What was ignored was that, although the gun shop owner had taken down information from several of Jackie's IDs, he couldn't identify her picture.

Eddie Swaine's heated argument on Sunday night with the police was also ignored. He unsuccessfully had insisted that the police reopen their investigation when he found out that, upon examining Jackie Messer's body, they had not found the bullet wound he was certain her leg would have.

But the weakest rumor, also traced back to Barbara Sexton, was that Robert had uncovered something strange about the Atlanta Nishizaki restaurant and that maybe the two bodies found in the aquarium at Nishizaki's New York offices were related to his investigation.

That was as close as any of the rumors ever got to the truth, but each of the rumors was kept alive for months.

No one knew the facts. No one could satisfactorily explain the deaths of two senior associates, one wife and the teenage son of an Initial. And there is no better culture available for nourishing and sustaining rumors than confusion surrounding a tragedy.

Stuart's frustration, caused by not being able to publicly explain the true story, and his anger at the excessive attention these rumors were receiving, flashed through his thoughts, making him realize that he had been looking down, probably for only a few seconds, at the speech he had prepared. He looked up again.

Patrick Davis, sitting among the Initials in the front pews, caught his eye, reminding him of their short conversation 30 minutes ago in front of the church. Before they had talked Stuart had assumed that PHD must have also lost a son, but when he had asked that question PHD had answered that he had lost dozens of sons, and then had walked away, as he always tried to walk away from pain. There was something, however, in Patrick's resonant but raspy voice which seemed intentionally designed to remind Stuart that PHD had worked on a helicopter ambulance crew in Viet Nam. In addition to those dozens PHD had watched die, Stuart was suddenly sure there must be some who had survived because an intense man had whispered in their ears, "hang in there kid, you're going to make it."

Stuart's clear vision then sought out Tim's friend, Steve, the one who had been driving when Andy had been killed. Stuart had seen him outside before the service but had not had a chance to talk to him. He noticed him sitting next to an older couple whom he did not recognize at first. Then he remembered. They were the Blairs, Sandy's parents.

Those three were sitting further back than the rest of Tim's friends.

Stuart refolded his speech slowly with his left hand, and slid it back into his suitcoat pocket. He looked at Catherine one last time and then began to speak.

"For the life of me, I cannot summon the strength I would need to tell you the stories I wanted to tell you about my son, about *our* son. Often I misunderstood Tim. Often, I'm sure, you misunderstand those you love.

"Time passes. Each generation has its own language. It's as if we are doomed to misunderstand our own children.

"But my son made an effort to bridge my stupidity. And I tried, almost too late, to meet him halfway. Fortunately, I was not too late. And that is what I most want to tell you—before it is too late for you. Because it is worth every imaginable effort.

"And I am very, very sorry that it is already too late for the Blairs. Their daughter, Sandy, whom I just found out was loved by my son Tim, died almost exactly two years ago. But it is not yet too late for her to share my son's service, so, please—"

Stuart closed his eyes, but no tears fell from them. He was making every imaginable effort to prevent that.

"I am also very sorry to say that I have no idea whether or not we pray here today in vain," Stuart continued after a minute's silence, "but I can say that I touched the depths of my dying son's soul. And that gives me hope.

"And pride. Because for years my son Tim tried to minimize others' pain, although he was in great pain himself. He even tried to minimize the suffering he knew his own death would bring, senseless as it was.

"And that makes him, in my eyes, a hero. One his mother and I, and our children Stu and Ashley, hope will inspire you to find the courage to minimize your own suffering so that you can more effectively minimize others'."

Stuart took one step away from the pulpit and then turned back, pointing to the young man sitting next to Sandy's parents. "And Steve, Tim would have wished that most of all for you."

After the funeral service was concluded, Stuart and Stu, as pallbearers, led Tim's coffin down the red-carpeted aisle and outside the church, assisted by Catherine's brothers and two of Tim's friends. Catherine and Ashley followed numbly.

Stuart made a point of stopping the procession briefly twice, once to shake Eddie Swaine's hand, and the other to reach out to Sally Thompson, who was standing at the other edge of a pew near the back.

After Tim's coffin was slid into the long black hearse waiting in the parking lot near the rectory entrance, Stuart and Stu walked the few steps behind it to the old Volvo station wagon with which Tim had had a hate-love relationship. Stuart opened the back door for Catherine and Ashley with his free hand, and then sat down in the front on the passenger's side.

As the hearse pulled away a few minutes later, to begin the ten-mile trip to the Craxton family plot in Woodlawn Cemetery, Stu revved the Volvo's old engine in imitation of his brother's habit, and then slid it gently into first gear, following in the hearse's wake.

Five black stretch limousines, carrying Aunt Lucy, Stuart's four cousins, Catherine's two brothers, their wives and Tim's five cousins, and Mohadi Sukemi, eleven of his aides and Christine Lava, pulled into line behind the Volvo, followed by 60 white 1991 Lincoln

Continentals, the entire fleet of the White Shoe private cab company, which had been engaged by Ted Swaine to transport almost 200 Tilden & Hayes lawyers and staff to Scarsdale in a show of support for their colleague, Stuart Emerson Craxton III.

The formal portion of Tim Craxton's funeral procession was complemented by an assortment of late model Jeeps and sportscars which had never before been driven so slowly on the Bronx River Parkway by Tim's teenage friends.

Chapter Forty Eight

Two days later, early on Thursday morning, May 2nd, Stuart and Stu waited together at the Mamaroneck station for the New Haven train. Stu had decided to return to Yale in time to prepare for his final exams, rather than make them up as he could have arranged. Stu felt uneasy, as if returning so quickly was a crime, but he really wanted to get back. To study, he thought, but mostly it was to avoid seeing the despair in his mother's eyes.

Stuart waited with his son silently. He had no idea what he could say that would ease his son's obvious discomfort. It was Stu who finally broke the silence.

"I don't know if this is a good time to tell you, Dad, but I have been accepted at Harvard Law and I've told them I'm coming in the Fall."

"Congratulations, son," Stuart said, trying to sound enthusiastic, but his attempt revealed his displeasure. He felt as though Stu had intentionally crossed him, just as he had when he had been accepted at Harvard four years earlier. Then it had taken a threat of no financial assistance to get Stu to compromise and attend Yale.

"Thanks, Dad," Stu said, but he felt that his hold over his father's affections was weak. He quickly pushed his way through the remaining resistance he had built up against giving his father the gift Stu knew he wanted.

"I also wanted you to know that I have not yet answered NYU Law. I've also been accepted there. So, what do you think, Dad? Should I accept their offer and tell Harvard to go to hell?"

Stuart's eyes just barely moistened as he looked at his son. He didn't answer, but his answer was clear in his eyes and in his inability to speak.

As the train to New Haven pulled into the station, Stu stood entranced by the emotions he had aroused in his father. Finally he picked up his bag, stretched out his hand to shake hands, and then held onto Stuart's hand tightly. As the train screeched to a halt, Stu leaned toward his father and whispered loudly into his ear, just as if he were now a partner in a conspiracy, "that's what I've decided to do, Dad. I want to be a Craxton, just like you and grandpa."

Stuart watched his son run down the platform and board the train. The picture of a tall young man, looking so much like Stuart himself had looked at 22, stayed in focus, though it blurred around the edges where the moisture had collected in Stuart's eyes. Stuart took off his bifocal glasses and wiped his eyes with a handkerchief.

Before putting his new glasses back on, Stuart looked for his son, his only son, Stuart E. Craxton IV, and couldn't make him out among all the blurred figures. He slipped the glasses back on and there was Stu, hanging off the train, waving goodbye to him.

My son looks happy, Stuart thought as his son's words, and the gentle feeling of his son's breath in his ear, echoed through his mind. But his heart suddenly felt very tight, gripped by a deep, wrenching pain. An unfamiliar emotion surged through him. Standing on the platform, Stuart E. Craxton III could no longer control himself. He began to cry.

As the tears streamed silently down his face, Stuart imagined his conversation with Stu continuing. He did not want it to end. He heard himself saying that the family tradition was a stupid one, that Harvard Law was an excellent choice, the best choice to make. So what if it was in Massachusetts? Stu then protested that NYU was where he really wanted to go, but in his imagination Stuart could suddenly see his son more clearly, could see he was just saying that because he meant to say "I love you, Dad," but couldn't. He was a Craxton, after all, Stuart suddenly thought furiously, a ridiculous Craxton.

Even better, he thought he would say to Stu, go to Medical School, Harvard Medical School. Or better still, buy a textile factory in Massachusetts and run it well.

Run it well, Stuart thought, and realized he would soon be the Managing Partner of Tilden & Hayes. Well, he would run that well. Better than ETS had. Even better than his father had. He would insist on the traditions and resist the temptations while rooting out those weaknesses that had grown under ETS.

He imagined giving Frank DeSocio, the 45-year-old Harvard graduate and tax partner he trusted, his old power office on the 43rd floor. And that made Stuart realize that, come October, he would be moving up to the 47th floor, to the highest of the power offices.

Maybe, he thought, he should move DeSocio directly into the 46th floor power office, but he decided there was no reason to rush, no reason to irritate Jack Kendall further. Kendall would retire in five years anyway. Then he could move DeSocio up, making it clear he was the heir apparent in spite of being a tax lawyer.

Then Stuart thought of Sally Thompson and realized how impressed he had been with the firm but gentle way she had assisted him at the Anniversary Dinner. He surprised himself by imagining her in his old power office five years from now, following in DeSocio's path, becoming the first female Initial at 41, and then maybe even following DeSocio to the top. A woman Managing Partner, a University of Pennsylvania graduate! Stuart imagined laying the groundwork for making that double heresy possible. He wondered if Sally had the ambition. She certainly had the intelligence, skill and class required for the job.

And next year, Stuart then thought, returning to the near future, I will lower the Managing Partner's annual draw by $400,000 and distribute it among the other partners. Catherine will agree with me, I know she will. I'm sure we can live on $1.1 million a year, even if half of it does disappear in taxes.

Stuart's thoughts of his imminent financial sacrifice were suddenly interrupted by the realization that his family lived extremely well on less than a million a year now. He became violently indignant with himself. We don't have to be any richer than we already are, he thought. I'm not an investment banker, after all. No, I'm certainly not.

And then his mind was flooded with remorse for having ever entertained dreams of being really wealthy, dreams which had been stirred by Sydney Brewster, and he felt like a fool, like a complete idiot. He realized that throughout his entire life he had always had more than enough money.

And in his mind he was talking to Stu again, telling him never to be a lawyer, that it had carved too large a chunk out of his soul. Be a doctor. Be a doctor, Stuart nearly yelled in his imagination to his son. But then he thought of the doctors he knew and he took it all back. Some were even less humane than lawyers.

So in his imagination he told Stu, no, son, be poor. Your mother is right, be poor. But then he thought of the homeless in Grand Central, and was repulsed by the idea.

A face drifted into Stuart's sad daydream, a young face, but out of focus. Stuart tried to see that face clearly, but instead saw himself telling Stu, be a good lawyer, son, a good lawyer like Frank DeSocio. Stuart had almost thought of Robert Kim, but that thought had not been allowed to form.

Or be anything you want son, he saw himself telling Stu, but whatever you do, minimize the pain. And if not for yourself, at least for others.

Stuart was suddenly struck with how badly he had failed his father's advice, with how much suffering his folly had caused. And he remembered how soiled he had felt, how terrible the recognition had been, when Sydney had made it clear that his Swiss bank account was filled with Mohadi Sukemi's money, because he had known immediately she was telling the truth. And what was much worse, he realized he had known it before she had told him, but had never admitted it to himself.

He decided to call Stu immediately, to leave a message on his answering machine telling him to go to Harvard Law. He imagined his son's protest, "but I want to be just like you and grandpa." And he imagined his heartbreaking response, "you already are too much like us."

Then Stuart imagined Stu looking forgivingly into his eyes, and felt his son's breath whispering very, very softly in his ear, "it would not be so bad to be you, Dad."

Stuart suddenly felt much better and much sadder. But he had to agree. It would not be so bad.

Stuart felt the dull pain in his right shoulder from the bullet wound become sharper as the image of Tim's pale face against the white sheets of the ambulance bed suddenly came into focus in his mind. And then he remembered distinctly the reality of Tim's death, and realized why he had been crying, and whose breath was lingering in his ear.

Stuart intentionally prolonged the imagined sensations. So much so that when he finally opened his eyes he was surprised to find he was still standing on the platform.

He looked straight ahead, seeing all too clearly that his son's train had already left the station.

Available From

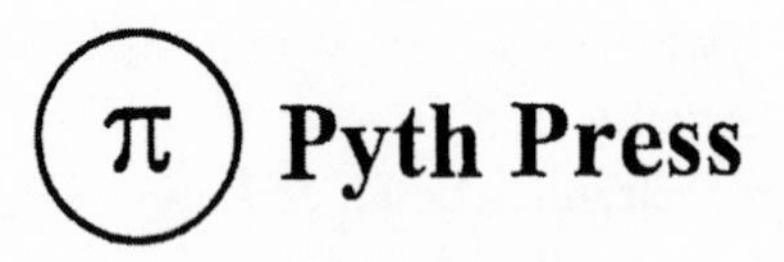

By
George Hammond

Philosophy

Even More Relativity

A philosophical essay on theoretical physics analyzing the fundamental concepts of mass, energy, the speed of light, the atom, space and time and proposing both a comprehensive revision of the basic principles of physics and alternative solutions to individual problems (1995).

The Gospel According to Andrew

A retelling of the story of Jesus's life, and the early years of the new faith, through the eyes of the apostle Andrew, who does not find Paul's theological speculations persuasive (1979).

Conversations With Socrates

Philosophical dialogues between Socrates and Plato on the nature of virtue, happiness, justice and the absolute (1979).

Rational Idealism

Why no one, not even God, can be omniscient—and fifteen other essays on the purpose of life, the Eternal Ideas, our emotions, intelligent desiring, educational theory and theoretical physics (1981).

Fiction

Bob and Charlie

A humorous novel about two 50-year-old Manhattanite dreamers, one an energetic pessimist and the other an exhausted optimist, who pool their resources to build Captain Bob's Casino ("Where Everyone is a Winner") in Las Vegas (1996).

The Senior Partner

A legal thriller about four crucial months in the life of Stuart E. Craxton III, a senior partner at Tilden & Hayes, and how his flirtation with greed nearly destroys his law firm, his family and his life (1994).

The Morning Light

An idealistic, philosophical novel about a Roman Senator's doomed stand against slavery in the 2nd century B.C. (1977).

Mark Twain's Visit To Heaven
And Other Short Stories

Twenty-two short tragedies, comedies and parables, including two novellas: The God Desire and Christopher O'Connor's Romances (1978-1996).

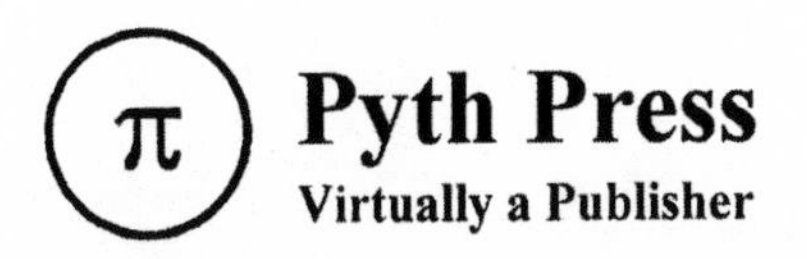

HAMM

90000>
9 780738 804071